The Touch of a WOMAN

KG MacGregor

Bella BOOKS

2015

Bella Books, Inc.
P.O. Box 10543
Tallahassee, FL 32302

Printed in the United States of America on acid-free paper.

First Bella Books Edition 2015

Editor: Katherine V. Forrest
Cover Designer: Sandy Knowles

ISBN: 9-781-59493-465-0

Other Books By KG MacGregor

Acknowledgment

This page is always the last one I write, and it's squeezed into the document by formatters as it goes through typesetting. During the window after I finished this book, the Supreme Court of the United States issued their historic marriage-equality decision, a ruling that will forever change the way I approach writing lesbian romance. Though marriage between two women has been accessible in certain states for several years, it's different now that all of us can celebrate. Not every romance ends on bended knee, but it sure is nice to have that be a genuine possibility.

I'm grateful to my editor, Katherine V. Forrest, for pointing out all the places where "it was in my head but not on the page." Fingers crossed that I've filled in all the gaps. Thanks also to the rest of my cleanup crew—Jenny, Karen and all the staff at Bella.

Lastly, I'm so happy for the chance to give a big shout-out to JJ Crabb, who steps up every single time I offer something for a charitable donation. Her generous response on my behalf to the Starship Children's Hospital in New Zealand is an inspiration. I love knowing people like JJ read my books.

PROLOGUE

Ellis Rowanbury snatched the leather folio from the waiter's hand before he could drop it on the knotty pine table. "Don't even think about it, Roxanne."

Her friend leaned back and folded her arms. "My, my. When did you get so aggressive?"

"You left me no choice. You've paid...what? Three months in a row?"

"If you say so. I certainly don't keep track." Roxanne pulled a compact from her purse and touched up her lips with pink gloss that gave the outward impression she was soft. Nothing could be further from the truth. "They probably wouldn't appreciate a wrestling match over the bill in the middle of their dining room."

On the contrary, Ellis thought. Who wouldn't enjoy watching a pair of women in high heels get down in a hair-pulling catfight? Smart money would be on Roxanne because her hair wasn't long enough to pull. And because she'd cheat.

Ellis fished a small stack of bills from her wallet and tucked them inside the folio, smiling with the knowledge that it was *her* money, not part of what Bruce gave her for the household budget. "Did you catch my feature last month on chiropractors? I was amazed at what they're treating these days with spine adjustments." She ticked the ailments off on her fingers: "Obesity…depression…addiction. I had no idea."

"I have a copy of *Vista* on my credenza. I'll check it out when I get back to my office."

As if someone in Roxanne Sternberg's position had an extra minute in her busy day to peruse a city magazine. It was a testament to their thirty-year friendship that she still made time once a month to meet at Buck's in Woodside, halfway between her Silicon Valley office and Ellis's home in San Francisco.

Ellis looked forward to their monthly dates, relishing the chance to step out in a stylish business dress or suit, something she didn't often have occasion to do. Her part-time work for the magazine was freelance. There was no reason to dress up when she worked at home, but she knew Roxanne would be decked out as usual in something that said power.

"Your assignments always sound so interesting, Ellis." This coming from a woman whose job title was Vice President of Leisure Innovations at a dot-com company. "I'd give anything to have the freedom you have. Other than a frantic trip to Beijing, I haven't been out of my office in a month."

It was hard to feel sorry for Roxanne. At forty-seven, she was a millionaire several times over, thanks to timely career moves that always included stock options. Petite with dark hair and brown eyes, she hardly looked her years. Plus she had perks that added to her cosmopolitan image—a personal shopper who dressed her in the finest career wear, a trainer who came to her house, even a woman who did her nails in her office while she busied herself with conference calls.

A glamorous, high-powered career had been one of Ellis's dreams too, but she wouldn't have lasted a year in a pressure-cooker job like Roxanne's. Deadlines didn't bother her. Nor did she mind taking on intellectual challenges. Where she would have struggled was with demanding personalities. Too easily intimidated, too quick to defer—the total opposite of Roxanne, who took on everyone in her path.

Ellis was better suited to freelance work, where she rarely encountered office politics or power struggles. Still, she could have had a successful career at *Vista*. With easygoing publisher Gil Martino on her side, she could have been editor by now had she not stepped away to raise her children.

"Less than a year to go, Roxie. Then Allison's off to college and I go back to full-time at the magazine. Gil's been begging me to do that for years but I promised myself I'd wait till my last one finished high school."

"You should go for it. Allison will be fine. She's a tough cookie…like her Aunt Roxie."

In many ways, that was true. Allison had long looked up to Roxanne as a prime example of how women could rule the workplace.

"I can't. I promised myself to be there for her. Every volleyball match, every drama club skit. I did it for the boys, so it wouldn't be fair to bail on her."

"Who do you think you're kidding, Ellis? You're only following her around so she won't sneak off and get anything else pierced."

The studs in her daughter's chin and brow had horrified her, but at least the holes would close once she outgrew her rebellious phase. "Believe it or not, I can handle her putting holes in her body. It's the tattoos I'm worried about. I've put my foot down over that one but she's counting the days till she turns eighteen. That happens in May."

"Just don't let them spell something wrong. She'll end up going viral in one of those Internet memes everybody posts on Facebook."

Ellis groaned with exasperation. "Let's just hope she doesn't try to outdo Jeremy." Her son's neck and left arm looked like someone had left their crayons on a hot sidewalk.

"At least you have one child who hasn't defiled his body."

That would be Jonathan, Jeremy's fraternal twin, younger by eighteen minutes and his polar opposite in every way imaginable. A political science major at Stanford, he was bent on getting into law school.

Roxanne stood and straightened her gray sheath dress, then swung a blazer around her shoulders. "I'd give anything to stay and hang out, but I have a call this afternoon with the Tokyo office." She dropped a twenty-dollar bill on the table. "You can give this to Pete for me."

Ellis collected their leftovers in a cardboard container the waiter had left behind. For the past several years, she'd been feeding Pete Proctor, the homeless man who'd claimed the corner of Diamond Heights Boulevard and Gold Mine Drive.

As they left, she returned the polite smiles of two middle-aged men, appreciating the fact that, even as she and her friend neared the half-century mark, they still turned heads.

"Our time always goes by so fast, Roxie. What are you doing for Thanksgiving?"

"Mom wants me to come to Palm Springs, but I don't think I can stand being with Arthur all day. He'll have Fox News blaring in the background."

"Ugh. I don't blame you. Jonathan's started watching that crap too. We make him go to his room and close the door."

"Amazing. You and Bruce are about the most liberal rich people I know. I can't imagine how that nonsense crept into his head in the first place."

Their liberal roots had been planted as students at Cal-Berkeley in the early nineteen-eighties. The rich part came much later through Bruce's work as an investment planner. Still, they were hardly rich by Bay Area standards, not with all the dot-com billionaires buying up San Francisco's real estate.

Ellis donned her sunglasses as they stepped outside. "Come to the City. I'm doing a big turkey. We can hide in the kitchen and drink wine."

"Now you're talking. Let me look at my calendar and make sure I don't have a call to Mumbai or something. They don't celebrate the Pilgrims, you know."

Walking through the parking lot arm in arm, they reached Ellis's car first, a black Lexus SUV.

"Is this new?"

"You know how Bruce is about buying cars, whether we need one or not. I'd just gotten used to which button did what on the Escalade."

"Hard to begrudge a husband who spoils you like that." They shared a final hug, and as Roxanne walked away, she shouted over her shoulder, "If there were more Bruces in the world, I might have gotten married too."

Roxanne was already married—to her job. Yet another reason Ellis couldn't handle having such an ambitious career. Bruce wasn't perfect, but he'd always supported everything she did job-wise, including her decision to turn the sitting room in their master suite into a home office. She was happy with her life just the way it was.

As the driver's seat hummed to her programmed position, she lowered the mirror on her visor to check her appearance. No wonder the men had smiled. Like Roxanne, she wore her years well. Though she had to work at it—facials, waxing, moisturizers…whatever it took to keep her skin looking young. She'd been blessed with thick dark hair, which Antoine had tinted with auburn highlights and cut in a long bob that curled into a point below her chin. She still was a woman men noticed.

With a touch to her steering console, she activated her phone. "Call Bruce." He'd like hearing that Roxanne was considering joining them for Thanksgiving. As regional manager for investment giant Kerner-Swift, he found her expertise on the world market for technology invaluable.

Four rings, then voice mail. Probably in a meeting.

The ride home was gorgeous along Interstate 280. Hills and meadows on both sides, green from the autumn rain. The Crystal Springs Reservoir sparkling in the sun, the San Francisco International Airport peeking through the trees from Millbrae. As far as she was concerned, the Peninsula was the most beautiful place on earth—except for the traffic, which was building as she approached the City.

Another button on her wheel turned on the AM radio, set to a local news channel with traffic reports every ten minutes.

"...dozens of emergency vehicles swarming the area. No other traffic is being allowed in at this time."

Jolted by the urgency in the announcer's tone, she turned up the volume.

"If you're just joining us, police are on the scene of what they're calling an office shooting in the Financial District. Witnesses report hearing shots inside the Transamerica Pyramid, but it's unclear at this time exactly which floors are involved. Tenants of the Pyramid include Merrill Lynch, URS Corporation, Kerner-Swift..."

In a panic, she redialed Bruce, only to get his voice mail again. "Bruce, I'm just hearing the news. Call me the second you get this. I mean it!"

Traffic had slowed to a crawl, pinning her on the freeway more than half a mile before an exit that could take her close to downtown.

The City had suffered this horror before, twenty-some years ago when Gian Ferri had killed eight people at the Pettit-Martin law firm. She and Bruce had been vacationing with their toddler twins at his mother's house in Napa, and she'd felt no guilt at all for being grateful it was someone else and not Kerner-Swift.

The bulletins came quickly. Conflicting reports of casualties. Still nothing on the specific location inside the building.

At the risk of missing an update, she placed a third call, this time to the main number at Kerner-Swift. That too went to voice mail.

"Of course," she said aloud. "They've probably evacuated the whole building."

"The scene here is still tense, Marty. I'm calling from behind a police barricade that's been set up on Jackson Street. What I can tell you is that heavily armed SWAT teams entered the building about ninety minutes ago. They've been clearing floors and evacuating the occupants through the emergency exits. I spoke moments ago with one of the workers who says she was trapped in her office for over an hour. She reported hearing sporadic bursts of gunfire..."

The sound of sirens in the background drowned out the reporter's words.

"Tamara, did the woman you spoke with indicate which floor the shots were coming from? I know our listeners are anxious about loved ones who work in the Pyramid."

"Excuse me, Marty...we're just seeing several emergency medical teams rush inside the building. That would seem to indicate the shooting has stopped."

"Goddammit! What floor?" Ellis screamed and pounded her steering wheel.

She was midway through another call to Bruce when she had a horrible thought: What if he'd been hiding from the shooter and his ringing cell phone had given his position away?

"Marty, police are now confirming that at least six people have been killed, but that number may go higher. Also, they're saying the shooter is reportedly among the dead. No word yet on whether he was killed by police or took his own life. SWAT teams continue to sweep the building in search of victims and people who may have been hiding throughout this horrifying episode."

Her hands shook so hard she could barely hold the wheel. Somehow she made it to the freeway exit and raced through the Mission District to Market Street. Too much traffic. A jog up Gough and she could take California all the way downtown.

With the assurance the shooting was over, she dialed again, and nearly cried with relief when the call connected after only two rings. "Bruce? Thank God! I've been listening to the news. Were you anywhere near the shooting?"

"Hello?" It was a woman's voice, unfamiliar. "This is Sergeant Lynn McLeod of the San Francisco Police Department. To whom am I speaking?"

CHAPTER ONE

"Uh-oh." The last thing Summer Winslow expected to see in her quiet apartment complex on a Sunday night was flashing blue lights. With above-average rents, River Woods was an enclave of young families saving for the down payment on their first home, white-collar professionals just starting out, and established singles like herself, stuck between relationships and not ready to commit to another mortgage.

So which of her neighbors also represented the criminal element?

Courtney Meyer stopped her car near the gate. "I'll let you out here if that's okay. I don't want to get mixed up in that."

"I hear you," Summer said. "Thanks for the ride."

"Thanks for the movie. Next time it's my treat."

She hobbled across the parking lot, careful not to put weight on her pinky toe, which she'd broken two weeks earlier in a game of Twister with her friends. The sidewalk in front of the adjacent building was blocked by the ramp of a moving truck. She noted dismally that her new neighbors, the ones unloading the truck, were young, early twenties. That likely would mean friends, parties, cars and noise.

The Sacramento Police Department cruiser was parked behind her car, but it was the sight of the familiar Jeep Cherokee in a nearby guest space that set her on edge. What did Rita hope to accomplish by showing up uninvited? She couldn't possibly think she'd be welcome, not after their last confrontation.

Cringing at the obnoxious flashing lights, she continued gingerly toward her door. As she passed Rita's car, she anticipated the face-off.

No, you can't come in. No, I don't want to talk.

A police officer intercepted her, shining a flashlight into her face. "Excuse me, are you Summer Winslow?"

She looked away to avoid the glare and only then noticed Rita sitting in the backseat of the cruiser. *Shit.* So that's why he was here. What had she done? "I am."

"And do you know Rita Finnegan?"

For an instant, she considered saying no. "I'm afraid so. What has she done?"

The muffled sound of Rita yelling interrupted his reply. Clearly she was under the mistaken impression they could hear her plainly through the rolled-up windows of the cruiser.

Summer knew in an instant she was drunk. Her wavy red hair had come loose from its tie and was hanging around her face, streaked with mascara from her tears.

The stone-faced officer drew her away from the car, ostensibly to get out of Rita's earshot. "We got a complaint from one of your neighbors that she was banging on your door and yelling. Some pretty bad language, apparently. She told me she lived here and lost her key. Your neighbor didn't think that was right."

Oh, the temptation. If she told the truth—that Rita was her ex and was stalking her—then he might haul her to jail for the night, which would serve her right. As much as that would have pleased her, she couldn't let it go that far. Rita worked as an auditor for the State of California, and an arrest could get her in a lot of trouble.

Still, a part of her wondered if it would take something as drastic as getting arrested for Rita to finally see herself as Summer did. After fifteen years of sobriety, she'd convinced herself her drinking was under control. *It's about moderation, Summer.* Except moderate drinkers didn't get rip-roaring drunk at least once a month, and they didn't end up in the back of police cars.

"Let me make this easy for you," the officer said, dropping the businesslike tone in favor of a folksy cadence. "It's obvious your friend's been drinking. Now I didn't actually see her drive so I can't charge her with DUI, but I can't take a chance of her getting back behind the wheel tonight. If you're willing to take responsibility, I'll release her to you. But *do not* let her drive."

She didn't want to be responsible for Rita. That's why she'd walked away after twenty-one years together. Caught between a rock and a hard place, she persuaded him to let her make a call. She'd put Rita's fate in the hands of their mutual friend, Queenie Sullivan. If Queenie thought she needed a night in jail, so be it.

"Jesus," Queenie said, echoing Summer's frustration. "I had no idea she'd end up at your place. She was over here late this afternoon. Sam told me she smelled alcohol on her breath, but she wasn't drunk." It was clear she didn't want to be dragged into this.

"She's plastered now and sitting in the back of a police car. Apparently she's been outside my apartment screaming at me for the last half hour. I was at the movies with Courtney. She must have seen my car and figured I wasn't answering the door. No wonder my neighbors called the cops."

"What do you expect me to do?"

Queenie and her wife, Sam Lotti, were probably the only ones who cared enough about Rita to consider the consequences. "I need you to come over here and drive her home. I'll follow and bring you back."

"Why can't you take her?"

Limping along the sidewalk as she paced, Summer held up a finger to let the impatient-looking officer know she'd only be another minute. "You know I can't be around her when she's like this. Not anymore. I've had it. There's no point in talking to her. She's too drunk to be rational. Besides, that's what she wants—to talk to me—and if she gets it this time, she'll do it again."

Queenie groaned, but Summer knew she agreed with her. They all knew Rita too well.

"Man, I wish you guys could work this out. It's getting to be such a drag."

Summer decided not to push back on that one. She was well aware how inconvenient it was for their friends to arrange parties and get-togethers, always having to be careful not to invite both of them. The only way they'd ever "work it out" would be for Rita to get professional help. Even then, the best anyone could hope for civility. Their romance was over.

"Look, my only other option is to let the police take her away. I'm okay with that if you are."

After a string of muttered expletives, Queenie agreed to the deal.

As Summer waited for the officer to escort the stumbling Rita from the patrol car to the passenger seat of her Jeep, she strolled along the sidewalk to get another look at the moving van next door. A woman walked out of the apartment, apparently to retrieve something from her car, a black luxury SUV. From the golden-hued lights in the parking lot, she appeared to be older… Summer's age, perhaps. Maybe this was her new neighbor, not the youngsters. Either way, it made for a lousy first impression to have a police car in the apartment complex.

The whole episode was embarrassing as hell. Which of her neighbors had called it in? Rita had a foul mouth, especially when she was drinking, so it must have been quite a show.

The woman, only twenty feet away, glanced in her direction to find her staring, and momentarily froze.

"Sorry about this," Summer said. If only she could add that it wouldn't happen again. Unfortunately, Rita was too unpredictable to guarantee it.

She returned to the Jeep, where the officer met her with the keys. "Hold onto these, and hide them from her when you get her home. You can call her in the morning and tell her where they are."

"Wait, you're not leaving her with me," she pleaded. "Can't you wait until my friend gets here?"

He shook his head. "She just threw up in the back of my cruiser. I need to get it cleaned out before it sinks into the upholstery."

If history was an indicator, that actually was good news. Summer tentatively approached the passenger side of the Jeep and confirmed that Rita had passed out.

* * *

Eighteen-year-old Allison, now a freshman at UC-Davis, crammed the kitchen drawer full of tea towels, potholders and linen napkins with no regard for how they wrinkled. Not surprising, since she handled her clothes the same way. Her long blond hair was pulled into a ponytail and looped through the back of a denim ball cap that matched her ragged jeans. Every time she raised her arms, her T-shirt rose to reveal a dark green vine crawling diagonally from her hip, its edges still red from the trauma. The tattoo she'd always wanted.

"You should sleep under your mattress, Mom. That would give you an extra layer of protection from flying bullets."

Her brother Jeremy snorted before covering his face.

"Stop it, both of you," Ellis snapped. Ever since the police car had pulled up out front, they'd been teasing her about her new crime-ridden neighborhood. For all she knew, they were right. "It's probably some kind of domestic issue. Those are just as dangerous as drug deals."

"I didn't see anyone get arrested. The cop let that woman go."

It didn't matter to Ellis. Civilized people controlled their behavior. They certainly didn't drag their dirty laundry out for everyone to see.

Jeremy swung his colorful arm around her shoulder and squeezed. "I'm sure it's not that bad. At least your neighbor had the courtesy to come over and apologize."

They'd actually only met in passing. The woman had looked embarrassed.

Bruno Peretti, Jeremy's boyfriend of two years, joined them from the master bedroom, where he'd been hooking up her second TV. "Just be glad she was nice about it. Some people don't care about their neighbors at all." Though he worked as a legislative aide at the capitol, in his free time he always wore shorts—regardless of the weather—and an open shirt with a T-shirt underneath. He was clean shaven and buff from working out.

Ellis liked Bruno, as he was a calming influence on her son, who'd asserted his wild side in high school as a way of grappling with challenges to his masculinity. Since moving in with Bruno after dropping out of college two years ago, Jeremy had stopped adding tattoos and given up his motorcycle.

They made an attractive couple. Jeremy took after her side of the family. He had her father's receding hairline and kept his hair short so no one would notice when he started to go bald. Blue eyes like hers, and he even had the same brown spot in the iris of one. Though he'd been raised in San Francisco, he loved Sacramento and had every intention of making his life here.

Ellis was resigned to her move from the City, where she'd lived since graduating from Berkeley twenty-six years ago. With her finances in utter disarray after Bruce's death—and two kids still in college—she'd jumped at Gil's offer to be assistant editor of *Sacramento Vista*, an offshoot of his San Francisco franchise. She'd desperately needed the steady income. Plus it was cheaper to live in the capital, and she was closer to Jeremy and Allison. However, it was farther from Jonathan, who was now a senior at Stanford.

She peered out the window and was relieved to find the parking lot clear of trouble. "River Woods might turn out to be a little dicey, but I guess it's better than the Tenderloin."

"Or the Financial District," Allison muttered.

"Not funny," Jeremy said sharply.

"That was irony, dipshit. Look it up."

"Three months in college and now you know everything."

"Yeah, so I can drop out now, just like you did."

"Enough, you two," Ellis said. She was used to playing referee between Jeremy and his brother, but Allison rarely pushed anyone's buttons.

The shooting had changed all of them, but it had been especially hard on her daughter in her final year of high school. Spurts of anger, extended bouts of self-pity. Even with a fresh start in college, she was still struggling to escape the nightmare.

Jeremy too had suffered with depression, but Bruno steered him into a community counseling program and stood by his side with comfort and support. Only Jonathan had managed to hold it together, losing himself in his studies.

"I think we've done enough damage for one day," Ellis said. "That's everything off the truck. Let's call it a night."

Boxes of clothes, dishes and miscellaneous household items remained stacked in the small living room, but she didn't want anyone else putting those things away—she might never find them again. Besides, she had plenty of time on her hands after work and no extra cash to go out, even if she had somewhere to go. Tomorrow was the first official day of her grind toward retirement.

Allison immediately slung her backpack over her shoulder, as if she'd been waiting hours for permission to quit. "Can you take me back to campus, Mom? And I could use a few extra bucks if you have it."

Before she could answer, Bruno spoke up. "We can take you, but we need to swing by and drop off the truck."

After something between a whine and a groan, Allison slogged toward the door like a child being marched to the principal's office.

"Hold on, honey. I'll get you some spending money. Jeremy? Bruno?"

"None for us, Mom. We're good."

She'd figure out another way to thank the boys for their help. A home-cooked dinner, or maybe Jeremy's all-time favorite oatmeal raisin cookies. Allison had gone vegan and was too picky to feed. She wanted cold hard cash.

Ellis walked back to her bedroom for her purse and immediately noted her next task was getting sheets on the bed so she'd have a place to sleep. Though it was only nine thirty, she needed to be fresh for her first day at her new job.

"You ought to make time to come see Mom on the weekends," Jeremy said, his voice carrying clearly all the way down the hall. "I know you're busy at school, but she needs us right now."

"I see her all the time. Jon's the one who can't be bothered."

"I'll talk to him too. We all have to step up. I'm worried about her. This is a big change. She's done everything for us but nobody's been there for her."

She felt guilty for listening but the conversation was mesmerizing. A woman of forty-eight had no business expecting her grown children to take responsibility for her.

Allison sniffed loudly, a sign she was ready to burst into tears, something she'd done often since the shooting.

"I know, Allie. It's been harder on you than anybody. But you're going to love college. Put those dweebs from Balboa High in the rearview mirror."

"It's already easier…just being away from there." Normally she pushed back against the boys when they tried to give her advice, but there was nothing in her voice this time that gave off defiance.

"And I'll try to slip you some money. It won't be much, but you can't keep going back to Mom, not till they figure out the settlement."

That was enough. She couldn't let Jeremy take over her obligations, no matter how strapped she was for funds. It wasn't his fault the lawyers were taking their sweet time with the negotiations.

"Here you go, sweetie. Eighty bucks."

"I don't need that much. Just twenty." She gave her brother a sidelong glance. "Or forty."

"Take it all. And now I want both of you to do me a big favor. I need some space. I know I'm closer now and you're going to be tempted to drop in. But how about giving me a couple of weeks to get myself sorted out here? Make some friends, learn my way around, get a new routine. Can you do that for me?"

Jeremy looked surprised. "Are you sure, Mom?"

"Absolutely. I'll call if I need help with anything. But I want all of you here for Christmas dinner. No excuses." She shooed the three of them out and walked with them to the truck, rubbing her arms against the night chill as they drove away.

At the building next door, a car pulled up where the police car had been earlier. Two women got out, and one of them left immediately in another car. Ellis recognized the other as the woman who'd apologized.

She'd turned to go back inside when the woman called out.

The sound of her approaching footsteps was firm, but uneven. Boots with heels, and she was limping.

Ellis paid closer attention this time. The woman had on jeans with a white shirt, its starched collar standing up and out of a dark pea coat. A nice look for someone her height, which she guessed at barely five feet. Light curly hair with wispy bangs she pushed from her eyes, and wire-rimmed glasses. It was only when she was a few feet away that Ellis noticed her age—late forties, she guessed. Not the scruffy sort she might have expected to be involved with the police.

"Hi, I'm Summer Winslow."

Ellis nodded. She didn't need friends who attracted trouble.

"Was it you who called the cops?"

"It was not."

"I guess that's good...except now I have to go find whoever it was so I can apologize to them too." She smiled sheepishly. "I'm sorry I made such a rotten first impression. That's not a normal thing, I swear. It's never happened before...and I hope to hell it never happens again."

What could she say? That it was all right? It wasn't. That it didn't bother her? It did.

"Anyway...I just wanted to tell you again that I was sorry. I think you'll like River Woods. Just hit the reset button tomorrow and start over."

It was rude to stand there in silence. The least she could do was acknowledge the woman's obvious embarrassment and pretend not to be judging her. This was her neighbor, someone she'd likely see again. "Thank you. I'll give that a try."

CHAPTER TWO

Sacramento Vista occupied the third floor of the Crawford Building, one of the oldest business complexes in the city. Situated only two blocks from the capitol, it was, at five stories, dwarfed by the office towers on K Street.

Ellis waited nervously in a hard vinyl chair for the official start of her workday. A close examination of her nails revealed chips in the pink polish from handling the cardboard boxes as she unpacked. In the old days, she'd have dashed out to her manicurist for a quick touch-up, but her budget didn't cover such frivolities anymore.

Her first full-time job since she left the San Francisco magazine on maternity leave twenty-four years ago. Assistant editor, though she had no clear idea what duties that entailed. Her anxiety had more to do with meeting her coworkers and bosses than tackling a new job.

Gil had offered the position when it became obvious she'd never support herself on a staff writer's salary in San Francisco, one of the most expensive housing markets in the country. A two-bedroom apartment like the one she'd rented in River Woods would have cost four times as much in the City, five times if it included parking.

She'd always considered Sacramento a cow town. Now it was home. To be fair, most places were sleepy when held up to a world class city like San Francisco. But she was committed to the move. She'd get to know the capital in short order once she immersed herself in the magazine. It would be fine. She'd *make* it fine.

"Ellis Keene?" A curvaceous Hispanic woman, her long hair dyed burgundy, appeared in the hallway behind the receptionist. Her face was blank, and she made no effort at eye contact. "I'm Angie Alvarez. I'll be your supervisor. Follow me."

It was odd to hear her maiden name spoken aloud after all these years. Though she'd used it professionally for her *Vista* articles, it was only in preparation for her move to Sacramento that she'd made the legal change, right down to her social security card. All to avoid having to talk with strangers about the shooting. How long would it take for the world to forget?

The hallway led to a large room of cubicles with windowed offices lining the outer walls. Many of the nameplates on the office doors included their job titles. *Advertising Manager*, *Creative Director*, *Finance Officer*. Around the corner, the offices got bigger, but Alvarez steered her into a labyrinth to a cubicle, naked but for the dust on the gray laminate desk and a 49ers mug with a lipstick ring.

"This is you." She yanked open a drawer containing pens, pencils and paper clips. "Supplies are here."

No computer, no phone. Not even a file organizer.

"And whom do I see for my assignments?"

"Nobody. They'll come to you." Alvarez scurried across the hall to a larger cubicle bearing her name and returned with two document baskets. "I'll put the copy in your in-basket. Once you verify everything in it, you put it in the other and I'll pick it up."

So assistant editor was another name for fact checker. Fine, she'd be the best fact checker *Sacramento Vista* ever had. "I suppose I'll need some reference materials. A style manual. A computer, of course, with Internet access. And a phone."

Alvarez shook her head. "There's a computer you can use in the conference room. That'll have to do until we get another one in the budget."

Left alone in the tiny space, Ellis took a seat in the armless office chair, immediately noticing that it wobbled. Ignoring the fact that she was wearing nylons and a skirt, she knelt on the carpeted floor and flipped the chair upside down to find the loose connection. Using a dime, she tightened the bolts that attached the seat to its stem.

The din of conversations in the surrounding cubicles didn't concern her. She'd managed to work in a house with three teenagers amidst their video games, music and friends, so she could work anywhere.

She tested her seat again. Workable.

Alvarez reappeared with a cardboard box of miscellaneous desk implements. "Take whatever you want from here and leave the box in the break room. But first, Marcie wants to see you."

She was shown to a corner office, where a woman sat with her back to the door as she talked on the phone. The expansive windows beyond afforded an enviable view of the tree-lined street below with its pedestrian walk and light rail. Had Ellis stayed at *San Francisco Vista* all these years, she might even be editor by now, and looking out on the Bay from a corner office on Telegraph Hill.

She seated herself in a pedestal armchair that was more style than comfort. All of the furniture around her was modern, including the L-shaped desk of black graphite and glass. At the far end was an iMac; at the near end, a laptop. And an iPad. No wonder there weren't enough computers to go around.

"That's great. I'll see you Thursday in LA." The woman spun around as she signed off. Long straight hair of champagne blond, understated makeup, and wearing a black wrap dress that had to be a size zero. She couldn't have been a day older than thirty-five. Marcie Wagstaff, executive editor. Her boss. Everyone's boss.

"Ms. Wagstaff, I'm so happy to finally meet you. Gil has told me wonderful things about your work."

"Call me Marcie," she said, flashing perfect teeth in what appeared to be a genuine smile. "Gil says good things about you too. It's obvious he really likes you."

"The feeling's mutual. I've actually been with *Vista* quite a long time…in San Francisco, that is. I like to think I know the magazine really well, so I'm eager to help in any way I can."

Marcie nodded along, still smiling. "Arts and special features. That's the thrust of San Francisco. And LA has the entertainment industry covered, but we're the capital. Here we have a special focus on state politics. Do you follow the statehouse?"

Ellis was embarrassed to be caught flatfooted. "I…I can't say I do. But I will."

"Here, take this." She scribbled a note on a pad and tore off the top sheet. "That takes you to California-dot-gov, the state website. Get to know the departments, the legislative committees, the high-ranking legislators and the cabinet. Their names will come up a lot in our stories. Photos too. Nothing riles me more than getting a call from an assemblyman who's mad because we spelled his name wrong."

Yes, she would go at once and memorize the organization tree…on her nonexistent computer.

"And you should go to the archive and read Rex Brenneman." She snatched the sheet back and made another note. "He's our political columnist. There isn't one thing that goes on in the capitol that he doesn't know about."

Rex Brenneman, check. The archive on her nonexistent web account. Fortunately, she already was somewhat familiar with his work, since it was syndicated in the *San Francisco Chronicle*.

"We welcome your contributions. I really like that you're older than most of the people working here. We need that perspective from time to time, especially when we're reaching out to our mature readers."

Mature. So that's what the Gen-Xers were being called now that the Millennials were rising into positions of power. Ellis didn't know whether to feel revered or humiliated.

"We value all of our readers, Ellis, and our employees too. Assistant editors aren't required to attend the editorial meetings, but if you have any story ideas, feel free to pass them up through Angie. And let me know if there's anything you need."

"There is one thing." It was worth a shot to ask. "It would help if I had a computer on my desk. I understand there's a shortage, but maybe I could get it on the budget list?"

"Pfft." Marcie waved her hand dismissively and spun around to pull the plug on her iMac. "Take this one. I never use it anyway."

Ellis returned to her cubicle balancing the computer, keyboard and mouse. Along the way, she noted the outdated hardware on the desks of her new colleagues. Mismatched peripherals and low-resolution monitors.

She was setting up her prize when Alvarez returned.

"I got you the phone from the break room. Your extension is—" Her jaw dropped. "Is that Marcie's iMac?"

"It was. She gave it to me."

"That's not fair."

It didn't seem fair to Ellis either, but she wasn't going to look a gift horse in the mouth. Nor would she offer to trade with someone else. "I can't do my job without a computer. And since Marcie gave me a couple of links to study, she must have thought I needed one too. It's possible she'll order another and want this one back."

Alvarez's lips pursed in an angry pout. "Nothing personal, but I don't get why they hired you without even giving me a say. I have two copy editors who already paid their dues. Both of them deserved to be promoted instead of bringing in somebody new. Obviously you know somebody pretty important if you didn't even have to interview. And now you go in there and walk out with the best computer in the whole office. You're already making more than anyone else on the line when you haven't proved yourself at all."

That explained the resentful vibe she'd felt since the moment she arrived. A showdown with Angie Alvarez, who apparently was her supervisor, didn't strike her as a good idea.

But she wasn't going to shrink from the accusation that she was unfit for her job. Especially since their conversation had caused everyone around her to go quiet.

"You have every right to be upset if they left you out of the loop, Ms. Alvarez. But rest assured, I *have* proven myself. I was copy editing for *Vista* in San Francisco before you were born, and I have at least three hundred bylines of my own. That kind of experience usually warrants a higher salary than the one I'm making now, but you don't hear me complaining." She lowered her voice to keep the others from overhearing the rest. "And I'm sorry you felt disrespected about my hiring, but I had nothing to do with how anyone treated you. I'm very glad to be here, and my number one concern is making the magazine the best it can be. I hope you won't work against me."

Alvarez stared at her in silence for a long, tense moment before dropping a document on her desk. "There's your first assignment. And everybody calls me Angie."

* * *

Summer settled into a steady pace on the recumbent exercise bike, the only machine in the fitness center that gave her a decent cardio workout without causing her toe to hurt. Not as good overall as the elliptical but better than she'd expected.

She worked rigid hours—eight to five—and always hurried home to get the jump on others who tried to squeeze in a workout before dinner. She had the fitness center to herself until the woman she'd met the night before came in and claimed a treadmill at the far end of the room. Not even a nod, which Summer tried not to take personally, since the woman hadn't actually looked in her direction.

Nice body from the back. Firm calves and butt, pulled even tighter in spandex leggings. After about five minutes, she removed her warm-up jacket to show off broad shoulders that rippled with every step. Like Summer, she was dedicated to her workout. No headphones, no TV, no cell phone.

Unlike Gene Steele, a hefty man in his sixties who appeared right on schedule at six o'clock sharp. As usual, he grabbed the TV remote, took the treadmill next to their new neighbor and turned on Fox News.

Within seconds, the woman stopped walking and scanned the room, seeing Summer for the first time. The only other cardio machine was the elliptical next to her bike, and it was clear she was weighing which was the lesser of two evils—Fox News or her hoodlum neighbor. She chose the latter.

Summer decided in that instant she liked this woman and wanted to be her friend.

"Obnoxious, isn't it?" she said with a wry smile.

"Such utter nonsense. Amazing how quickly your view of someone is set when you see them hanging on Bill O'Reilly's every word."

Or how quickly it was set by seeing a police car in someone's driveway. Either of those was a good clue in most cases. This lady just happened to be wrong about the police car.

"That's Gene. I've learned to stay on this end if I want to work out at six. But he only goes for twenty minutes, so you can get back to the treadmill when he's done."

"Good to know." She began pumping her arms and legs in alternate rhythm, quickly reaching the same pace she'd managed on the treadmill. "I'm Ellis. Ellis Keene. Just moved over from San Francisco."

"Great city, isn't it? I was born there. In fact, that's how I got my name. Summer…since I was born during the Summer of Love."

Her admission brought a hint of a smile.

"I don't mean to keep beating a dead horse, but I really am sorry about last night. I was as shocked as everyone else when I got home. That was my ex in the cop car. We split up last year because of her drinking, and what does she do? She gets drunk and comes over here to make an ass of herself. How's that for irony?"

Ellis showed no reaction, which Summer took to mean she wasn't helping her cause.

"These days I have to ask myself what I ever saw in her."

Still no response. Maybe she was put off by the mention of a girlfriend, but that was hard to believe of someone from San Francisco. Especially one who knew Fox News was nonsense.

"Did you get everything moved in?"

"It's all there, but don't ask me where."

"From the looks of it, you had lots of help. I couldn't tell at first who was moving in, you or one of the kids." Were they her kids, or people she'd hired?

No reply. In fact, Ellis picked up her pace on the elliptical and appeared to be tuning out the conversation. She couldn't have made her disinterest much plainer.

Perhaps it had nothing to do with the police, Summer thought. It might very well be that Ellis Keene was the sort of person who kept to herself. Or maybe she was slow to open up to new people. Whatever the reason, she didn't bolt back to the treadmill when Gene left, and Summer took that as a good sign.

Her legs were burning from the resistance on the bike, and she slowed her pace to start her cool-down. She'd already stayed ten minutes beyond her usual workout, but hadn't wanted to leave while there was still a chance her new neighbor would talk to her.

Ellis began to ease up as well. Though her face was red from exertion, she didn't seem to be struggling for a breath. Definitely not a stranger to the fitness room. "Is there a place where I can recycle my cardboard boxes?" she asked.

Another reason to like her. She hated Fox News and she recycled.

They walked out of the fitness center together as Summer relayed the directions to the nearest recycling center. "But you have to break them down."

"I'd have to do that anyway. Otherwise they wouldn't fit in my—" Ellis's face fell as she stopped short.

Summer followed her gaze to a black Lexus SUV, its rear tire fully flattened. "Oh, that sucks. Time to call Triple A."

"Except I don't have Triple A."

Here was her chance to make a better impression. "I do. Let me call them."

"Can you even do that? I thought it had to be *your* car."

"It can be anybody as long as I'm here when they arrive. I get three service calls a year, and I've only used one. And it's December."

Ellis shook her head warily. "I don't know...what if something happens and you end up needing it for yourself?"

"Then you can pay me back. Wait here. I'll go call them and get my card."

She hobbled to her apartment as quickly as she could. Her good deed wasn't only to make up for Rita's disturbance. A new neighbor in need of a hand...she was glad for the chance to come to the rescue. Once they got past their rocky start, they might even be friends.

* * *

Ellis licked guacamole from her fingers in what Summer had called the best kept secret in Sacramento, a hole-in-the-wall taqueria less than half a mile from River Woods. She'd offered to treat as a way of saying thanks for the AAA, and couldn't believe her luck—two giant burritos for just eight bucks.

The tiny cafe had only four small tables, as most of its business appeared to be carryout. And nearly all of it was Latino. Summer assured her that was its stamp of approval.

Summer had finished her burrito and was tipped back precariously in her chair, explaining her job with the California Department of Health and Human Services. "I keep track of programs that serve the homeless. The state gives out grants to shelters and soup kitchens. I'm there to keep everybody honest, make sure they aren't spending your tax dollars on bonuses and perks for the higher-ups. Basically your run-of-the-mill paper pusher. Twenty-six years with the state. That pretty much makes me a lifetime bureaucrat."

"Are you from Sacramento originally? Oh, stupid question. Summer of Love. That was what? Sixty-seven? Haight-Ashbury. That's quite a claim to fame."

"That's nothing. I'll have you know I was also at Woodstock. My mom has a picture of me sitting on Dad's shoulders with Jimi Hendrix on stage in the background."

The more they talked, the more she grudgingly came to realize she'd grossly misjudged Summer. There was nothing in her manner to imply she was prone to run-ins with the police. She was mild-mannered with a steady job, and had quickly come to her aid without asking for anything in return. Plus she was good company.

"My folks are old-time hippies," Summer went on. "Matter of fact, we lived in a commune in Mendocino until I was six. Then my grandfather died and left us a farm in Hollister. Just a small one. They grew organic herbs. Supplied all the best restaurants in the Bay Area. Not so much anymore though. Too much competition from the corporate farms. They're into artsy stuff now."

Chatty...and she had a natural look about her. Not the shaggy, tie-dyed hippie fashion of the Sixties. Just a casual style that suggested she didn't fuss much over how she appeared to others. Nor did she need to. Her blondish hair was graying naturally and she had a smooth complexion for someone her age. And the glasses were cute.

"Okay, you're looking at me funny," Summer said, "like I just told you I was from Mars."

Ellis laughed. No way would she confess to her musings. "No, I was just thinking how odd that I've lived in Northern California all my life and never met anyone who grew up in a commune. You'd think they'd be everywhere. How did your folks feel about you going to work for the Establishment?"

"I guess they were glad I went into social work instead of something like marketing, or God forbid, finance. To them, the Establishment meant the elite, the powerful. Still does. What I do is about helping people. Sharing the wealth. That tracks with their values."

Finance. She'd never hear that word again without thinking about Bruce, and she didn't want a casual conversation with a virtual stranger to devolve into a discussion of him. Her move to Sacramento was an opportunity to leave behind the horror of the shooting. She didn't know Summer well enough to talk about it, and besides, she couldn't stand to look at one more person who didn't know what to say.

"And what about you, Ellis? Where in Northern California?"

"My story isn't as interesting as yours, I'm afraid. Born and raised in Modesto. My dad worked in shipping at the Gallo winery and my mom was admissions coordinator at the junior college. They retired a few years ago and bought a gigantic motor home. Come November, they drive it down to a campground near Scottsdale. That's where they ride out their winters."

"Living the dream."

"*Their* dream. More power to them."

"What took you to the City? That's a big jump from Modesto."

She liked that Summer had called it the City, just like the locals. San Francisco deserved its lofty image.

"I majored in English lit at Berkeley and got my first job at *San Francisco Vista*, the magazine. Left after three years when I had the twins—my boys—but then I started freelancing again when Allison started school."

"Three kids. So you must have gotten married young."

It wasn't a question. More like an invitation to elaborate. At some point, she needed at least to mention Bruce. "Yes, my husband died a little over a year ago."

Summer frowned and reached over to pat her arm. "I'm so sorry."

Ellis didn't want to dwell on it. "It's been an adjustment. I think Sacramento will be good for me. One of my sons lives here, and my daughter's a freshman now at UC-Davis. That's Jeremy and Allison."

"I bet that's who I saw helping you last night."

"And Bruno. That's Jeremy's boyfriend." Her admission brought a huge grin, which wasn't surprising at all since Summer had mentioned a girlfriend.

"You have a gay son. How cool is that?"

"He's a wonderful young man. Calls himself a landscape designer...I think of him as a creative gardener. And he's probably my best chance for grandchildren because the other two insist they aren't interested."

They bused their table and walked out into the chilly night air to Ellis's car. She'd been tempted to trade her Lexus for something downmarket, but the boys had convinced her to hold onto it since it was already paid for. It was well built, Jonathan said, and good for another ten years at least. Perhaps by then she'd feel financially secure again.

"You remember how to get home from here?" Summer asked.

"I think so. Don't let me miss any turns."

"So now that I've introduced you to Julio's, do you forgive me for last night?"

"I suppose." Ellis chuckled. "And I guess this would be a good time for me to confess that I might have misjudged you."

"I'd like to think so, but I don't blame you for having your doubts. I freaked out too when I saw those blue lights. Next right."

She signaled and turned simultaneously. "And that was your ex-girlfriend?"

"Of twenty-one years...give or take all the times we split up and got back together. That's why she keeps coming around, I guess. Because I've always ended up taking her back. Not this time though. I'm done. In my lifetime, I've quit drinking, I've quit smoking. But Rita's always been the hardest to quit. Sometimes it feels like one step forward, two steps back."

That was a dynamic Ellis couldn't understand at all. If they'd broken up over and over, they must have fought with each other all the time. How could anyone live that way?

There were many aspects of her life with Bruce that were less than ideal, but very few had led to serious fights. Even disagreements were rare, since he didn't believe in overlap of responsibility. He handled their finances and made all the decisions about the house, while she managed their children and social life. That was their deal, and it settled potential conflicts before they could erupt.

While it had spared them the usual sources of friction for couples, the end result was in fact cliché—a wife left behind with little skill in managing money and a mountain of turmoil. It would have been far better had they shared responsibility for their finances through the years. Maybe then she wouldn't have been blindsided.

CHAPTER THREE

Ellis would have bet the farm the deep male voice outside her cubicle belonged to Rex Brenneman. It was serious, confident and even a touch acerbic. Just like his political columns, which she'd digested over the past three days.

He was chiding Angie about a change one of the assistant editors had made to his recent submission. "All I'm saying is her official title is director of the Lottery Commission, not commissioner. So it wasn't a correction. It was an *in*-correction."

"That isn't a word, Rex."

"Well it should be." He slapped the side of Ellis's cubicle in obvious frustration, and then swung around to look inside. His angry look faded instantly, replaced by an unmistakably flirtatious smile. He looked exactly like the small photo next to his byline, ruggedly handsome with brown hair parted on the side and a neatly trimmed mustache. He wore a tie with a brown leather bomber jacket, and in his hand was the trademark suede trilby from his photo. "Sorry. I didn't realize anyone was in this cubicle. You're new."

"I started on Monday," she said, rising from her chair.

"Please don't get up." He held out his left hand to shake and made a point of turning hers over as if checking for the presence of a wedding ring. "I'm Rex Brenneman, political writer. And you are?"

"Ellis Keene, assistant editor. And no, I wasn't the one who *in*-corrected your piece."

"I would have forgiven you anything," he said smoothly. Lowering his voice, he went on, "Nice to see they finally hired another adult. How did you end up in our merry little crew?"

"I wrote for *Vista* in San Francisco for years. Freelance... mostly features." She handed him one of her temporary business cards, on which the receptionist had typed her name and extension.

"I'm not seeing a cell number on this." His green eyes twinkled with anticipation.

She was hardly a stranger to men's come-ons, but this was the first time in nearly thirty years she found herself without a foolproof way to deflect their interest. It was unnerving to realize she was free to respond any way she wanted. Right now, that was with apprehension.

"I, uh...I check my messages regularly on that extension."

"Fair enough, then." He held her gaze for several seconds before finally stepping away.

Within moments, Angie came in to take his place, her eyes wide with dismay. "I can't believe he was flirting with you!"

She decided to take that as a commentary on his behavior rather than an assessment of her appeal to the opposite sex. "Is he always like that?"

"Never. The only time he ever talks to any of the lowly assistant editors is to complain. You must be his type."

Clearly he liked women his own age, and she was practically the only one in the office who fit that bill. The thought of dating again hadn't crossed her mind until this very moment. It would be crazy to go out with someone from her office, let alone a man who had her coworkers walking on eggshells.

"Do us all a favor and go out with him," Angie said. "Maybe he'll realize we're people too and start treating us with a little respect."

"Or we could have a terrible date and it could be worse."

"True dat."

Angie had softened over the past week, apparently convinced by Ellis's first assignments that she was more than capable of doing her job. In fact, she was making it a regular habit to ask Ellis's opinion on the other editors' work as well.

That goodwill wouldn't last long if her peers thought she was getting special favors just because Rex found her worthy of his attention. Roxanne always said it was harder to work with women than men because they were prone to focus more on the personal than the professional. Ellis had no desire to test that theory.

* * *

By virtue of seniority, Summer had an office with a window. Granted, it was the smallest office—and smallest window— on the entire third floor of the Health and Human Services building, but it was her own space. Best of all, it had a door to close out the hubbub of chatter and clacking keyboards. She'd decorated in a Southwestern motif with a Zapotec rug, two Gorman prints of Navajo women, and by her coveted window, a dreamcatcher. The space was cozy but serviceable for the mountain of paperwork that crossed her desk.

After five on a Friday afternoon, the third floor was a virtual ghost town. With her work put away until Monday, she passed the time searching Google for Bruce Keene's obituary. And feeling guilty for it. If Ellis had wanted her to know how her husband died, she would have told her. Not that it mattered. She'd found only one Bruce Keene in San Francisco, and he was very much alive.

The night before, she'd researched Ellis's bylines, getting literally dozens of hits on the *Vista* website alone. Her Facebook and Twitter accounts were purely promotional, linking only to her articles, and they hadn't been updated in over a year. Perhaps about the time her husband died. Something like that would upend a person's whole life.

Hearing footsteps in the hallway, she closed the search screen.

Alythea Cooper, her immediate supervisor and closest friend at work, appeared in her doorway. With her short Afro and vibrant jewelry, she looked at least a decade younger than her fifty years. "I'm giving you one last chance to back out of this, Summer. No questions asked."

"No way, I'm psyched. Bring it on."

A whistle brought the sound of a small stampede and the excited arrival of Alythea's grandchildren, six-year-old Nate and his sister Bree, four. A few steps behind was their mother, Nemy.

Summer opened her desk drawer to reveal a modest stash of candy, inviting the children to serve themselves.

"You'll be sorry you did that," Nemy said. "I've just gotten them down from their Halloween sugar highs. They're going to keep you up all night."

"We'll manage," Summer said. She'd known both kids since they were born and had babysat before. This was their first overnight stay, a plan to allow their mother and grandmother to go Christmas shopping. "I'm fixing sloppy joes for dinner, and I've got *The Princess and the Frog* set to go on Netflix. We're going to have a great time."

"If you hear an echo during the movie, it's Nate. He knows Prince Naveen's lines word for word."

Truth be told, she wasn't as enthusiastic as she let on, but there was nothing she wouldn't do for Alythea. The woman had seen her through tough times with Rita—several of them over the last ten years—serving not only as a sounding board, but as a well of courage and wisdom. If not for her support, Summer might still be stuck in that punishing cycle.

In the parking garage on the lower level, they moved Bree's booster seat into Summer's Mazda sedan. After repeated admonitions for both children to behave themselves, Alythea and Nemy left.

And Bree began to cry.

"Is something wrong? What is it?"

Her sobs worsened to wailing with still no explanation, and soon turned to hiccups. Nate tried to calm his sister, but she refused to be comforted.

The ten-minute ride to River Woods felt more like a week. As they exited the car, Summer spotted Ellis on her way to the fitness center.

"Do an extra couple of miles for me, will you?"

"Looks like you've got your hands full." Ellis approached beneath the streetlight, no doubt curious about the small visitors.

"This is Nate." She held out a hand to coax Bree from the car. For the moment, the girl had gotten her tears under control. "And this is Bree. Their grandma is one of my best friends—and coincidentally, my boss. She and their mom needed some private time to discuss a few things with Santa. I'm sure they'll be calling later to double-check on how good these two are being so they can let Santa know."

Emotional blackmail of a child. Probably a criminal offense, but it was better than having Bree work herself into an anxiety attack.

Ellis stooped low in front of the little girl. "Where did you get those beautiful pink shoes?"

"My mama bought them for me at the Payless."

"Mine are black and purple," Nate interjected, planting his foot forward to show off his sneakers. He was uncommonly patient with his sister most of the time, but not willing to let her have the spotlight all to herself when a stranger was passing out compliments.

"Wow, those are nice too." She pointed to Summer's boots. "Yours, on the other hand, could use a shine."

"Ouch. Are you guys going to let her pick on me like that?"

From the way they were giggling, the answer was yes.

"Just for that, I'm going to make sloppy joes and eat them all by myself."

Nate made the motion of zipping his lips.

"Well, okay. I guess you can have one." She turned back to Ellis. "There's plenty if you want to join us."

Ellis scrunched her nose. "Not my favorite, but thanks."

Summer was surprised by how disappointed she was. And how giddy just from sharing a two-minute casual conversation with her new neighbor.

* * *

Only one week into the exile of her children, and Ellis already was wishing one of them would drop by. Why had they picked now to start being so obedient?

She'd taken a couple of hours each night to arrange her apartment and was satisfied it was the best it could be. There wasn't nearly enough storage space, forcing her to part with household items and clothing she wasn't absolutely certain she would use.

The apartment wouldn't have felt so cramped had it not been packed with oversized furnishings she'd selected for a three-story home with spacious rooms. The china cabinet that had belonged to Bruce's grandmother. The sectional sofa from her family room. If only she hadn't brought the king-sized bed. New furniture wasn't an option and wouldn't be for several years.

The oven chimed, and she scraped the last batch of oatmeal cookies from the sheet. She hadn't made these in years, but something told her a certain boy and girl in the next building would appreciate her effort.

The sight of Summer with two African-American children had been a pleasant surprise. She appreciated diversity in her friends and liked knowing Summer did too. Her deer-in-the-headlights look was hilarious, probably brought on by the little girl, whose face had been swollen with tears. Separation anxiety, if she had to guess.

She briefly considered changing from her exercise tights, but thought it silly to dress up just to dash over to her neighbor's.

Summer answered the door with a wide grin and immediately crossed her eyes. "I hope you brought the straitjacket. I'm going to need it."

"I had an inkling you were in over your head." She held out the plate of cookies.

"Way over. Uh-oh, their mom warned me about sugar."

"Trust me on this," she whispered. They were sweetened with applesauce and raisins. Ellis had fed them to her kids to stave off hunger pangs through the night. "Just add milk."

"You're my favorite person in the world right now. Come on in."

The children were already in their pajamas and lying on a queen-sized air mattress in front of the TV. Nate craned his neck to see what was happening. "Cookies, Bree!"

Summer directed them to her small dinette and poured milk. "Decaf?" she asked Ellis.

Ellis spotted the one-cup coffeemaker on the kitchen counter. "Make mine high-test. It doesn't faze me." It was then she noticed Summer too wore pajamas, plaid flannel pants with a long-sleeved T-shirt. And no wonder—eight-thirty was bedtime for children as young as Nate and Bree. "Are you sure it's okay? It looks like you're ready for bed."

"Actually, we're *prepared* for bed…just in case we happen to fall asleep. That was the deal. But I promised to let them stay up as long as they wanted if they settled down."

The apartment had the same institutional look as hers. Off-white walls, beige carpet and vertical blinds. It was somewhat smaller, apparently a one-bedroom unit since there was only one door off the hallway. Same kitchen with barstools, same dining nook, same compact washer-dryer. The similarities ended there.

By the look of it, Summer's furniture had been purchased to fit the space. An overstuffed sofa in synthetic leather, the kind you fell asleep on while watching TV. A matching captain's chair with a halogen reading light peeking over its arm. Judging from the tablet computer on the ottoman, that was Summer's chair. The room's centerpiece was an enormous TV mounted on the wall.

"We just finished *The Princess and the Frog*, and now we're going to start it over from the beginning. Want to join us?" She lowered her voice. "Or maybe you'll show some mercy and rescue me from having to watch it again. Sit here at the table and we can have our coffee."

After two cookies each, the children dutifully brushed their teeth and returned to the air mattress to start the film again.

Having raised three children, Ellis knew all the tricks. "Now go back over there and turn the TV down really low. They'll have to be quiet to hear it, and they'll fall asleep."

Summer followed her tip and took an extra moment to tuck the blankets around them and lower the lights.

"They seem like good kids."

"You weren't here when they were fighting over whether or not frogs needed underwear. So glad I was an only child. I hate to fight."

"Speaking of which…" Ellis wasn't asking just to be nosy. Summer was starting to feel like a friend. If they were going to hang out together, it would be nice to know the issue with the ex-girlfriend was over and done. "Any more problems with your ex?"

"No, but this is her usual MO. Rita makes an ass of herself and then disappears for a while hoping I'll forget. The next time she shows up, she'll be stone cold sober and tell me she's turned over a new leaf. I can set my clock by it."

Ellis didn't have much experience with drunks, though she had a good idea what it was like to have an addict in the family. "My nephew on my husband's side had a cocaine problem. Went into treatment twice before he finally got clean. I wasn't around Michael all that much, but I know he put his family through hell."

"That's pretty much what it's like." Summer stared at her coffee mug, twirling it slowly. "We gave up alcohol together about sixteen years ago. I never felt like I had a problem with it—not personally—but I thought it would help her if we just cut it out of our lives. It worked for a long time, but then she started sneaking around. Drinking out of other people's cups at parties…stopping on the way home from work. Eventually she had a little stash in the garage. If she was going to cheat and lie about something, I wish it had been an affair. But that kind of betrayal…it's got to be the worst."

No it wasn't, Ellis thought. Not even close.

"Rita's biggest issue is that first step. She won't admit she has a problem. She'll say the words sometimes, but then she convinces herself she has it all under control. I wish Donita— She lives in the apartment above me. She's the one who called the cops last week—I wish she'd gotten the whole thing on video so I could show it to her. Hell, I'd have posted it on Facebook so everybody could see it. Maybe then all our friends would quit nagging me to take her back."

"Oh no, you don't want to take her back." Seeing the gloomy effect the subject had on Summer, she regretted bringing it up. "Listen to me offering you advice on your girlfriend, and I don't even know her. It's not any of my business. We don't have to talk about it if you don't want to."

"No, it's okay." Summer smiled weakly. "There aren't a lot of people I can talk to. Most of our friends just want us to work everything out so it won't be so awkward for everybody. I get that. They like both of us and don't want to have to pick sides."

"But they don't have to put up with it every day."

"Exactly. And they don't have to worry what she might do to somebody when she gets behind the wheel like that. God, if Rita had hurt somebody…I couldn't have lived with myself."

With every word, Ellis was struck by how much they had in common.

"I've been asking myself if I made a mistake the other night," she continued. "I thought I was helping her by getting our friend to come over and take her home, but maybe I should have just let her go to jail. That could have been the wakeup call she needed. If something happens, I'm going to kick myself over that."

"Why? You aren't responsible for what she does." The sharpness of her tone surprised even her, and she caught Summer looking to see if the children had heard. "I'm sorry.

I...I just remember how Michael's parents blamed themselves. You can't do that to yourself."

"I know that intellectually. It doesn't stop me from worrying about it though." Summer got up to peek in on Nate and Bree. "Amazing. They're both sound asleep. I'm officially hiring you as my babysitting consultant."

Ellis didn't want to risk a return to the unpleasant conversation. "I probably should go and let you wind down. Don't think for a minute you're going to sleep in tomorrow. I'll bet you anything those two are up by six a.m."

"Thanks for the warning. And the cookies. And especially the company." Summer surprised her by hooking elbows as they walked toward the door. "I like having a friend close by to talk to. Feel free to stop in anytime."

She'd come to Sacramento for a fresh start. A new job, a new home. New friends. Was Summer Winslow someone she could trust? The next few days would tell—either she'd open up about the person she used to be or retreat back into her shell.

CHAPTER FOUR

"Eight-ball, side pocket," Summer said, tapping the side rail with her cue stick. With a gentle tap, the eight dropped and the cue stopped well short of the corner. "That's all she wrote, ladies. Who's got next?"

Courtney slapped her hand with a high five, celebrating their third win in a row as partners. Courtney took her eight-ball seriously. It also didn't hurt that it was her billiard table. No doubt she practiced every night and knew all of its quirks.

Summer relished the twice-monthly potluck nights at Courtney's, which usually drew about a dozen women, most of them couples. The food was nice, but the real attractions were the raucous games they played after dinner. Billiards, ping-pong, Twister, poker…whatever struck their fancy.

As luck would have it, Rita didn't enjoy games, so there was never a concern about her showing up. That made it one of the few places Summer could hang out with friends and know she could totally relax.

Of all her lesbian friends, Summer liked Courtney in particular because she was hospitable to everyone, no matter who was on the outs or why. She didn't involve herself in other people's drama. From a practical standpoint, it meant Courtney wasn't one of the voices clamoring for her to take Rita back.

"I guess no one else is brave enough to take us on," Courtney said. She gestured toward a pair of barstools from where they could watch the others play Pictionary. "How's your toe?"

Shouting so everyone could hear, Summer replied, "My toe is better, but I'm never playing Twister with Norma again."

That got the attention of Norma Serrato, whose sliding foot had sent Summer's into a table leg. "Can I help it if you're fragile? You need to drink your milk, build up those bones." She flexed her biceps.

"I'll show you fragile," Summer threatened. "Next time I'm wearing steel-toed boots."

"Speaking of next time," Courtney said, her voice low, "I went out to dinner last week with Norma and Vicki. They had a new friend they wanted me to meet, a woman Vicki works with at the convention center. Tracie Carlson. She just moved up here from the LA area."

"Interesting…did you like her?"

Courtney rolled her eyes sheepishly. "It wasn't a date. Besides, you know me."

Indeed she did. Courtney's partner Janine had died in a foggy freeway pileup nearly ten years ago, and she'd been single ever since. If not for her unapproachable vibe, Courtney would have a line of suitors out the door. She had a lively look, with short silver hair and sparkling blue eyes. As chair of the social sciences department at the local community college, she also was well-read, meaning she could converse intelligently about anything. But her most prominent personality trait was that she never seemed to relax. Everything she did was in high gear—the parties, the games, the outings. Most of their friends thought she was overcompensating for her loss by surrounding herself with people.

"I got the idea she's already feeling homesick for Southern California," Courtney went on. "That's why they wanted to introduce her around, so she could start making some friends.

I think she's going to fit in really well. She was supposed to come tonight, but Vicki said her niece was in town from San Francisco."

At the mention of the City, she thought of Ellis Keene, also new to Sacramento. Sacto, they called it. For the briefest moment, she wondered if Ellis would ever consider coming to one of Courtney's potluck game nights. It wouldn't be the first time someone had brought along a straight friend.

Courtney scooped a handful of nuts and offered her the bowl. "Anyway, I thought Tracie was nice. Cute too. Early fifties, but she looks a lot younger. Blondish hair, a little darker than yours, big brown eyes. One thing I liked about her was that she had a genuine look…you know, she didn't go overboard with the makeup or frilly clothes. Reminded me a lot of you."

Summer took that as a compliment. She liked thinking of herself as genuine, even though her fair complexion and light hair left her looking washed out unless she wore a touch of foundation and a little eyeliner. "Sounds like Tracie made an impression."

"Not like that," Courtney reiterated, this time with a backhanded swat.

"That's too bad. She sounds like a catch." All of their friends would be thrilled to see someone work her way into Courtney's heart.

They stopped to watch Vicki drawing a hideous rendering of what turned out to be a pastry chef, which made her think of Ellis showing up at her apartment with cookies for the children. Truth be told, lots of things made her think of Ellis—the copy of *Vista* at her hair salon, the AAA renewal notice, and even the woman buying Lean Cuisine dinners at the supermarket, with her pink fingernails and designer workout gear.

"That's why I'm telling *you* about her. I talked with Norma and Vicki, and we all thought you two might like each other."

The suggestion took her completely by surprise, especially coming from Courtney. It wasn't like her to get involved in other people's personal affairs. "Wow, I didn't see that coming. All I've heard since Rita and I split up was how everybody wanted us back together."

"That's because you were good for Rita and everybody knew it. But she's not so good for you, and you shouldn't have to be responsible for somebody that way. It's been what, a year?"

"A year and a half since I moved out. It's my own fault people keep expecting us to get back together. I move out—she stops drinking—I move back. Rinse and repeat."

Courtney tossed a peanut and caught it in her mouth. "Plus the fact that Rita tells everybody things are going great and she thinks you're going to work it out any day now."

"Oh, for Christ's sake. Is she still doing that? She's delusional."

"Forget her. You want to meet Tracie?"

Summer could honestly say she hadn't given a thought to starting a new relationship. It was ironic in light of their conversation that she continued to feel she wasn't free of Rita. "I don't know. I almost hate to subject somebody to Rita. She'll probably start stalking her. Do you know she still shows up at my house when she gets drunk?"

"I heard about that from Queenie and Sam."

On the other hand, there was no better way to demonstrate once and for all that she was finished with Rita than to start seeing someone else. And there was no one among her lesbian friends she'd consider dating. Why not meet someone new?

"You know...maybe I should meet her. Yeah, let's go for it."

With that settled, they turned their attention back to watching the game. Norma had drawn a crescent moon with stars, a plus sign and a four-legged creature that, from its crude saddle, appeared to be a horse. Her teammates shouted possible answers to the puzzle. Star horse. Moon ride.

Summer recognized it immediately...and hoped it wasn't an omen about meeting Tracie. "Nightmare!"

* * *

Ellis tucked the phone under her chin as she wriggled into her pajama pants. "Mom, don't you dread having to drive that monstrosity all the way home?"

"The only thing your father dreads is being back in Modesto. It wouldn't surprise me if he decided to stay right here in Scottsdale."

Oliver and Susan Keene, now in their late seventies, had been married fifty-six years. It wasn't what Ellis would call a love story for the ages, but they were undeniably companionable.

"What will he say when the thermometer hits one-fifteen?"

"I honestly don't think he'd care. They have a clubhouse here with a pool, and I swear, he knows everybody in the place. He comes in practically every afternoon and tells me so-and-so is coming for dinner, or we're going to their place. I have to drop whatever I'm doing and get ready."

Though it sounded like a complaint, Ellis recognized the familiar dynamic. Her father was king of the castle—his plans, his preferences, his rules. In all her life, she couldn't name a single time her mother had pushed back.

Her brother Stan, two years older, ruled his family the same way. While his wife Peggy acquiesced to his dictates, they'd struggled with their four children, all of whom resisted the rigid discipline. It was a constant source of friction in their home, one Ellis had worried would spill over with her own children.

She told herself often she was nothing like her mother, that she would have stood up to Bruce had he been too strict or selfish. As it was, he'd left the major child-rearing decisions to her.

"You should think about staying then, Mom. Or at least consider parking the RV and driving home in the car."

"It's up to your father...whatever he wants to do."

It was silly to worry about her parents. Though her mom was quick to harp on her life, she didn't want advice on how to make it better.

"I wish you could be here for Christmas. All the kids are coming to Sacramento. Bruno too. You remember him...Jeremy's boyfriend." She added that just to get under her mother's skin. They'd never accepted the fact that their grandson was gay.

"Your father's smoking a turkey. Did I tell you he bought a smoker?" She completely ignored the reference to Bruno, and launched into a detailed description of their latest cooking fad, followed by a rundown of their menu and the various neighbors who would be in attendance.

Ellis set her phone to its speaker function and listened politely, all the while touching up her nails with a fresh coat of polish. The monthly call gave her a chance to keep track of her parents' well-being. Though her father repeated himself more often and her mom complained of arthritis, their health was generally good.

"That's all I have on this end, Ellis. Tell everyone Merry Christmas from us, okay?"

She ended the call, noting as usual that her mother hadn't asked how she was doing. Her parents had erected a wall between themselves and the shooting and its devastating aftermath. No regard for the suffering of their daughter and grandchildren, no concern for their financial struggles. As if it hadn't happened at all.

Waving her hands to dry the polish, Ellis returned to the living room and peeked through the blinds. Summer's car was in its space. She'd missed their workout, which was unusual for a weeknight. What else was there to do in Sacramento on a Monday evening?

Her interest in Summer had grown over the weekend as she considered whether or not to confide in her about what brought her to Sacramento. Sometimes she wished she could follow her parents' cue—forget it all, pretend it never happened. In a way, that's what she'd intended when she reverted to her maiden name. Gil had promised not to share her story with anyone at *Vista*, so there was no reason for her to bring it up.

Except the suffering continued, and would until every single party involved in the shooting agreed on a financial settlement. The insurance adjusters, the building management, the security company. The attorneys seemed hellbent on dragging out the process, whatever it took to justify their fee. All she really needed was enough to provide for her children—get Jonathan and Allison through college, and help Jeremy get his business off the ground. A nest egg would be nice. Until the lawsuit was settled, she faced nothing but grief and uncertainty.

Summer had known misery too, and surely had grieved her relationship with Rita. No matter how serious their problems, a person couldn't spend that many years with someone and not feel a hole once she was gone.

It was interesting that her first new friend was a single lesbian. Besides Roxanne, her closest friends in the City had been women she met through school activities, particularly the mothers of her children's friends. One had been a stay-at-home lesbian mom, a distinction that was easy to forget, since she was otherwise like all the other mothers.

On a whim, she scrolled through her contacts and hovered her thumb over Summer's number. She had nothing pressing to say. The plate of cookies had been her invitation for friendship, something more than their casual interactions in the fitness center. Summer had responded that evening by talking in personal terms about her relationship with her ex. While Ellis hadn't yet reciprocated that openness, she'd begun to feel that she could. But that was three days ago, and Summer had made no move to follow up.

"Hello! I was just thinking about you," Summer said when she answered, her breath coming in short gasps.

"You sound like you're out of breath."

"I was doing sit-ups. I always feel guilty when I miss my workout. How are you doing? Did you have a good weekend?"

Ellis was glad to get such an enthusiastic response. "I dropped in on two of my kids. It's amazing how excited they are to see you when you're holding a plate of cookies."

"Tell me about it. It was all Nate and Bree could talk about when their mom came to pick them up." She went on to describe her weekend, which consisted of house cleaning, laundry and last-minute Christmas shopping for the office gift exchange.

"I got my Christmas shopping done before I left the City. But I had to pack everything in boxes labeled 'lingerie' so my kids wouldn't open them when they helped me move. They must think I bought out Victoria's Secret."

They chatted for half an hour before Summer got around to the reason she'd missed her workout. "One of my friends has a bunch of people over for potluck every other Monday. After dinner we shoot pool, play cards…and sometimes the games can get kind of wild. That's how I broke my toe—playing Twister with these crazy people."

"Sounds like my family playing Spoons. You should come over sometime when they're all here."

"Careful what you ask for. I can dish it out too."

Ellis let out her best evil laugh. "We aren't scared of you."

"In that case, I'm dragging you along next time I go to Courtney's."

"Oh, I don't know about that." It was one thing to have a lesbian as a friend, and quite another to immerse herself into a whole network. "Not so sure I'd fit in."

"Hmm, you might be right. Someone as pretty as you would draw too much attention at a lesbian party." Her compliment had come without a second's hesitation.

"Aw, thank you."

"Just telling it like it is. Do you like sushi? I know a great place we could go tomorrow after our workout. Cheap too."

The quick transition to the subject of dinner meant Ellis didn't have to take her compliment too seriously. "I'd love that."

As she readied for bed, she considered Summer's flattering remark. It was a sweet thing to say, and at the same time, lighthearted. She'd found it delightful. So different from her wolfish impression of Rex Brenneman as he'd examined her hand for a wedding ring.

The biggest difference though—Rex was serious. Summer wasn't.

CHAPTER FIVE

Nothing beat the turkey gumbo at Muntean's on a rainy winter day. Wednesday's special—tender white meat, okra and tomatoes, all cooked together in Cajun spices. Worth the walk, even in the rain.

Most days, Summer picked up lunch to go and ate in the break room but a prime table by the window made her rethink her habit. Gumbo was best when it was piping hot.

She was engrossed in a second-hand copy of *USA Today* when a familiar voice greeted her.

"Is it all right if I sit here?" Lunch tray already in hand, Rita waited for permission to pull out the other chair. Tall and big-boned, with ginger hair that tumbled about her shoulders, she was imposing as always. Today, an olive green pantsuit brought out the color of her eyes.

Rita worked in the auditor's office on Capitol Mall, only six blocks from the Health and Human Services building. Muntean's used to be one of their favorite meeting places, so it was only luck they hadn't run into each other more often.

"Sure." Summer didn't feel trapped this time, not like when Rita had shown up at her apartment. One wrong word, one hint of agitation, and she could walk out.

"Love this rain, huh? Not that it'll do much for the drought. Things going okay at work?"

"Work's work."

This was their usual verbal dance. Talk about the weather, work. Next would be friends, and finally, Rita would offer up her version of an apology for the last shitty thing she'd done.

"End of year's a grind, isn't it?" She grinned, showing off a double dimple that Summer had always adored. "I hung out with Queenie and Sam over the weekend. Did you catch the Niners game?"

"Nah, I braved the mall and got some Christmas shopping done."

Three seconds…two seconds…

"I guess I ought to apologize for coming over to your apartment that night and getting your neighbors so upset."

"You think?"

"Come on, it wasn't that bad. I couldn't believe it when the cops showed up. That's the problem with apartments. Everybody's so close, they get in your business. That was flat out ridiculous. All I did was knock on your door."

Summer tried her best not to take the bait, but she wasn't going to let Rita get away with shifting the blame onto one of her neighbors. As evenly as she could manage, she replied, "That's not the way I heard it, Rita. I know how you get when you've had too much to drink because I've heard it a million times. You yell, you curse. You call me names. People don't like having to explain those words to their kids."

Rita's face reddened.

"And just so you know, 'I guess I ought to apologize' isn't an apology. You need to do way better than that."

"Would it do any good?"

"Some people say it makes them feel better."

Rita dropped her sandwich on her plate and ran her hands through her hair, leaving behind a small piece of shredded lettuce Summer decided not to mention. "I know you're pissed and I don't blame you. It got away from me again. Some days I go home and have a drink—one gin and tonic or a glass of wine—and that's it. It makes me feel like I'm in control again."

"That's your first mistake, Rita. The only thing you have control over is whether or not you drink that first one. After that, all bets are off."

"That's what I'm trying to tell you. I *do* have control. I haven't had a drink since that night. I poured it all out the next day, I swear. And I'm not going to drink anymore." She held up her hand as if taking an oath. "It was a close call. I would have been arrested if you and Queenie hadn't taken me home."

"Don't think I didn't consider it." Her soup had gone cold, but she no longer had an appetite. Their conversations nearly always came to this. Rita would promise to quit, and then blame her eventual relapse on Summer for not coming back.

"I'm sorry, Summer. Very, very sorry. Give me a chance to prove that to you."

"You don't need to prove it to me. Prove it to yourself." She shrugged into her raincoat. "It's different this time. I know you don't want to believe that, but I mean it. I'm not part of this equation anymore."

"Please don't go. Just talk to me." Rita's eyes were clouded with tears. Surprising since she wasn't normally a crier. Could this time actually be different? "I feel like I'm finally on the right track. That was a wakeup call. Can you just be my friend? I'm not sure I can do this without you."

It wasn't quite the same as threatening to hurt herself—she'd done that before too—but it was every bit as emotionally manipulative. "You *can* do this, Rita. All you have to do is decide which person you want to be. The one in control of her behavior, or the one making a drunken spectacle of herself. You can't go back and forth between those two people. It's got to be one or the other."

Rita nodded and wiped her nose with her napkin.

"I'm willing to bet you don't like yourself very much right now. Nobody likes regretting things they've done. And nobody likes feeling scared about what could have happened. You should seriously consider talking to somebody…a substance abuse counselor. They know how to help you deal with this."

"I don't need that kind of help," she said sharply, before looking around to see if anyone had heard. "All I'm saying is this would be a lot easier if I knew getting sober meant you'd at least consider taking me back."

"No. I'm over you." Summer rose and slung her purse over her shoulder. Leaning close so she could keep her voice low, she added the message Rita most needed to understand. "I have no intention of being your reward for doing something you have to do for yourself. That's the bottom line here. The only guarantee you have for turning your life around is how *you're* going to feel about it. Stop trying to make it sound like I have anything to do with it. Because I don't."

* * *

Ellis pinched a slice of California roll with her chopsticks and dipped it in soy sauce. Not the greatest sushi she'd ever had, but hard to beat at four dollars a roll. Summer knew the best neighborhood places to grab a cheap meal. Cheap also meant casual, so they'd come straight from their workout wearing exercise tights and sneakers. Tucked in a booth under the dim light of a Japanese lantern, they could have worn pajamas and no one would have known.

"I can't believe Rita still thinks her guilt trip's going to work on me. Like it's my responsibility to keep her sober." Summer took a bite of her Dynamite roll and chased it with a gulp of ice water.

"So just between us…is there any chance you'll take her back if she cleans herself up?"

"No way. I'm always going to care about what happens to her, but we won't ever be in a relationship again. And we won't ever…you know."

Her sheepish look was charming. Apparently, "you know" was code for having sex.

"This time it finally feels like *never*, especially after we sold the house. We were so angry about everything...we didn't even speak to each other for about six months. But then I ran into her last April at a wedding, and I went and gave her a hug. Huge mistake. She took it as an invitation."

Ellis caught herself eating the edamame as if it were popcorn. "Here, we're supposed to be sharing this."

"We're supposed to be sharing the conversation too, and all I've done is talk about Rita. What's going on in your world?"

She'd rather listen to Summer than grouse about the fact that her kids were too busy to visit. That left work, where the only thing worth talking about was Rex, who had dropped by her desk again to invite her to lunch.

"There's this guy at the magazine...Rex Brenneman. He's the political writer."

Summer peered over her glasses with a pensive look. "I know who he is. He wrote that column on the legislators who raked in campaign cash from the utility companies and then pushed through the rate increases. I bet something like that goes on in every single department."

"Then you can also bet he'll find out about it. He's really sharp." She was glad to hear Summer read *Vista*. It was validating to know her friends thought the magazine was worth their time. "It seems Rex has taken more than a professional interest in yours truly. He asked me to lunch today but I'd already eaten, so he promised to give me more notice next time."

"Hunh." A grunt that sounded like disapproval.

"I take it you think that's a bad idea."

Summer sighed and shook her head. "Don't pay any attention to me. I'm kind of a hard-ass about stuff like that."

"About dating coworkers?" Something felt wrong about Rex asking her out, so she was interested in getting Summer's perspective. "I've heard that old dog maxim...about never going to the bathroom where you eat."

"That's part of it, because you don't want to end up having a bad relationship with somebody and still have to look at them every day at work. But I can see how tempting it is. That's the number one place you meet people. Plus you already have plenty to talk about because you know all the same people. Where I have a real problem is when there's a power differential. This Rex, he's a big shot, right?"

She nodded.

"Suppose you tell him no. Next thing you know, he goes to your boss and complains about your work. Not because you actually did anything wrong, but because he's an asshole, and his opinion of you is colored by the fact that you turned him down."

"And if I say yes?"

"If you say yes, you'll never get credit for anything you do because everybody will say, 'Oh, she only got promoted because she's dating Mr. Big Shot.' And again there's the issue of what happens if it goes south later. *Awk*-ward."

The subject had definitely touched a nerve. In fact, Summer was actually putting into words some of her own reservations. Ellis knew from a few of her friends in the City about the potential for disaster, but hadn't experienced anything like that herself.

Summer went on, "I saw it happen in our office a couple of years ago, and the woman—it's never the man, you know—she nearly lost her job over it. She probably would have if she hadn't hired a lawyer." She took off her glasses and rubbed the bridge of her nose, as if she were sorry she'd brought it up. "There must be happy stories too. Whatever you told him, I'm sure it's fine."

"I didn't answer one way or the other. To be honest, I was just floored. It never occurred to me someone would be interested in me that way."

"I hope you're kidding, Ms. Keene. Take it from a woman who appreciates attractive women. You're a prize."

Ellis couldn't stop her lips from turning upward in an embarrassed grin. It was the same sort of compliment she'd been given on the phone the night before.

"I'm serious. You're smart, you're *very* pretty. And you've got yourself together."

"I…thank you. That's a first."

"A lesbian telling you you're pretty? I might be the first one who said it, but trust me—I'm not the first one to think it."

She fanned herself, knowing her face was turning red. Summer's flattery was even more open than Rex's. "What surprises me is you thinking I've got myself together."

"At least it looks that way on the outside. That's half the battle, isn't it?"

If Summer only knew how chaotic her life was, how hard she had to work to keep from wallowing in self-pity. How the smallest word or gesture that evoked her former life could trigger a stream of tears. She was many things but "together" was not one of them.

The turmoil seemed to pervade every aspect of her life—home, work, family and friends. If she dared forget, something would remind her. An unexpected bill, a letter from the attorneys. What's more, it had been going on so long, she no longer considered it a disruption. It was the new normal.

"Did I say something wrong?"

Ellis had no idea how much time had passed while she ruminated on her mental state, but she knew from Summer's look of concern that her own face had fallen. "No, not at all. I just...my battles are definitely on the inside."

"Of course they are." Summer reached over and took both of her hands. "You lost your husband. You left your home. I bet you lived in that house twenty years."

"Twenty-two."

"And you started a new job. Those are all pretty high on the stress list. I'm sure you've already got lots of friends to lean on, but if you could use one here in Sacto, I'd like it to be me."

Could it? Most of her other friends had drifted away, never quite knowing what to say. Or more important, what not to say. Even Roxanne had stumbled because of her work demands. On a particularly challenging day, Ellis had launched into an emotional tirade and told her to forget it, that she didn't need any part-time friends.

But Summer didn't share the history her other friends did. She hadn't known Bruce, hadn't been to dinner parties in their home, hadn't watched their kids grow up. It was awkward for everyone. Ellis wondered if she herself would have known how to respond had one of her friends suffered the same tragedy.

What she knew right now was that a sushi restaurant wasn't the place to pour her heart out.

"I'm sure we'll be friends, Summer. You have no idea how much I appreciate that. This past year has been a living hell."

"You know what they say. Only one way to go from here, and that's up."

Ellis hoped she was right.

* * *

"Oh, for Christ's sake! I can't believe she's pulling this crap again," Summer grumbled when they turned into the parking lot at River Woods. Rita's Jeep was parked in the guest space next to her car. "When is she going to get it through her head that no means no?"

"Do you think she's drunk again?" Ellis asked.

"I doubt it...not this time. She thinks being sober's the only way to get me back. She probably wants to make some kind of elaborate deal, where I take her back if she does everything on my list."

"Or maybe she just wants the last word."

"Could be. One thing I know for sure is she's going to go apeshit when she sees me getting out of another woman's car."

"So get out on this side. She won't even see you. Then when you think she's not looking, sneak into my place. I'll leave the door open."

The plan worked to perfection, and Summer found herself inside Ellis's apartment for the first time. It was exactly the same layout, but with a wider hallway between the kitchen and dining nook that led to a second bedroom. "I'm jealous. Look at all this space."

"That's funny. I was jealous when I saw your apartment because it wasn't jam-packed with furniture. Every time I walk through this living room, I worry I'm going to fall over something."

It was indeed crowded, but the furniture was tasteful. The modern sectional sofa was upholstered in rich green linen, with cream and gold accent pillows. The room's décor included a couple of signed lithographs, and an abstract wall sculpture. Everything looked expensive.

Just like the Lexus outside. For the first time, Summer wondered what Ellis's husband had done for a living. Obviously something lucrative. But from the way Ellis appeared to pinch pennies, she'd suffered a drastic lifestyle change.

Or maybe they were like so many other families of the Great Recession era—caught living beyond their means.

She peered out through the blinds and groaned to see Rita's Jeep still parked. "I promise not to stay long. If she isn't gone in a few minutes, I'll suck it up and go out there."

"There's no hurry." Ellis went behind the counter to the refrigerator. "This is normally the time I have a glass of wine, but I'll skip it tonight if it bothers you."

"I don't mind. I have nothing against people having a drink. Just the ones who don't know when to stop." She took a seat on one of the barstools while Ellis poured a glass of chardonnay.

"I have to admit, if I didn't get a splitting headache after two glasses, I swear sometimes I'd drink myself into a coma."

It was obvious something had been bothering Ellis ever since their conversation in the restaurant. There were even a couple of moments where Summer had thought she might cry. No wonder she took a drink at night. With all the upheaval in her life, it truly was amazing she didn't drink all the time.

Before Ellis could sit down with her wine, her cell phone pinged and she excused herself into the master bedroom at the end of the hall. She left the door open though, and Summer was glad to hear her animated voice.

From her barstool, she noted a framed photo on a corner table—two guys in their late teens and a younger girl. Probably her children. Nothing of an older man who might have been her husband.

Ellis was grinning when she returned. "That was my son Jonathan, the one studying poli-sci at Stanford and trying to get into law school. He finally confirmed he's coming for Christmas dinner, so that means I'll have them all here. I asked for a little space after I moved in, but I didn't mean for them to jump off the face of the earth."

"It's nice to see you smiling."

Ellis winced slightly and nodded. "I'm going to try to do that more often."

"I'm sure it's tough for you sometimes. When Rita and I split up, I was miserable. I mean, let's face it—we were together a long time and it hurt not to have her there anymore. I went a long time without smiling too."

Ellis stared blankly at her wine, her cheerful spell broken.

"Not that I went through anything as bad as what happened to you, Ellis. I can't imagine how you've managed at all after your husband died."

Those were the words that spawned the tears, which Ellis quickly wiped away.

Summer patted her forearm. "I'm sorry. I didn't mean to upset you. It's just that I can see it's bothering you. If you want to talk, I'll listen."

Ellis squeezed her eyes shut, and for a moment it appeared she was burying her emotions. "My husband...he worked at Kerner-Swift. The financial services company."

The baritone voice of their spokesman played in her ear. *Kerner-Swift—So it's there when you need it.*

"But then last year...you probably read about it...the office shooting."

"Oh, my God! At the Transamerica Pyramid."

She'd imagined cancer, a heart attack. Nothing as horrific as a murder. That bastard had slaughtered seven defenseless people, all trapped behind their desks.

"Ellis, you poor, poor thing." Her eyes stung with tears of compassion. She rose to offer a hug but Ellis stiffened her shoulders and pulled away.

"No, no sympathy. I don't deserve it."

For a moment, Summer was confused—until she saw Ellis's look of utter horror.

"My husband was Bruce Rowanbury. The shooter."

CHAPTER SIX

Ellis waited for the look of shock and disgust on Summer's face, knowing it would come as soon as her news sank in. People could guard their words but never their face or manner.

As Bruce's survivors, she and her children were forced to carry his guilt. How could he have hoarded all those handguns and ammunition without the family knowing about it? Couldn't they see he was dangerously mentally ill? Why had they pretended so long nothing was wrong?

The shooting had turned the whole family into pariahs.

Instead of revulsion, Summer's gray eyes were brimming with tears. "I can't imagine how horrible that was for you. It doesn't matter how it happened. You suffered a terrible loss." She ignored Ellis's resistance and hugged her anyway.

Bruce had died in a barrage of gunfire when cornered by the SWAT team, a fact that was roundly cheered by the media, and even by many of their friends. Virtually alone in her grief, the only thing that kept her going was her kids, especially Allison. The poor girl had been forced to finish out the school year, her days filled with whispers and taunts.

"Please don't tell anyone," Ellis pleaded. "I'm sick of dealing with their hateful looks and the gossip behind my back."

"I won't say a word. There's no reason for people to treat you that way." Summer held her embrace, swaying as if to music. "No wonder you moved here. You needed a fresh start."

Ellis savored the comforting warmth of her hug. The shooting had robbed her of this kind of friendship. Everyone saw Bruce's horror, but none her humiliation. In Summer, she had a friend who didn't judge her. Who sympathized not only with her shame, but with her loss.

Summer finally returned to her barstool but held fast to her hand.

"They asked me if I'd noticed any changes in Bruce…if I knew he had those guns. I had no idea of anything, I swear. He kept everything locked up in the garage with his tools."

"That's so awful."

"He'd been lying to us for three years about his job." Her voice rose with agitation. "We finally pieced it all together after he died. It started when they brought in a new regional director at Kerner-Swift. That was Bruce's job. He got put back into the field as a client manager, but he never told any of us. One of the men who used to work for him said Bruce had given up all his contacts years ago to his reps—the guys who worked for him. Why would he need them if he was the regional manager, right?"

She was ashamed of her ignorance about their money situation. If only they'd shared responsibility for the finances, she would have known.

"So thirty years building up the branch and all of a sudden he's back to cold-calling for commissions that are only a fraction of what he used to make. Entry level."

"That's so unfair."

Those were probably the first sympathetic words anyone had said about Bruce since the shooting.

"He worked like that for two whole years and we never even knew he'd been demoted. Hell, I thought he'd gotten a raise because he was bringing home more money. Turns out he was drawing it out of our 401K. And then after two years, he wasn't bringing in enough new clients so they let him go. Fired him! Can you believe that?"

Summer was shaking her head.

"But we didn't know that either. He was getting up every morning, dressing in a suit and tie and leaving the house. Every day for another whole year. Apparently he was looking for another job. Interviewing all over town, but he couldn't find anything that wasn't cold-calling. At least that's what the investigators said."

She was getting herself worked up again and paused to take a sip of wine.

"The part that's so hard for me—all of it's hard...those poor people. What I can't understand is why he didn't tell me they put him back in the field. Why would he feel like he had to keep that from me? We were married for twenty-six years. We loved each other. We trusted each other. It's not like I was some spoiled wife who demanded things. Hell, we could have moved to Modesto and started over together for all I cared. I could have gone back to work."

With every new detail, the creases in Summer's forehead grew deeper. Shared pain, not judgment.

"You can't beat yourself up about it, Ellis. It was probably his pride. People who go off like that...it's hardly ever because of somebody else. It's because there's something wrong in their head. Their brain chemistry gets screwed up, and something happens to push them over the edge. I'm sure it had nothing to do with you."

Ellis wanted to believe that, but there were too many others pointing fingers her way. "Would you please tell that to my attorney? According to the law, I'm as culpable as Bruce. All because California's a community property state. I had to put all of our joint assets on ice while they negotiate the wrongful death claims. I don't expect to have a dime left when it's all over. No investments, no pension. Just a pile of debt and whatever I earn from my job from this day forward."

They went a full minute without talking, and all the while Summer tenderly stroked her hand.

"I wish I knew exactly what you needed to hear right now so I could say it. I think the best I can do is tell you I'm on your side. If you need to talk about it…if there's any way at all I can help, just ask." She drew Ellis's hand to her lips and lightly kissed her knuckles. "I'm a pretty good friend to have. You're going to find that out."

Ellis felt a wave of relief wash over her. Bit by bit, she'd put her life back together here in "Sacto." So much easier with a real friend beside her.

* * *

Summer was horrified to find herself so close to such a tragedy. But where everyone else had pushed Ellis away, she felt drawn to her side.

She remembered exactly where she'd been when she heard of the shooting—sitting beside Alythea in a budget briefing from the Secretary of Health and Human Services. The event was of such significance that an aide had interrupted to relay the news.

In the back of her head, a voice reminded her that she'd cast her own doubts about the Rowanbury family. They had to have known he was disturbed, had to have seen his collection of guns. No one could have lived an outwardly normal life while plotting such mayhem.

Now she felt guilty for those thoughts. Ellis and her kids were victims too.

"Feeling any better?" she asked.

They'd migrated to the sectional sofa, where Ellis had sat curled into a ball for the past hour.

"Marginally. I knew I needed to tell you before you got too invested. If it makes you feel weird to be hanging out with the widow of a mass murderer, I understand." It was a quiet aside, the way a waitress warned you off the meat loaf. "No one else wanted to either."

Sitting within arm's reach, Summer gently rubbed her shoulder. "You can't possibly think it makes any difference to our friendship. You didn't do those things. Bruce did. As far as I'm concerned, the only thing that's changed is I now understand where your head goes sometimes."

Ellis caught her hand and squeezed it. "I appreciate that so much. I'm serious—you're the first friend who really gets what it was like."

And probably the first one who didn't feel betrayed by Bruce. Would she have stood beside Alythea if her husband Julius had done something so awful? "Of course I would."

"What's that?"

"Nothing…I was just thinking how much we have in common. Not that I've been through anything remotely close to what happened to you. Just that my friendships have changed too. They don't really get what I've been going through with Rita…her lies and manipulation. Oh, shit! That reminds me." She scrambled from her seat to check the parking lot.

"Is she gone?"

"Finally!" Her relief was tinged with regret. After more than an hour of hiding out, she had no more excuse to prolong her visit. "I guess I should go…give you back your home. You're a lifesaver."

Ellis waved her off. "No big deal. It was good to get that off my chest."

"I'm glad you did." Summer held out a hand and pulled her to her feet. "I meant what I said. I'm here for you…whatever you need. And I won't tell a soul."

As they shared a hug, sympathy gave way to new feelings— the desire to comfort, and to protect Ellis from a world too angry to see she was a victim too. And something else…a faint flicker that Ellis could be more than a friend.

CHAPTER SEVEN

Summer and her boss had the break room to themselves and were sharing a chicken casserole Alythea had brought from home. As it was Casual Friday, both were dressed down, though Alythea's casual was slacks and a cashmere sweater set, while Summer wore black jeans with a cable-knit pullover.

"Question for you," she said. "As a straight woman, do you ever feel put off by any of my mannerisms…like the fact that I tend to touch people when I'm talking to them?"

Alythea chuckled. "I might notice if you grabbed my boob."

"If I ever do something like that, you have my permission to slap me." Summer set her fork down and took Alythea's hand. "If we were having a serious conversation and I took your hand like this, would it bother you?"

"Apparently not, because you do it all the time."

"Really?"

"You're just a touchy-feely person. I noticed it the day we met. I don't have a problem with it. You do it to everybody. Even Julius."

"As in your husband Julius? I never took his hand."

"You most certainly did. The very first time we all met at that barbecue place in Rosemont. You and Rita, me and Julius. I came back from the restroom and you were holding his hand and telling him some story about how you got in trouble at school because you took a bunch of your daddy's herbs in a plastic bag for show and tell and your teacher thought it was marijuana."

"That had to be totally subconscious because I don't remember doing it."

It wasn't subconscious where Ellis was concerned. Her dramatic revelation two nights ago had brought out Summer's primal urge to soothe the heartache, to show her sympathy and share her strength.

She hoped she'd covered her shock. The news that Ellis's husband was the notorious Bruce Rowanbury—arguably the most hated man in San Francisco after Dan White, who'd killed George Moscone and Harvey Milk—had nearly knocked her off the stool. But the sight of Ellis breaking into tears had overridden the horror.

The moment she'd returned home, morbid curiosity got the better of her, leading her to revisit all the news articles related to the shooting. The police report revealed the savagery of Bruce's rampage—five men and two women brutally murdered as they cowered behind their desks—and his death, the result of thirty-one bullet wounds to his head and chest. Unspeakable pain for the families left behind imagining their loved ones' final moments.

Ellis's version rang true—she was absolved of culpability after investigators pieced together the paper trail of Bruce's deception. It showed the regular withdrawals from his 401K to simulate a continuing paycheck, and the fruitless interviews with financial services companies all over the City. The weapons, three semiautomatic handguns, had been purchased in Reno, Nevada, charged to a credit card that was in his name only.

Those facts didn't stop the public vitriol. If anything, the aftermath for Ellis was even more grim than she'd let on, with victims' families suing her personally for tens of millions of dollars, their lawyers insisting the family was culpable for not treating Bruce's mental condition. No wonder she'd left town. It must have felt like barbarians at the gates.

"What's up with you, Summer? Why are you so all-of-a-sudden concerned about holding hands with people? You get told off?"

"No, nothing like that."

Had she gotten carried away with her compassion? As Ellis poured out her grief, she'd meant only to give her solace. To let her know there was someone on her side, someone who cared about her suffering. Ever since, she'd worried obsessively about what Ellis must have thought when she kissed her hand. Her worry rose to panic the night before when Ellis didn't show at their usual workout time.

Her feelings of empathy had been overpowering. Emotions so strong she wanted to wrap Ellis in her protective arms and shield her from anyone who might cause her more pain. But then came the attraction. "I think I might be falling for somebody…a straight woman."

"Hmm…I see."

Summer knew delight when she heard it. "It's nothing to celebrate. Crushes on straight women usually end badly."

Alythea tipped her head back and peered skeptically down her nose. "You know what I always say. Under the right circumstances, everybody's a little bit gay."

"I don't believe that, because it would mean everybody's a little bit straight too. I don't have a straight bone in my body."

In her deepest voice, Alythea chuckled and said, "Who said anything about bones?"

* * *

What on earth had possessed Ellis to say yes to dinner with Rex? It wasn't a burning desire for male companionship. The thought hadn't even crossed her mind until his persistence made it impossible to ignore.

Yet here she sat in Firehouse, purportedly one of the city's finest restaurants, sharing an intimate booth with the first man to ask. And in a clingy knit black dress with a plunging neckline, no less. She'd wanted to feel sexy but had second thoughts when Rex's approving smile suggested he'd read her display of cleavage as an invitation. In an effort to dampen his expectations for the night, she made it a point to order the least expensive entree on the menu. Unfortunately, that was Cajun chicken, and the spices made her eyes water.

Rex, meanwhile, was feasting on a scrumptious-looking rack of New Zealand lamb, and practically moaning after every bite. He'd worn his bomber jacket with a gray shirt and matching tie, and in fact looked even more handsome than usual. A man's man with his square jaw and deep-set eyes. All evening, he'd been charming and attentive, peppering her with questions about her political views and her impressions of Sacramento and *Vista*.

"I took my eldest daughter to a place like this when she was six years old and she ordered the escargot," he said, shaking his head. "Big mistake. She loved them. Next thing I know I'm paying market price for snails every time they're on a menu."

"How old is she now?"

"Twenty-seven. With two little girls of her own. Cutest angels you ever saw, but I'm biased." He drew out his wallet to show off the sisters in matching lavender dresses. "Grandpa here plans to introduce them to lobster, caviar, truffles. You know what they say about paybacks."

She liked how proud he was of his four grown children. The mom, the chemist, the dental student and the US Marine Corps corporal. They had that pride in common.

He was twice-divorced, accepting the blame for both. "I was married to my job. Having grandkids, though...it puts everything in perspective."

"I hope to find that out for myself someday, but I'm not sure it'll happen. My husband—he died last year—he told me once he'd make more time when the grandchildren came along."

"It's easier to do when you don't feel responsible for them."

She'd heard a tremor in her voice as she brought up Bruce. All evening, she'd been wishing the person across from her was someone she could talk to without being anxious over every word. Someone she could trust with her secrets and emotions. Someone who wouldn't judge her, who'd take her side. Summer Winslow.

"So where do you see yourself five years from now, Ellis? Staff writer? Associate editor? Or touring the morning talk shows talking about your Great American Novel?"

"Ha! I have a feeling my chances for writing a bestseller are greater than my chances for moving up at *Vista*. From the looks of our office, youth is valued more than experience."

He shook his head. "Wish I could argue with you but you're probably right. Marcie has a thing for hipsters. Have to give her credit though. With her focus on the capitol, she got me syndicated in all the major papers in the state. That's money in the bank."

"It's good for your profile too. Before you know it, someone else will come knocking."

"Not a chance. I'm happy right where I am," he answered, and then launched into a chronology of his career. *The Record* in Stockton, the *Mercury-News* in San Jose, where he'd been downsized after the paper was sold. His work as a stringer for the Associated Press brought him to Sacramento. It was an exemplary résumé, made even more impressive by the way he downplayed his accomplishments. "What I like best about *Vista* is not having an editor standing over my shoulder telling me what stories I ought to be writing about. That's the ultimate freedom for a columnist."

"I always liked that about freelancing. I never ran out of ideas."

"I went online and read some of your work," he said casually.

She waited several seconds for his assessment, but he went about carving his lamb. "And?"

"And...I found them to be...well structured." His eyes darted back and forth nervously, clearly aware of his clumsy word choice.

"That's possibly the very best example I've ever heard of damning with faint praise."

They stared at one another, she with her sternest look and he as though he'd swallowed his foot, before they both burst out laughing.

"I didn't mean to imply that your stories weren't good. It's just that…well, I'm not that big on features." He gestured toward his plate. "Sort of a meat and potatoes guy."

Not even when those features shined a light on teachers who found innovative ways to deal with brutal cuts to their classroom budget? Or single mothers who raised two children on minimum wage?

"You had me terrified I'd said something horribly insensitive," he went on.

"You actually did. Lucky for you, I have enough self-esteem where my writing is concerned to survive your feeble compliments." In fact, she was proud of her work and confident she could tell an engaging story. While her ego didn't require glowing accolades, it still was nice to get respect from other writers and people she actually knew. "For your information, I've read your work too—everything in the *Vista* archives. Marcie insisted on it. And I shall swallow my indignation and confess that I find it extremely well written and quite compelling. I'd say you have the unique ability to engage readers' interest in what might otherwise be a boring topic."

"Thank you very much. And I owe you an apology for—"

"Forget it." She doubted it would be sincere. "But it would be nice if you stopped to consider once in a while that the policies you write about impact the people I write about."

"Touché, madame." He offered a toast with his wine glass.

Despite Rex's falter, she'd begun to enjoy their conversation, especially as he shed light on the inner workings of the capitol—the alliances and adversaries, the naked ambition and the personal secrets all the players held close. It was especially nice when he probed her for ideas on how to make his stories more meaningful to readers like her.

Still she couldn't seem to relax.

He was hardly behaving like a rogue. He'd complimented her dress with a momentary leer when he picked her up, but hadn't said or done anything else she considered flirting. No effusive flattery or touching. It was almost as if getting her to say yes to dinner was his sole conquest. He'd given her little reason to worry about his intentions. Though he showed no sign he expected more than company and conversation, she was prepared to be firm in her refusal. Friends. Anything else was too soon, too complicated.

So why had she come at all? Since the moment they'd met, he'd made no secret of his interest. Interest usually led to desire. Had she come in search of a similar spark? Or had she failed her first test of independence by meekly giving in to the first man who came along?

The more her mind raced with questions, the more she believed she'd made a huge mistake. She was leading him on. Summer had warned her not to do this. Rex could make her job a living hell if he turned on her the way he had on the other assistant editors. What would it take? Would a simple no when he pressed to come inside for a nightcap be enough?

"Is your dinner all right?" he asked, gesturing toward her plate.

Lost in thought, she'd barely touched her food. "It's wonderful, but it's such a large portion. I guess I filled up on salad and bread. That's easy to do when everything is so good."

He shrugged. "I'm sure they'll let you take it home."

She was forced to do exactly that rather than admit the chicken was too spicy.

When the valet delivered his luxury sedan, Rex held her door, offering his hand for support. It was surprisingly callused for a man who made his living as a writer. Bruce's hands had been soft...enough that she'd once teased him about never having worked an honest day in his life. How cruel those words must have seemed to a man who secretly wasn't working at all.

"Have you seen much of the city since you've been here?" Rex asked.

"Not really." Her knowledge of Sacramento was largely limited to the route between her apartment and the office, though Jeremy had driven her around the capitol once when she came to visit. That didn't mean she wanted a tour now. She was ready to go home despite her anxiety over how their evening would end. No, she wouldn't invite him in for coffee. She dreaded his suggestion to do this again, but not nearly as much as the possibility he might try to kiss her goodnight.

"Then I insist on showing you a few things. We'll start with the Christmas lights at the Capitol Building."

The statehouse, bathed in white lights, was admittedly striking with its marble columns and majestic dome. A single Norfolk pine stood in front, decorated with thousands of twinkling lights that gave it a purple glow.

"This is lovely," she said.

"I love the city at night. Especially over by the river. The buildings reflect off the water, and everything seems...I don't know, brighter. Livelier."

They weren't far from *Vista*'s headquarters, but Ellis usually skirted the capitol to avoid traffic. She'd never seen this side of the mall before, nor ventured toward the Sacramento River.

"Here's a treat for you," Rex said as he rounded a curve. Before them was a bridge lit with golden floodlights aimed upward at two tall structures in the center. "It's not as majestic as your Golden Gate, but it's still interesting. This is our Tower Bridge." He slowed as they drove across, explaining how the segment between the towers lifted like a platform when boats passed underneath.

"I'm impressed." Though nothing was as splendid as the Golden Gate Bridge.

He smiled proudly, as if he'd built the bridge himself. "And there's another sight for you."

She followed his gesture to a glowing building, also golden, on the opposite side of the river. It was built in the triangular shape of a Mayan temple.

"You have your Transamerica Pyramid. We have the Ziggurat."

The words jolted her. Did he know?

"That's the headquarters for California's Department of General Services. I spend a lot of time over there roaming the halls trying to get somebody to talk to me. It's surprisingly easy. All I have to do is tell them I've been talking to so-and-so, and I'm going to run with that unless they want to set me straight."

Of course he knew. All those years as an investigative reporter whose specialty was connecting the dots and telling stories people didn't want told. If he'd been determined to find out who she was, it was buried there in the public records—her marriage license, Bruce's death certificate and her petition to revert to her maiden name.

And now he was fishing, hoping she'd confess that her husband had worked in the Pyramid. That he'd murdered seven of his coworkers. What was his angle? The tragedy one year on. The spinelessness of politicians who refused to pass meaningful gun control. Who refused to fund mental health programs. Or maybe an invasive look into the lives of the survivors. An inventory of her guilt.

Surely he wasn't entertaining the idea of writing a column about a coworker. That was a breach of journalistic ethics. It just wasn't done.

"I'd like to go home now."

"You sure? We could stop in Old Sacramento…walk around a bit. They've preserved the—"

"No." It came out more sharply than she'd intended. On the off chance she was jumping to conclusions, she softened her reply…with a lie. "My daughter is coming by first thing in the morning and I have some things to do to get ready."

They rode home in silence, with Ellis growing more convinced Rex knew her whole story. That meant he also knew why she'd suddenly canceled the rest of their evening. She was perfectly happy to have him stew on that, and if it made him think twice about asking her out again, so much the better.

She was already out of the car by the time he reached her door. "Thank you for dinner," she said cordially.

"Oh, that reminds me." He retrieved her doggie bag from the back seat.

"Great." She forced a smile. "I'll have this tomorrow and you'll have bought me dinner twice."

Wordlessly, he insisted on walking her to her door. When they reached the doorstep, he took her key, pushed the door open and stepped back, clearly having gotten the message that he wouldn't be invited in. "Ellis, would you mind if I asked you a question?"

She froze, imagining myriad possibilities, nearly all of them unsettling.

"Was tonight your first date since your husband died?"

That wasn't the one she'd expected. "Yes."

"I thought that might be the case." He pushed his hands in his pockets in a gesture she found pleasantly disarming. "I enjoyed your company very much. I hope I didn't push anything too far. I'd like it if we could do this again…but I understand if you think it's too soon."

Under the circumstances, it was probably the best thing he could have said, and she felt the tension that had been building over the past fifteen minutes begin to dissipate. "I appreciate your sensitivity. It's definitely a big change and I'm still getting my bearings." She reached out for his hand and shook it firmly.

His response…it wasn't exactly a smile. But it was a kind look, more compassion than pity. "I'll leave it in your hands. Whatever feels right."

"Thank you, Rex."

Once inside, she made a beeline for the refrigerator and removed a bottle of chardonnay that she'd corked the night before. The clock on her stove said nine twenty.

But it wasn't really wine she wanted. She needed to unwind, to talk about her feelings with someone who'd give her sound advice, someone who wouldn't judge her. In the old days that would have been Roxanne. They hadn't spoken in months, not since Ellis had called on the verge of tears to mourn the sale of the house she'd lived in for more than two decades. Roxanne couldn't talk—she was hurrying onto a plane to Tokyo. Ellis's self-pitying tantrum over being cut off had ruined their thirty-year friendship.

Summer was her refuge now, the only one who'd promised to be there when she needed someone. All evening, she'd found herself wishing for the comfort of their friendship, the ease of their conversations. That friendship mattered more to Ellis than she'd realized, certainly more than a premature romance that brought more risk than reward.

CHAPTER EIGHT

"Come in, come in." Summer was both surprised and delighted to find Ellis at her door, smiling and holding out an empty coffee mug. "I take it you want me to fill that?"

Ellis removed her thigh-length overcoat to reveal a skin-tight black dress that boasted more than a little cleavage. Clearly she'd been out on the town.

"Holy wow, woman! You look amazing. But if you ask me, it's a little fancy to be out slumming for coffee." She fanned her face with both hands. "Not that I'm complaining. You can wear that over here every day as far as I'm concerned."

She couldn't help her effusive compliments, especially when she saw Ellis wasn't bothered by their pseudo-sexual nature. Or maybe her smile meant she was happy to stand on the receiving end of a lesbian's gushing about her appearance.

"I'm a big believer in making myself presentable when I drop in unannounced."

"Just don't expect me to dress like that when I pop over to your place." Summer looked down at her bedroom slippers and flannel pants. "By now you've probably noticed that I wear pajamas at home. Almost exclusively."

"I have, and I'm jealous. Now I'm wishing I'd taken the time to change."

"I'd offer you a pair of my sweats, but they wouldn't get past your knees. Why don't you run back home and change while I make your coffee?" She liked the dress—she liked the dress a lot—but also wanted Ellis to stay awhile. She'd be more likely to do that if she were comfortable.

"You've got a deal," she said, her high heels clacking as she left.

It appeared she'd followed through on her date with Rex, and now she was coming to dish. Summer felt a twinge of guilt for being glad she was home so early.

She liked knowing Ellis valued their new friendship enough to come here first to share her news. Unfortunately, that also meant she'd have to feign enthusiasm if Ellis was happy with how the evening had gone.

"I think you're onto something," Ellis announced when she returned. She'd changed into worn jeans and an oversized white Henley, its sleeves rolled to the elbows. But thanks to her elegant makeup, she still looked far from casual.

"Pajamas are my uniform. I'd wear them to work if they'd let me." She handed Ellis her mug and guided her into the living room, where she'd been huddled under a Navajo blanket on the couch getting ready to watch a movie.

Ellis held the coffee to her nose and inhaled deeply. "Ahhh. This'll take the chill off. It's turning cold out."

"That's nothing. Watch this." Summer scrolled through the channels on her TV until she reached one with an ambient fire, complete with crackling and popping.

"I've seen those before but I never knew anyone who'd admit to using one."

"Because all your friends had real fireplaces, I bet."

They sat facing one another on opposite ends of the couch, and Ellis helped herself to the blanket, stretching her legs out alongside Summer's. "So I did it. I went out to dinner with Rex."

Her recounting of the evening sounded mostly mundane until she got to the part about him mentioning the Transamerica Pyramid. "Do you think I'm just being hypersensitive?"

"It's a helluva coincidence if you ask me."

"Especially since he used to be an investigative reporter. I bet he knows everything there is to know about me. And instead of saying something, he manipulated the conversation so I'd tell him and he could act surprised."

Summer chided herself inwardly for being glad the date had ended on a sour note, though she felt a tad guilty for not wanting Ellis to have a good time. "I guess that means Rex is history."

"I don't know what to think." Ellis sipped her coffee. "Other than that, he was very nice. And I don't know for sure he was baiting me. Turns out we actually have a lot in common. It's just that…it's been so long since I dated, I've forgotten what a farce it is. Everything feels so artificial. If we were talking in the break room at work, I wouldn't have any trouble thinking of what to say. But there's something about the whole premise of dating that turns everything into theater. The moment the doorbell rings, you freeze up and stop being yourself."

"And when you do talk, it's like a sales pitch where you emphasize all the good points and pretend there aren't any flaws."

"I can still hear my mother saying, 'Let the boy talk about himself, Ellis. That's what they like.' I can't believe that hasn't changed in all these years. Lesbians have it so much easier. Just tell me where to sign up."

"You'll be welcomed with open arms. Mine included." *If only*. "But if you think lesbians have it any easier, I've got bad news. Dating is just as much a pain for us as it is for everyone else. Maybe even worse because first we have to figure out which women are into other women. That's harder than it looks."

"I thought you all had gaydar. That's what Jeremy calls it."

"It's an imperfect system. Unfortunately, mine goes off around people I *want* to be lesbians. People like you, for example." In the context of their discussion, that was surprisingly easy to admit, and it evoked a blushing smile. Summer wouldn't go so far as to divulge her fantasies, nor the fact that she'd studied Ellis's figure in the fitness center and imagined how she looked beneath that clinging Spandex. "But once we sort that part out, the rest of it's pretty much the same."

"But I bet you look at women sometimes and see a potential friend. Men *never* see it that way. You don't have to watch their preening struts where they puff up and act like they're God's gift to women."

Summer laughed cynically and shook her head. "Whatever gave you that idea? Some of the lesbians I know can strut with the best of them. Trust me, plenty of women out there are interested in only one thing—just like men. Notch that headboard and move on."

Ellis's eyes went wide. "Are you like that?"

"No! But then I haven't been cruising in over twenty years." On that night, it was Rita who'd strutted so confidently, and Summer who'd fallen victim to her charms. Their chemistry— the raging fire that kept them entangled for twenty-one years— had erupted within moments and they'd gone home together. "I'm not even sure cruising is still in my repertoire."

"Tell me about it. I don't have a clue what I'm supposed to be looking for, but dinner still feels like the preamble. Once you say yes, they assume everything else is a possibility. I'm not going to jump into bed with someone I hardly know." She blew out a breath that sent one side of her dark hair flying. "Like I said, Rex was nice, but the whole night felt so clumsy."

"Did you feel pressured?"

"Not really, but…" Ellis stared pensively into her mug and then set it aside on the coffee table. "I make him sound so awful, but he really wasn't all that bad. It was just…blah. I didn't feel anything."

"Which is a perfectly reasonable response to a first date. Maybe you're just not ready." Her natural inclination was to reach out a comforting hand, but this time she held off.

"I sat there all night getting myself worked up about what was going to happen next. And then when we got home, I could tell he wanted to kiss me. He must have read my body language though because he didn't even try. Kissing's personal to me. On the lips, I mean. I kiss people on the cheek all the time, but I don't go around lip-locking people I hardly know."

Summer studied those lips as she spoke, wondering how they'd feel. Wondering if Ellis had ever kissed another woman. Or would ever consider it.

"I bet you still think I'm stupid for going out with him."

"I never said you were stupid. I was worried about the balance of power, but maybe that won't be a problem."

Ellis tipped her head and shrugged. "Let's hope not. I suppose I'll find out on Monday if his nose is out of joint." She looked up coyly but made only brief eye contact. "I have a confession. I skipped my workout yesterday because I didn't want to tell you I was going out with Rex."

"Aww." Summer kicked her playfully beneath the blanket. "Why would you go and do something like that?"

"Because I care what you think about me."

It was an interesting way to sum up their nascent friendship, because she felt the same way. "You don't have to worry about something like that. I liked you the minute you moved away from Gene Steele and his Fox News, and it's only gotten better since."

Ellis laughed. "And considering I wasn't too sure about you at the time, you know how much I must hate Fox News."

"Yup, that told me all I needed to know." Since Ellis had gotten up the nerve to confess how she'd skipped her workout, Summer figured she ought to come clean as well, no matter how embarrassing it was. "I have a confession too…a silly one. At least I hope you think it's silly. If you don't, then I could be in trouble."

"This already sounds good."

"Yeah, well…I had my own theory about why you skipped your workout. I thought I'd freaked you out the other night… because I might have gotten a little…" She drew her hands from beneath the blanket and wiggled her fingers. "Alythea calls it touchy-feely. It's a habit of mine. I was worried I'd sent you off screaming and running for the hills."

Ellis's smile faded instantly, replaced by an overly dramatic glower. "You know, I wasn't bothered at the time, but now that you mention it…"

"Oh, great. Now you're going to terrorize me. I pour my heart out and you use it against me."

"You call that pouring your heart out?"

"I didn't want you to think I was an evil lesbian stalker trying to lure you into my bed. Honest, I do it with everybody."

"You try to lure everyone into your bed?" Ellis craned her neck to look down the hall toward the bedroom. "Must be some bed."

Summer closed her eyes and shook her head, an outward show of indulging Ellis's weird sense of humor. On the inside, she felt nothing but relief. "It's a fabulous bed. One owner, low miles. No dents, dings or notches."

"None?"

"It's new. Actually it was from our guest room. Rita kept the other one, which was fine by me."

"Hmm…" Ellis closed one eye and tilted her head, clearly pondering something profound. "Maybe I should get a new bed. Beds are a lot like kisses. They symbolize intimacy. I think it would be weird to share a bed I've shared with somebody else. Not that I have any idea what that's like. The last time I slept with anyone other than Bruce, it was in a dorm at Berkeley. I hate to think how many people banged on that old mattress."

There was no stopping the mental image of Ellis writhing beneath a fumbling college dude, though in Summer's vision, she looked the same as now. Eyes closed, mouth open. Long arms and bare shoulders visible above the sheet.

"…a new bed anyway," Ellis was saying.

"I'm sorry, what was that?"

"I said I can't afford a new bed right now. Maybe I'll use that as my marker. No more dates until I get a new bed." She visibly shuddered. "I can't believe I'm even talking about it."

"You're allowed, Ellis. It's not like you're a hundred years old. We're sexual beings. That's human nature. It doesn't mean you should do something you aren't ready for, but don't feel like you have to fight it because of some arbitrary timeline." Summer looked down and realized she was doing it again—stroking Ellis's hand as she talked. "Sorry."

Ellis smiled as she intertwined their fingers. "It's okay. It's *your* human nature, so don't feel like you have to fight it."

* * *

It was after midnight when the movie ended and Ellis shook herself awake for the short walk home. A cheery end to what earlier had been a miserable, anxiety-filled day.

"I'm waiting right here until you get home and flash your porch light," Summer said sleepily.

"In case someone's ex-girlfriend is hiding in the bushes and decides to take me out?"

"Don't even joke about that. There's no telling what that woman is capable of."

With both of them standing in the open doorway, Ellis stepped into a hug. Summer was small in stature, and her soft blond hair nestled warmly beneath her chin. Kissing the top of her head felt like the most natural thing in the world.

But then she closed her eyes and tightened her embrace, imagining for a moment how it would feel to have Summer's lips brush against her neck.

Separating abruptly, she shook her head and blew out a deep breath to make sure she was wide awake. The thought hadn't been conscious at all. Probably just a fleeting dream triggered by their earlier discussion of Rex walking her to her door.

When she reached her apartment, she flicked her porch light and watched Summer do the same.

The small light over the stove cast a soft glow throughout her kitchen and living room. Everything had been scrubbed and straightened on the possibility she'd invite Rex in for an after-dinner drink. It seemed almost silly to imagine such a scenario. Nothing about him made her wish to feel his arms around her waist, kiss him or have him touch her in an intimate way.

Whereas the thought of doing those things with Summer was arousing. A part of her had already picked up on what

Summer had confessed. Her attention, her flattery. And she liked it.

Which was just the oddest sensation.

The black dress lay across her bed, along with the slimming bustier that had tightened her torso and pushed her breasts up and in to form a deep cleavage. Yes, she'd considered changing clothes before showing up at Summer's door with a coffee mug. But she'd known her sexy look would dazzle. That Summer would appreciate her towering elegance in the Zanotti heels she'd bought especially for opening night at the San Francisco Ballet.

What she didn't know was why Summer's approval mattered so much. Or why she was deliberately pushing those buttons.

It wasn't the same feeling as when she'd met Roxanne for lunch. Back then she'd labored over what to wear, knowing Roxanne would show up in something her personal shopper had found in Union Square using an unlimited credit card. She'd needed to hold her own against someone like that. And it was nice to imagine she was turning heads in the restaurant tonight, though by the end of their date, she'd cared little what Rex thought of how she looked. But she'd wanted Summer to appreciate her, to fantasize about being with someone so beautiful.

She'd wanted to hear Summer tell her she looked "amazing."

CHAPTER NINE

Ellis counted out eight dollars and change, and dropped another dollar in a jar by the cash register. This had to stop. She couldn't afford fifty bucks a week for lunch.

The tiny cafe catered to workers in her building, offering morning pastries and coffee, pre-made sandwiches and salads, and energy drinks for that last desperate burst needed to get through the afternoon. Nothing she couldn't bring from home.

Tray in hand, she scanned the room for a vacant table. Finding none, she interrupted another woman sitting alone at a table for two. "Do you mind if I join you?"

"Please do." The woman scrambled to move her purse and put away her e-reader. "There's never enough room in here when it's raining. I'm Nancy Singleton. I'm sure you've seen my office, Singleton Insurance. Life, home, car." At first glance, she'd looked to be in her late thirties—slender, with golden highlights in a stylish medium cut—but the lines on her face quickly added another ten or fifteen years. Like Ellis, she wore a business dress with low pumps.

Ellis introduced herself and explained she'd just started at *Vista*.

"I usually meet my husband for lunch over in the Renaissance Tower." Lowering her voice, she added, "Their cafe is much better than this one."

"I'll have to try it sometime." Though she had a feeling it was way more expensive.

"What does your husband do?"

That was a question she'd have to learn to handle in a way that deflected curiosity. Had Nancy not seemed so kind, she might have bristled at being defined by her husband's work. "He was in finance. He passed away last year."

"Oh, you poor thing. Do you have children?"

That set the conversation in a new direction, where they compared notes on their families. The Singletons had two daughters in school at Pepperdine, and a son at West Point.

It was a treat for Ellis to find someone in Sacramento with whom she could relate. Nancy was charming, though a bit old-fashioned, with an effusive personality and delightful sense of humor. In San Francisco, she would have added to the diversity of the mothers from Ellis's circle. Exactly the sort of friends she wanted to make, a new network that wasn't connected to her old life with Bruce.

The lunch break flew by and Ellis reluctantly announced she needed to get back to work.

"We have to do this again," Nancy said. "I'd love for you to meet Alvin. I know…I'll set up a dinner party. Have you found a church yet?"

The question struck her as presumptive. She wasn't usually put off by anyone's religion unless they tried to push it on her. "I'm not much of a church-goer."

"You should think about it, Ellis. It's a wonderful place to meet the right kind of men."

Another presumptive remark, but harmless—as long as the dinner party invitation wasn't meant to introduce her to someone. That she wasn't ready for, churchgoer or not.

As they left the cafe, a woman pushing an overloaded shopping cart, her hair wet from the rain, stopped to peruse the trashcan. Ellis thought of Pete, the homeless man who spent his days on the corner near her house in San Francisco, and regretted not saving part of her lunch to share. She immediately drew her wallet from her purse.

"That's so disgusting," Nancy said, not bothering to lower her voice. "I bet you thought you were leaving that kind of filth behind in San Francisco. At least we haven't been completely overrun by the gays—not yet anyway."

Ellis froze, feeling her back stiffen. She couldn't remember the last time she'd heard such a bigoted remark. It simply wasn't tolerated in the City.

At that moment, she hated Sacramento for its small-mindedness. Hated that she'd taken her beloved City for granted, for not recognizing how much it spoke to her soul. Hated the world for forcing her back in time to a place that hadn't yet evolved.

And she detested people like Nancy Singleton who thought God was whispering to them about how they should run the world.

"Nancy…I believe I'll pass on that dinner party. It turns out we may not have as much in common as I thought."

Nancy's momentary look of confusion was soon replaced by one of prim understanding. If she realized her comment had offended, she clearly didn't care. Her religion, apparently, commanded her to judge others.

"And it'll give me more time to spend with my son and his boyfriend."

She whipped past the small bills and handed the homeless woman a twenty, her own lunch money for the rest of the week. Well spent.

* * *

Pumping the elliptical alongside Ellis, Summer marveled at the woman's ability to talk without showing even the slightest drag on her breathing.

"I couldn't believe she'd say something so hateful right in front of that poor woman," Ellis said. "Does she honestly think people eat out of garbage cans because they *want* to? And that whole 'gays are taking over the world' business. What a crock."

"Welcome to my world," Summer replied bitingly. "Bigots like that, they're everywhere, but most of them crawl around like cockroaches in the dark. I had a coworker once—he didn't last long—who purposely kept sending back a grant application for a runaway shelter in LA because it targeted LGBT kids." Unlike Ellis, she had to pause her story to catch her breath. "He actually bragged about it, thought it was hilarious…how he'd circle the tiniest details on the form, like not being able to clearly read the signature. All he cared about was running out the clock on the deadline."

Ellis shook her head and groaned. "This lady was such a self-righteous bitch. At least we're finally getting to a place where opinions like that aren't acceptable."

"Sometimes I wonder if that's a good thing or a bad thing. It's kind of handy to know who your enemies are."

"Humph. I'd rather not hear it and pretend it doesn't exist. Then I wouldn't have to worry about my son living with so much hate around him."

With every conversation they shared, Summer liked Ellis more and more. She was the bane of every conservative's existence—a staunch San Francisco liberal in the mold of Nancy Pelosi, who wasn't afraid to stand up for her principles. Even with its own vibrant gay and lesbian community, Sacramento could use more transplants like Ellis Keene.

Her machine beeped when she reached thirty minutes and she began to slow. "Want to grab some dinner? There's a cafe on Freeport with California bistro."

"Sorry, my budget's whacked. I need to find something in my fridge."

"Funny you should say that. I was thinking the other day how I don't cook much anymore because it's so much trouble to fix for one. I could throw together a couple of omelets and a salad if you're interested."

She was moderately surprised when Ellis accepted and walked home with her, all the while insisting on returning the favor some other night.

Sitting across from her on a barstool as Summer whipped the eggs, Ellis asked, "Do you ever miss your house? I look around my apartment sometimes and it feels surreal, like I'm visiting my grandmother in assisted living."

Summer was afraid to laugh, though she found the comparison morbidly hilarious. "This is okay for now, I guess. I don't expect to be here forever." Nor did she expect to stay single, and it made sense to put off buying something until she knew where she wanted to live out her years and with whom.

"But you don't have anything to show for it. Rent money just goes down the drain. It scares me to think I'll retire someday and not have a place to call my own."

"I'll probably buy another place eventually. It might not be a house though…maybe a condo, something I don't have to keep up on the outside. When you think about it"—she poured half of the mixture into a warm skillet—"you don't really need a big house anymore, right? Your kids are gone, and you're going to spend ninety-five percent of the year by yourself…unless you get married again or move in with somebody."

"Now you sound like my parents."

"That can't be good."

Ellis laughed. "After my father retired, they bought a motorhome that was so big it hung over the end of the driveway. The first couple of years they drove it around the country from one campground to another. Now they just go down to Arizona in the winter. But he's talking about selling their house in Modesto and living in that tin can full-time."

Summer realized her face was contorted in pain just from imagining such a life. "It wouldn't be my first choice…"

"Or second, or tenth."

"Exactly, but more power to them if that's how they want to live. We all have to choose what makes us happy." She folded the omelet over sautéed vegetables and transferred it to a plate already containing a salad of strawberries and arugula. Passing it across the counter, she said, "Go ahead and eat while it's hot. Mine'll be ready in a minute."

"This looks fabulous." Ellis took the first bite and closed her eyes, humming with appreciation. Then her voice turned serious. "I'm not sure being happy's even on the menu for me. I'd be satisfied if I didn't hurt all the time, especially for my kids and the other families. What Bruce did…at least it's not in the news anymore. They bring it up every now and then when it happens somewhere else, but most people get to forget. We don't. We still live with it every single day, and we always will."

"I can't even imagine what that must be like."

"It was hardest on Allison, and then Jeremy because he's so sensitive. Jonathan was the strong one, the only one who didn't let it tear him apart. I knew he would be. He's always been so…" She frowned and raised her chin defiantly, as though she were imitating him. "Strident. He has everything so perfectly planned, and he never, *ever* loses control. So much like his father. Personality-wise, I mean. He doesn't have a violent bone in his body. Of course, I would have said the same thing about Bruce, so what do I know?"

It was fascinating to hear her ramble so candidly, as if spilling out reams of pent-up thoughts.

"When I think about the house, all the kids growing up there…how they would have come home someday with my grandchildren…it's selfish to say this, but I get nostalgic for the life I thought I'd have. It's almost unbearable. When Bruce retired, we were going to see the world. The opera in Vienna, the ballet in Moscow. Live in Paris for a summer. He didn't just die. He took all of our dreams with him. All of *my* dreams."

Summer waved the spatula emphatically. "You shouldn't feel selfish about that, Ellis. You have a right to mourn your old life. It was taken from you in the cruelest way possible." She turned back to the stove, flipped the second omelet onto her plate and came around the counter to take the other barstool.

"Maybe, but I hate to sound like I'm feeling sorry for myself. Those other families…they're all so angry. I don't blame them but I'm angry too. It was one thing for him to lash out at the people he thought were responsible for his problems. But he lashed out at the people who loved him, like it was our fault for expecting so much of him. The thing is though, he never asked us to settle for less. We would have been fine."

She wondered if Ellis had ever availed herself of a therapist who could help her process this tragedy. Probably not, and it wasn't because she was too proud to accept help. It was because she thought she didn't deserve it, that she needed to suffer to make up for the pain her husband had caused.

Ellis abruptly dropped her fork and rested her forehead in her hand. "I'm sorry. You're the first person I've actually talked to this way. Now that I've started, I can't seem to turn it off."

Summer stood, finding herself the same height as Ellis sitting on the stool. She hugged her and pressed her cheek to Ellis's ear, feeling a tremor that signaled tears might be on the way. "You don't have to turn it off. This is what friends do for each other."

The hug seemed to calm her, and after a long silence, Ellis patted her hand. "Thank you. It's amazing to me...people I've known for twenty or thirty years don't know what they're supposed to do with me, and you knew right away. I just needed somebody to listen."

"Anytime." She reluctantly let go and returned to her stool. Ellis's heartfelt confessions had sent her protective instincts into overdrive. "Don't write off those dreams just yet. There's still plenty of time to make them happen. But don't be surprised if they fade away when you find some new ones."

"You're right. Life's full of surprises." Ellis smiled with resignation and shook her head. "If anyone knows that, it's me."

* * *

"...and don't you dare change your mind and start thinking you're going to skip Christmas dinner, young man. You haven't even seen my new apartment."

Jonathan assured her he'd be there, though he couldn't commit to more than a few hours. He was working on an article for the *Stanford Law Review*, quite a prestigious honor for an undergraduate, and one that would practically guarantee his acceptance into law school.

"I love you, honey. Call us when you leave Palo Alto."

Ellis had phoned each of her kids after returning home from dinner with Summer. Her emotional outpouring had triggered a need to touch them all and make sure they were okay.

For a day that included a run-in with Sacramento's very own Church Lady, it was ending with her feeling amazingly upbeat. She was learning to count on Summer for the friendship she'd promised. In fact, she could honestly say—other than having Jeremy and Allison so near—Summer was the best thing about Sacramento, and the only thing that had proven one hundred percent reliable.

She readied for bed with a quick shower, rinsing away the salty residue of her workout. Motivating herself to get to the fitness room after work was easier knowing Summer would be there. Though her muscle-toning drills with a personal trainer were a thing of the past, she was satisfied that her focus on cardio would keep her fit. It actually relaxed her at the end of a workday, and helped keep her slim.

Twisting from side to side, she admired her figure in the mirror. Her breasts were large enough that gravity was the enemy, but they still held an attractive shape. A modest bit of extra flab around her belly, plus the faint remnant of her Caesarean scar. All in all, she was proud to look so good at forty-eight, but sexy wasn't a concept she entertained anymore.

Sexy for whom? She'd dressed up for Rex Brenneman, but her sexy feelings had evaporated almost the moment he arrived at her door.

Whereas...she'd gone out of her way to show off for Summer after her date.

She slid a satin nightshirt over her head and turned down the bed. A copy of the newest *San Francisco Vista* sat on her nightstand but she had no interest in reading tonight.

Her eyes gradually adapted to the dark, taking in the ambient red glow of her alarm clock.

Beneath the covers, she cupped both her breasts and began a sensuous massage, fondling her nipples until they were almost too sensitive to touch. Then a hand drifted lower...through her curls and into her warm, wet folds. With two fingers she spread the moisture all around, moaning softly each time she stroked her clitoris.

In her mind's eye, it was Summer's hand touching her for the first time and marveling at the slippery softness. Sighing when she found the swollen tip.

Ellis moaned again and tightened her butt in pulses as the sensations began to build. Faster, slower, faster. Up to the edge where she'd back off to draw it out. The fine, dangerous line between having a thunderous climax and losing it to the ether.

And all the while Summer telling her she was beautiful. She was hot.

Their skin together.

"Oh yes, that's it!" she cried to no one. A fantasy. A harmless trick of the imagination.

CHAPTER TEN

Queenie Sullivan was the last person a restaurant owner wanted to see at an all-you-can-eat salad bar. An elementary physical education teacher, she burned more calories in a day than most people did in a week. Though weathered and gray, she was as fit as women half her age.

She returned from her second trip to the buffet line with her platter piled high and placed a roll on the plate of her partner Sam. "They just put out fresh bread. I got you one."

"Sometimes I think you have a hollow leg," Summer said as she stole a stuffed olive. If she ate like Queenie, she'd be the size of a grand piano.

"We came here the other night with Rita and got a pizza. She said she wasn't very hungry and ended up eating half of it by herself."

It had taken them all of an hour to finally get around to bringing up Rita. It actually was an innocuous way for Summer to keep up with her, as long as they didn't pressure her to give Rita another chance. "How's she doing?"

"Believe it or not, I think she's finally starting to turn the corner."

Summer tipped her head in doubt, deciding not to mention that Rita had shown up at her house again only a few nights ago. "I'll believe it when I see it. And I don't mean just not drinking for a few weeks. Her changes have to come from somewhere deeper than that."

"Seriously, this time might be different," Sam said. Unlike Queenie, she was on the heavy side, with dark Italian features, the most prominent of which were gorgeous brown eyes. "She told us about running into you at Muntean's, and she said…how did she put it?"

"She said, 'I think it's really over with Summer this time.'"

That Rita finally understood was indeed big news. "And what do you think? Is she going to start drinking again?"

Sam shook her head. "She hasn't, at least not as far as we know."

"And we would know, I think," Queenie added. "Practically every time she has too much to drink, she calls us to talk. She convinces herself she's got it all worked out, and she has to tell us every little detail about what she's going to do. Always these great plans."

"We just pass the phone back and forth. I'm not even sure she remembers it the next day."

"And she hasn't done that?" Summer asked.

"Not since the night the police showed up," Queenie said. "I honestly think that scared the crap out of her. She called me the next morning to ask where I'd hidden her keys. Man, she was mad as hell, but I told her to shut up, that I didn't want to hear about it."

Sam held up a hand as she finished a bite of her chopped steak. "But that wasn't what finally did it."

Queenie went on, "A couple of days after that, she came over…acting like nothing happened. That was it for me. I told her I was through with her. All calm-like, not mad at all. I just put it out there that I was done picking her ass up and trying to help her patch things up with you. I said you were doing what was best for you and she needed to respect that…get herself together and think about what she wanted to do next."

"No kidding." Summer was awestruck. She'd been trying for months to get Queenie and Sam on her side. Instead, they'd been running interference for Rita, conniving to get the two of them back together. Maybe they were finally coming around because Queenie had seen the ugly side up close for herself, the side Summer saw all the time. "You guys have no idea how happy I'd be if she'd just accept that. I'd like to be friends with her again someday—the old Rita—but every time I try to be nice, she takes it the wrong way. And then if I don't respond to her, she threatens to go get drunk."

"She's not going to AA or anything like that," Sam said. "But Queenie said she was thinking about seeing somebody…a therapist. We thought you'd be happy to hear that."

"That would be so good for her." Maybe she'd taken the advice to heart. If anyone could use a therapist, it was Rita. She had a lot more to work on than her issues with alcohol. Her anger, for instance, and how she manipulated people with emotional blackmail.

It was obvious now that Queenie and Sam had arranged this dinner to update her on Rita's progress. Or were they running interference again? It didn't necessarily matter, not if Rita had finally gotten the message that she wasn't coming back.

Their waitress dropped off the check without offering to refill their drinks.

Sam nudged Queenie with her elbow. "She thinks you've had enough."

Summer counted out her part of the bill before deciding to pick up the tab with her credit card. "I'll get this. I've missed you guys." Their friendship was important to her, and she looked forward to the day when they could enjoy each other without Rita's problems sucking all the air out of the room.

"You're coming for Sam's world-famous lasagna on Christmas, aren't you? She's making enough for thirty."

Summer chuckled. "Only twenty if one of them is you."

That would mean seeing Rita again, but she'd be a lot easier to handle around a houseful of people—especially if she finally understood it was over.

* * *

Jeremy, fresh from his shower in jeans and a rugby shirt, dropped a kiss on Ellis's cheek as he walked past on his way to the refrigerator for a beer. "You don't have to do that, Mom."

"Somebody does." She'd gone through their closet and collected everything that needed ironing. "You could always buy permanent press, you know."

"Too stiff. Besides, Bruno won't even notice."

Though she liked her son's boyfriend, she relished the chance to have Jeremy to herself for a few hours while Bruno spent the day with his family. That was his tradeoff for getting out of Christmas Mass. The Perettis didn't accept that their youngest son was gay, and according to Jeremy, were particularly aggrieved by his choice of partners—the son of a mass murderer.

"How's it going with you and Bruno's parents? Any sign of thawing?"

"Ha! No, I'm still the bad-seed pervert who's leading their choirboy astray. Did I tell you about Gianni?" Bruno's older brother. "They let him plead no contest. The girl was fifteen! But at least he's on probation now and they made him register as a sex offender."

"And he's still their favorite son, I bet."

"You got it." He plopped down in an overstuffed armchair across from her and threw his bare feet over the side. "Bruno tells me all the time how lucky I am to have a family that loves me."

"Not only that, young man. You have a family that feels *lucky* to love you." She and Bruce had suspected from the time he was four that he might be gay, sparing everyone the drama of an emotional coming out. Still, she'd secretly mourned what she thought would be a life of hardship and danger until her motherly instinct to protect him kicked in and she became his greatest champion.

"I know I don't tell you this enough, Mom, but I appreciate how nice you are to Bruno." He gestured toward the ironing board and grinned. "Jeez, you're ironing his shirts. It means a lot to him to feel like he belongs."

"As long as he's the man you love, I consider him family." She'd always welcomed the special people in her children's lives, even the boy Allison dated for a while who'd done a stint in juvenile detention. Her daughter was a born rebel, but she'd predictably broken things off when it failed to get a rise out of anyone.

Ellis wondered if her children would return the sentiment if someone special came into her own life. What would they think of her dating? It hardly seemed worth mentioning her dinner with Rex, since she didn't plan on seeing him again. The more interesting question was how they'd feel about the time she was spending with a lesbian.

"You remember the night I moved in? The police car and the woman who walked over and apologized? She and I have actually gotten to be friends. Good friends. We work out together and she's shown me all the cheap restaurants in the neighborhood."

"You're friends with a criminal?" He said it in a teasing voice.

"She wasn't the one in trouble. In fact, she wasn't even home when it happened. It was her ex-girlfriend. Apparently she came by the apartment after she'd been drinking and started beating on her door and yelling obscenities. It was the woman upstairs who called the police."

"So the criminal's a dyke."

She was taken aback by the word. "That's ugly."

"Not when a gay person uses it."

"Well, *I* don't like it," she shot back. "You may get to meet her soon. She said her family was traveling over the holidays, so I'm thinking of asking her to join us for Christmas dinner. Would you be all right with that? And please don't call her a criminal—or a dyke."

"Why wouldn't I be? The more the merrier."

She could honestly say she loved all three of her children equally, but she'd always felt closest to Jeremy. More than the others, he'd needed her support growing up, and it had led to long hours of talking about everything from his emotional well-being to relationships. Even sex—in particular, his potential exposure to AIDS—but in a way that kept his private life private. She liked to think her fierce advocacy of his identity as a gay man had made him the grounded, confident man he was today.

What would he say about his mother being the target of another woman's interest? And to know she was flattered. Enough that she was considering a response.

"Her name's Summer. Summer Winslow. She works for the state...something to do with services for the homeless." She told him the origin of her name and added the tidbit about Woodstock. Talking about Summer gave her an odd feeling of excitement, as though it were somehow provocative.

"She sounds cool. Can't wait to meet her."

If Jeremy—her gay son—was troubled by the idea of her dating another woman, she needn't wonder how Allison and Jonathan would react. Not that she was willing to give them final authority over her personal life. But it would have to be a meaningful relationship for her to go against them. They were all she had.

If anyone had told her years ago she'd seriously consider getting involved with a woman, she'd have laughed in their face. But that was before she met a woman who'd openly expressed her interest. For whatever reason, she couldn't stop thinking about Summer's flirtations.

She'd never been attracted this way to Roxanne, nor any of the girls from college, women she'd known very well. Many of them were quite pretty, arguably prettier than Summer. They were smart, sure of themselves. Yet none had ever sparked her interest this way.

"Jeremy..." Her mind raced ahead, and she cynically acknowledged this could turn into the weirdest conversation she'd ever had. "Were you ever attracted to a girl?"

"Whoa! Where's this going, Mom?"

"Oh, for goodness sakes, don't read anything into it. Just try to answer the question. Was there ever a girl you thought was different from the others? Somebody who maybe made you think, 'Okay, if I *had* to be with a girl, this one would be okay.'"

He had a wide-eyed look of horror, as if she'd grown another head. "Never."

There went that theory. Had he said yes, her attraction to Summer might have made sense. A perfectly normal departure from her real self that said nothing about her identity.

"Fine. You're gay. A hundred percent."

"Is there something wrong with that?" he asked indignantly.

"No! I just was…" She'd stupidly backed herself into a corner, leaving herself no choice but to come clean, lest he think she was having doubts about him. "I wonder about people who live their lives one way, and then all of a sudden discover something different, something they didn't expect. What do you think causes them to change?"

"You mean people who get married and have kids, and then realize they're gay?" He scrunched his lips as he considered the question. "I think most of them were always gay but they felt pressure to conform…or they never knew the other was even an option. I don't think that happens as much as it used to. It's more accepted now."

"But what about those who didn't feel that pressure to begin with? They just went from being straight one day to being gay the next…or the other way around. Or maybe they're bisexual and don't know it."

"They probably always had that tendency but it never kicked in until a certain person came along." He laughed softly. "But it isn't going to kick in with me, so you might as well hang it up if that's what you're thinking."

"Sweetheart…" She perched on the arm of his chair and hugged him around the shoulders. "I'm not trying to change you. You're perfect the way you are. The person I'm wondering about…is me."

He swung his legs around and sat up straight. "You? What are you talking about?"

"Can we keep this between us? You and me. I don't want you to say anything to Allison or Jonathan, okay?"

"You're freaking me out now. What's going on?"

"It's about Summer. She's been flirting with me. Not in a bad way. Friendly, kind of teasing but maybe not...like if I actually responded, she'd be serious." She kept talking, ignoring how his jaw had dropped. "You'd think that would make me uncomfortable, but you know what? It doesn't."

It was clear after several seconds of silence that he wasn't going to respond unless she asked him a direct question. At least he wouldn't respond verbally—the tips of his ears were turning red.

"Jeremy, what would you think if I dated a woman? Would you be okay with it?"

He still took his sweet time to answer, setting her on edge with doubt. "I can't lie, Mom. It would be kind of weird. But I guess the idea of you dating anybody is weird, so I'm not sure it makes any difference who it is."

"Fair enough."

"That doesn't mean you shouldn't. It just means it'll take some getting used to. Nobody expects you to sit at home forever like your life is over."

She took the longneck bottle from his hand and helped herself to a slug of beer. "Believe me, it isn't nearly as weird for you as it is for me. I went out the other night with somebody from work. Rex Brenneman, the guy who writes all the political columns. My first date in twenty-six years, Jeremy."

She couldn't bring herself to tell him about the lack of physical attraction. A young man didn't need to think about whether or not his mother was getting aroused. Besides, her lack of sexual chemistry with Rex wasn't the main reason she'd labeled the night a bust.

"I was a nervous wreck all night. Couldn't wait to get home. And you know what I did? I went straight over to Summer's apartment to tell her all about it. I can talk to her about things. I have a lousy day at work...I go over there and just being with her makes everything better. Next to the three of you, she's the person I feel most comfortable with. We even hold hands when we talk…it's really sweet."

He sipped his beer in silence, clearly at a loss for words.

"I told her about your dad, and you know what? She was the first person *ever* who told me she was sorry for my loss."

Finally he answered with a grunt. "I know what you mean about that. I totally quit Twitter and Snapchat. All the people I used to keep up with from high school…probably the nicest thing any of them ever said was they knew I'd never do something like that. Bruno was the only one who really got that I was hurting because my father had died."

Her children's suffering broke her heart. They'd all wear the scars of Bruce's shooting for the rest of their lives.

"Honey, that's one of the reasons I like Bruno so much. I see how good he is to you. And it's why Summer's kindness means so much to me. She's a very dear person."

He rested his hand atop hers on his shoulder. "Are you sure she's talking about a relationship? Most of the gays I know steer clear of straight people unless it's just for a hookup."

The hookup culture of gay men was something she tried hard not to think about. It hadn't occurred to her Summer might only be interested in—

"No, honey. I'm not sure at all. But she was in a long-term relationship with that other woman, the one who came to the apartment and nearly got arrested." And she didn't collect notches on her bedpost, she remembered. "She hasn't come right out and asked me anything, but she made it pretty clear she's interested in something if I am. And ever since she said that, I can't stop thinking about it."

He took his beer back and guzzled the rest of it. "You want to split another one?"

"No, I need to go home. I have my own ironing to do." She couldn't shake the feeling that she'd made him uneasy, but there was more left to say. "Thank you for letting me talk this out with you. I know it isn't easy for a young man to think about that part of his mom's life, but you're special. I needed to know how you felt. And if I decide I want to get involved with Summer, well…I may need an ally."

His face softened and he pulled her into a hug that filled her with relief. "I'm always on your side, Mom. Just like you're always on mine."

"I love you." After several quiet seconds, she wriggled away and slung her purse over her shoulder. "And please, Jeremy… don't say anything to Jonathan or Allison for now. They won't be able to see this the way you do. It may not come to anything and I don't want to upset them over nothing."

"You just wanted to upset me?" His mischievous smile let her know he was teasing.

"Only you."

As she walked to the car, she was struck by the change in her attitude over just the last fifteen minutes. By giving voice to the question of whether she should get involved with Summer, she'd discovered the answer.

CHAPTER ELEVEN

Ellis waited at the dining table for Summer to exit her bedroom in her third outfit. Slimming pants, a scoop-neck top and casual linen blazer, all in earth tones. It was arguably her best look. A look that got under her skin. If Summer's intention was to make herself more attractive for her blind date, she was succeeding wildly.

"I guess I'll go with this one," she grumbled. "It's not my favorite…I hate not having any pockets. What do you think?"

"You look great," she confessed, albeit reluctantly. She chose one of the scarves hanging on a chair and draped it around Summer's neck. "Perfect, in fact. Where are you going?"

"It's called the Lemon Grass. Mostly Thai. Apparently it's only a few blocks from where Tracie lives, so she's going to meet me there. I said I'd take her home."

A short date, but one that might include going inside her apartment afterward. Coffee, conversation…it might even lead to more. "Do you know much about her?"

Summer stood before the hall mirror experimenting with different scarf knots. "I didn't talk with her long on the phone, but my friend Courtney liked her a lot. I know she works at the convention center with another one of my friends. A hotel liaison or something. And she's from somewhere down around LA."

"About our age?"

"Maybe a little older. Early fifties, I think."

Ellis was still dressed from her Saturday errands in a thin cardigan over a longer shirttail with skinny jeans. Not fancy enough for a date, but she was confident she could hold her own against other women her age.

It bothered her to realize Summer was dressing, not for herself, but to impress her date. Or maybe it bothered her to know Tracie would be impressed. "You know, if you want pockets, you should wear something that has pockets. It doesn't matter how you look if you aren't comfortable."

"These are okay, I guess," she said wanly. She wrapped the scarf twice around her neck and tucked the ends into her top.

"That's too much to have around your neck while you're eating. It'll drive you crazy." She draped it again, allowing the ends to hang loose. "Forgive me for saying this, but you don't strike me as someone who's excited to be going on a date. Are you even sure you want to do this?"

"I didn't at first," she said, her reluctance obvious, "but I guess it's time. I've been trying to fly under the radar ever since I split up with Rita because I didn't want to set her off. And I wanted to be by myself for a while."

"And now you're ready for a new girlfriend?"

"Who knows? You can waste a lot of time and energy looking for a new relationship." She spun away from the mirror and started pacing. "It's like a bear claw at the bakery. You don't go looking for one. You walk by the window and see it sitting there. And what do you do? You try to resist it. Except your mouth starts watering, and if you close your eyes, you can almost taste it. So you go back and get it."

"A bear claw."

"A relationship. The best ones are the ones you can't resist, the ones you can't stop thinking about no matter how hard you try."

Ellis decided not to point out the obvious—that Summer had trouble in the past resisting Rita, and she hardly qualified as a good relationship. "So which one is Tracie? The one you're looking for, or the one you happened to walk past when Courtney told you to call her?"

Summer's face contorted in a look of confusion. "Good question. I hadn't thought about it that way."

Ellis was confused too, but for totally different reasons. Why was she so annoyed that Summer looked so good? Why was she watching the clock, dragging out the conversation in order to make her late? Why was she challenging the premise that Summer was dating again?

Because she was jealous. Summer told her she'd be first in line if she ever wanted to date a woman. Now that she'd actually considered saying yes, she didn't want the invitation snatched away. What if Summer fell for Tracie?

"I guess I should go," Summer said, slinging her purse over her shoulder. "Don't want to be late."

Fighting the temptation to prolong her leaving, she took Summer by the shoulders and eyed her up and down. "You look fantastic."

"Thanks," she replied, looking down with a sheepish smile. "Let's hope Tracie likes it."

Ellis didn't hope that at all.

* * *

"Second thoughts" was putting it mildly. By the time she arrived at Lemon Grass, Summer was watching her phone and hoping for a text from Tracie. Food poisoning, a migraine… called in to work to deal with an emergency. Any excuse would do.

It wasn't anything against Tracie. She'd sounded very nice on the phone, and Courtney's recommendation carried a lot of weight.

The problem was Summer wanted to be somewhere else, with somebody else. The whole time she'd been dressing for her date, she'd imagined she was going out with Ellis. A five-star restaurant, both of them in their nicest clothes. Why hadn't they done that before? Hell, why hadn't they done that tonight?

Instead she was about to meet a stranger, someone her friends thought she'd like. How could she like anyone as much as she liked Ellis?

Ellis was the bear claw in the bakery case. From the very first night she'd seen her in the parking lot, Ellis was stuck in her head. If she closed her eyes—

The driver behind her honked his horn and she looked up just in time to dash through a yellow light, leaving the poor guy stuck for another cycle.

"Ellis Keene is not an option," she muttered aloud three times. That would be her mantra.

She recognized Tracie Carlson at the bar the instant she entered the restaurant. Blond hair with darker lowlights, big brown eyes, just as Courtney had described. She might also have mentioned her dark tan, as it was unusual in December. Either she was the outdoor type, fresh from the Southern California sun, or she frequented tanning salons. Surely it wasn't the latter, since Courtney had described her as natural.

"You have to be Summer Winslow," she said, smiling to reveal a tiny streak of pink lipstick on a prominent front tooth that slightly overlapped the other. "Tracie Carlson."

"Hi, thanks for meeting me."

They followed the hostess to their table and placed their drink orders, water with lemon for Summer and another white wine to replace the one Tracie had started at the bar.

Summer entertained a brief mental image of Ellis pouring a glass of chardonnay in her kitchen. Given what she'd been through, it was a testament to her character that she didn't drink all the time.

"I found this place right after I moved here," Tracie said. "Everything on the menu is fabulous."

She peeked over her menu for a closer look at Tracie, who seemed to fit Courtney's description of laid back. Very light makeup, understated jewelry and a blue denim pantsuit with a crisp white shirt. Next to her, Summer felt somewhat overdressed.

Since she'd been the one to extend the invitation, she felt it was up to her to drive the conversation. Besides, Tracie was new in town and needed to feel welcome. "I hear you work at the convention center with Vicki."

That was all it took to get the ball rolling. Tracie launched into a description of her career in the hospitality industry, from hotel clerk up the ladder to convention coordinator. Obviously a seasoned communicator, she had a knack for friendly conversation. Amusing anecdotes were sprinkled with just enough questions to show she wasn't in love with the sound of her own voice.

"My favorite convention, believe it or not, was the funeral directors. Trust me, they are not the somber people they appear to be. Those guys can party with the best of them. And the vendor room! Caskets lined up with all these extravagant flower arrangements, and everybody standing around laughing and sloshing wine. It was hysterical."

"You'll have to tell that at the next potluck. You know about those, right?"

"Second and fourth Monday at Courtney's. Except I don't drive after dark."

Alythea had experienced that problem before her cataract surgery, and it was a major inconvenience during Daylight Savings Time. "I'm sure somebody comes through this part of town on the way."

When the waiter delivered their dinner, Tracie ordered another glass of wine.

Hmm... Thanks to Rita, Summer was overly sensitive to other people's drinking habits. Even when she was out with Queenie and Sam, or among her potluck friends, she couldn't help but notice someone who had more than a couple of drinks. It annoyed her that she'd become the Alcohol Police. She barely knew Tracie...surely the woman deserved the benefit of the doubt.

"Courtney and Norma said I should ask you about your family," Tracie said.

"Everyone likes hearing about my childhood. You'd think I was raised by wolves." As they ate, she shared the story of growing up in a hippie family, including what she remembered of the commune. "I was only six when we left, but one thing I'll never forget was how cold it was when we took a bath in the Albion River. Still makes me shiver just to think about it."

"That is so cool—no pun intended. I know some people who claim to have been hippies, but none of them ever lived in a commune."

"Yeah, and everybody claims they were at Woodstock too. I actually was."

Tracie also had led an interesting life, which included a trans-Pacific voyage by sailboat with her father and brothers. Her tan, she explained, was left over from a trip down to Cabo just before she left LA.

"So you've only been here, what? Three weeks?"

"Two and a half. But I already know I'm going to like it. I was lucky to meet Vicki right off the bat. Because then I met Courtney…and then I met you."

Summer managed a brief smile as she grappled with a hint of alarm. Had something clicked already for Tracie? Because it definitely hadn't clicked yet for her. Granted, the evening was going better than expected, but she didn't feel even a flicker of attraction.

"Sorry if that came off as too much too soon. I've been in customer relations long enough to recognize panic when I see it." Tracie had finished most of her dinner. She pushed her plate away and leaned back to nurse her wine.

"Sorry, I…" Summer couldn't even finish the thought, let alone the sentence.

"No need to apologize. I have a bad habit of saying whatever's on my mind, especially after four or five glasses of wine."

Four or five? The first ones must have been at home, or in the bar as she waited. Indeed, her face and neck were flushed. Summer had seen that on Rita all too many times when she'd tried to pretend she'd had only one.

The moment the waiter cleared their dishes, Tracie leaned brazenly across the table, dangling her wine glass in a pose she undoubtedly thought was sexy. "Now that it's out there, I might as well own up to it. I hope I didn't scare you off. I was thinking it'd be nice to do this again…maybe at my place. I make a pretty mean veal scallopini, if I must say so myself."

Summer withdrew in time to avoid the scent of alcohol on her breath. It was stunning how quickly their date had gone south once the effects of Tracie's wine kicked in. An otherwise friendly, interesting, attractive woman reduced to an all-too-familiar caricature.

"Tracie…look, I have to be honest with you."

"You should always be honest." She slumped against the back of her chair, clearly bracing for bad news.

"My last relationship didn't end so well. We were together for a long time, and I'm not sure I'm ready to jump back into anything right now."

Tracie nodded pensively, and she squinted with apparent skepticism. "I can understand that…but you asked me out to dinner. I must have said something that made you change your mind."

Damn. She was perceptive for someone who'd had so many drinks. "The thing is, Rita and I had problems because…because she drank a lot. I'm not saying I think that's the case with you. So you like wine with dinner. Nothing wrong with that. It's my issue, not yours."

"I see." Her tone was more defensive than understanding.

"Don't get me wrong. I don't mind that my friends drink and have a good time. It's fine, really." That wasn't totally true, but it was a necessary fib to get through this conversation. "The thing is, I don't think I can handle it in someone I'm dating."

"So." Tracie pushed aside the glass, which had only a couple of sips left. "If I want to date you, I'm not allowed to drink."

A glass of wine would have been fine. The problem with Tracie was that she'd drunk four or five on their first date—and wasn't yet under the table. Someone whose body and brain tolerated that much was a habitual drinker.

"Who wants to live under somebody else's rules, huh?" Summer tacked on a weak laugh to lighten the mood, though it wasn't funny at all to remember how she'd gone through Rita's drawers and closet, and smelled her breath every time she came home. "The thing is though, I know myself. If we dated, I'd be nagging you all the time. Trust me, I've been through this before. You'd hate me within a month."

The waiter interrupted yet again, this time for their dessert order. They passed and he left the check, but his amiable chatter broke their tension long enough for Summer to plot her next move.

"Seriously, Tracie. I enjoyed meeting you tonight. You're going to make lots of friends here. You're fun to talk to, you're attractive." She had to be careful not to go overboard, lest Tracie redouble her efforts. "We could end up being good friends, don't you think?"

Tracie wrinkled her nose as she nodded. "I have to admit, you're pretty good at the old 'let her down easy' trick. We need to bring you into our office when it's time to fire people."

Summer laughed heartily as she grabbed the check.

"Oh no, you don't. Friends go dutch."

As Tracie tossed her bills across the table, her bracelet caught the edge of her wineglass and tipped it over, spilling what little was left. Yet the resulting mess was enough to confirm for Summer that she'd dodged a bullet.

* * *

"Merry freakin' Christmas," Ellis mumbled as she confirmed her online credit card payment. The holiday had taken a toll on her meager bank account, even though she'd cut back sharply on the extravagance of her gifts for her children. Everyone else—her parents, her brother and his family—had gotten only a Christmas card.

It didn't help that spring tuition was due, but at least it was the last time for Jonathan. She'd made it clear he couldn't depend on her help for law school. He'd have to get his own scholarships and loans.

January's bills wouldn't be much better. She'd blown way past her weekly grocery budget to stock the kitchen for Allison, who was spending the first week of her Christmas vacation at River Woods before heading off to visit her grandparents—Bruce's parents—in Napa. The extra cooking, lights and hot water would show up in the utility bill.

It was the emergency column of her ledger that had her most worried. She needed to build it up quickly. That could be anything—doctor visits, car repairs—not only for her, but for her kids as well. Thank goodness Summer had come to her rescue when she'd had the flat tire.

She resisted the urge to check the parking lot again for Summer's car. It was only ten after nine, hardly a late night for a dinner across town that started at seven. If she'd gone to Tracie's apartment for an after-dinner…chat, or whatever…she wouldn't be home until—

The doorbell caused her to jump, drop her pen and stub her toe on the table as she leapt from her seat. Summer smiled back at her through the peephole, still dressed in the outfit she'd worn to dinner.

"You're home early." Ellis realized too late she was grinning. There was no socially acceptable reason to be happy about her date ending so soon. "How did it go?"

"Two words—borderline disaster." After migrating to her favorite barstool, she told the story of Tracie's four or five glasses of wine, and how that led to an invitation to dinner at her place. "There's no way in hell I'm getting involved with someone else who drinks like that. I'm telling you, she wasn't slurring, she wasn't confused. Rita was the same way until all of a sudden she wasn't. She got so she could drink a whole bottle of wine and act perfectly normal. Then on the next glass it would hit her and she'd be shit-faced. No thanks."

Ellis took the other stool and raised her foot to see if her stubbed toe was broken. "Maybe she was just nervous."

"I don't think so. Most people get defensive. She didn't push back at all, except to ask if we could date if she stopped drinking. Then I found out when I took her home that she'd lost her license for driving drunk. The judge only lets her go to work and back."

From the sound of it, she was more sensitive to seeing people drink than she'd let on. "Does it bother you when I have a glass of wine? You said it didn't, but now I'm thinking you were just being polite."

"No, you're different."

Different...because they were just friends. "So you're okay with it in general, but not if it's someone you're dating."

"Right...no, wait a minute. I'm perfectly okay with you and your glass of chardonnay. It's one glass, not four. I don't want to date somebody who doesn't know the difference. I could date *you* in a heartbeat, girlfriend. All you have to do is say the word."

Ellis felt a surge of heat rush to her face as she tried in vain to hide her smile.

Flirting was like teasing—it was meant to be playful. If Summer really wanted to ask her out, she'd have done it already. She certainly wouldn't have invited her over to help her get ready for a blind date.

"Yeah, well...*the word*, as you say it, is I need to get back to work. I have bills to pay." Ellis bopped her gently on the nose and slid off her barstool. What she really needed was some space before she did something idiotic—like ask her what word she needed to hear.

CHAPTER TWELVE

The highway noise nearly drowned out Rosemary Winslow's voice. "Here, say hi to your daddy. You have to yell because he's driving."

"Hi, Daddy." Summer felt silly screaming so loudly in her apartment, but her folks were adamant about not holding the phone while driving, and their pickup was too old to have a Bluetooth connection.

"We're coming into Santa Fe right now," her mother went on. "Wish us luck. We could use a good show. We hardly sold a thing last week in Tucson. Lots of people out but they were holding onto their wallets. But we'll be back in Modesto next weekend. You'll come over, won't you? That's always been a good fair for us, especially your daddy. People actually spend money. What a concept, huh? Okay, we're here now, so I've got to go. You be sweet, Summer. Merry Christmas."

"Merry Christmas, Mama."

Summer grinned, imagining the sly look her father would have given her had they been together. Her mom was a sweetheart, warm and kind to everyone she met. She also was a talker, a woman who verbalized her stream of consciousness. Summer and her dad were used to it, and actually found it endearing, but that didn't mean they couldn't share a giggle every now and then.

After a quick check in the mirror—new jeans and a thin red sweater with a snowflake pin—she picked up her humble offering of spinach dip and walked to the next building. Ellis's invitation to have Christmas dinner with her family had come as a pleasant surprise. Her only other offer was the annual gathering at Queenie and Sam's, but she was reluctant to deal with Rita. Reports of her rehabilitation were often overstated.

The door was answered by a teenage girl with silver studs protruding from her chin, nose and brow. She was thin with dark blond hair that fell past her shoulders.

"You must be Allison."

"And you must be the neighbor who got arrested. Oops, I wasn't supposed to mention that." She covered her mouth for a second. "What's in the bowl?"

Summer was taken aback by the girl's manner until she noticed a hint of mischief in her eyes. "Spinach dip."

Allison twisted her mouth with obvious displeasure.

"Don't go making a face. It happens to be vegan because your mom told me that's all you'd eat. So I expect you to savor every bite."

"What's going on here?" Ellis appeared behind her daughter sporting a green apron that read *Dinner Is Ready When the Smoke Alarm Goes Off*. Beneath it, she wore an open-collared white shirt with black jeans and silver flats. Her hair was pinned back on both sides with tortoiseshell barrettes. "Is she giving you a hard time?"

"Yes," they answered simultaneously.

"Please come in, Summer. I'll get a tray for that."

Two young men rose from the couch and approached her. One was unmistakably her son, with the same oval face, wide blue eyes and slender nose. The male version of Ellis, twenty-five years younger. With tattoos.

"Hi, I'm Jeremy. Really glad you could come. Mom says you've shown her all the local food joints."

"Just a couple so far. Sushi Koi and Julio's."

He put a hand over his stomach. "Julio's! I hit that place every time I have a job in this part of town. Their burritos are gigantic."

"And cheap," Ellis added from the kitchen.

"This is my boyfriend, Bruno."

Bruno had a face for *GQ*. Dark eyes and hair, smooth olive skin. Despite the chill outside, he wore plaid Bermuda shorts and a crisply-ironed blue shirt with a gray T-shirt underneath.

Ellis carried in a tray and set the dip and crackers on the coffee table. When she returned to the kitchen, Summer followed and took a seat at the bar. That way they could talk and she'd still be tuned into the living room conversation.

"Sounds like you told them all about my run-in with the law."

"You forget, they witnessed it firsthand. And of course, they were worried about me falling in with the criminal element."

Allison spoke up, "Mom told us everything. She said your old girlfriend showed up drunk while you weren't home."

"And made a spectacle of herself," Summer cheerfully added. "Twenty-one years and still full of surprises."

"Were you guys married?"

"Nope, never took the plunge." She and Rita had been on the outs during the brief window in 2008 when same-sex marriage was happening in California. Then Proposition 8 put everyone on ice. By the time it came back around once and for all, she'd had too many doubts about their future to commit. "Turned out to be a good thing."

"I think a lot of gay people got married because they could," Jeremy said. "Some of my friends did it just to make a political statement. Now reality's set in and the divorces have started."

"Yeah, we're just as entitled to screw up marriage as everyone else. Equality!"

"I'm holding out for a man with a lot of money," Bruno said, grinning slyly.

Jeremy chucked his shoulder. "That's okay. I'd never marry a man who dresses like Dad on vacation." His comment brought a chorus of laughter.

"Oh God," Allison shrieked. "Remember those plaid shorts he wore when we went on that cruise to Mexico?"

"I bought him those shorts," Ellis said indignantly.

"Yeah, and the Hawaiian shirt too."

"How was I supposed to know he'd wear them together?"

Summer was so busy admiring the family dynamic, she almost missed the fact that Allison was wiping tears from her eyes. Even as everyone continued to laugh, Jeremy got up and gave her a tender hug. It was hard to fathom what this poor family had been through. Only with one another—and behind closed doors—could they reminisce about the good times.

She was humbled at being allowed inside this inner sanctum. Ellis's trust in her clearly carried weight with her children, enough to make her wonder how they'd feel if their friendship grew to something more.

* * *

Ellis missed her big kitchen. And her expansive cooking tools, her five-piece Lenox place settings and mahogany dining table beneath the elegant crystal chandelier.

And yet, she'd managed to pull together the Rowanbury traditional Christmas feast—bacon-wrapped beef tenderloin, wild rice and green beans amandine. For the past three years, that tradition also included a side dish of crispy fried tofu for Allison.

Bruno and Jeremy had brought extra folding chairs so all of them could crowd around the round table in her dining nook. All that was missing was Jonathan, who'd texted over two hours ago to say he was leaving his home in Palo Alto.

"I'm hungry," Allison whined.

"Your brother should be here in a few minutes," Ellis said.

"Am I the only one who's sick of having our whole world revolve around Jon? Is he really so busy that he couldn't leave until the last fu-freaking minute?"

She appreciated her daughter's effort to watch her language, and shot a wink toward Summer, who'd been keeping her entertained while she cooked. "They all love each other, honest. Just a few political differences."

It was a treat to have Summer there, and she was especially pleased Jeremy had been so welcoming. She couldn't wait to ask him later what he thought.

"Because Jon's turning into a right wing nut job," Allison added. "He wants to be Antonin Scalia when he grows up."

"More like Anthony Kennedy," Jeremy said. "He's the one who taught at Stanford. Say, if Jon makes it to the Supreme Court someday, you think they'll run everything on his schedule like we do?"

Ellis didn't want Summer to get a bad impression of Jonathan. "Now, *children*. We've talked about this before. His coursework is very demanding, especially at a place like Stanford. And he's stressed about getting into law school. He needs to focus. You guys should give him a break."

Allison studied her fingernails as she twisted on the barstool, an avoidance response to being scolded. "We've all been under a lot of stress. But Jon's the one who's going to roll in here like we're all beneath him. Then he'll eat and leave."

So much like his father, wrapped up tightly in his own life, often oblivious to how his actions affected everyone else. He'd started his rightward drift in the ninth grade, and family gatherings always meant him against everyone else.

"I really want to have a nice dinner today," she pleaded. "Can we please do that?"

The doorbell rang and Allison leapt to her feet, welcoming her arriving brother with a hug.

Ellis didn't care if she'd done it spontaneously or in response to her admonishment. It was their second Christmas since Bruce's death, and maybe this time they'd feel more like celebrating. Neither of her boys had come home for the holiday dinner last year, leaving her and Allison alone pushing food around on their plates. Now that her family was under one roof again, she was ready to renew their festive traditions.

* * *

Summer studied the jagged edge of her knife, wondering if it was sharp enough to cut the tension in the room.

Jon—Jonathan, he preferred—had greeted her politely, chatting longer with her than with Jeremy or Bruno. At first she wondered if it had anything to do with his brother being gay, but it soon became apparent their differences were across the board. Jonathan had a preppy look about him, with slacks and a crew neck sweater over a buttoned-down shirt, and a straitlaced personality to match. Quite the contrast to his colorful, jovial brother.

Like Allison, he had light hair, fine as silk, and a pronounced widow's peak, probably traits they'd inherited from their father. All three children had Ellis's blue eyes, but only Jeremy had the same mesmerizing brown spot in one.

"Mom says you work for the state. What do you do?" Jonathan asked.

"I'm a program analyst for homeless services. I keep track of whether or not programs are delivering resources according to the specifications of their grant. Not a money auditor. More like a hall monitor on the lookout for waste and malfeasance."

"Don't take this personally, but...how many layers of bureaucracy does the state need to run a soup kitchen?"

"A fair question." And though he'd asked her not to take it personally, it was hard not to notice it was a challenge to her usefulness as a bureaucrat. "Only three, I'd say, because it's never a good idea to consolidate too much authority. We have checks and balances, which I believe are necessary when you're spending the people's money. The service figures come to my office. Things like the number of meals, the number of individuals served, the number of paid workers versus volunteers, the ones who are working off a community service commitment because they got in trouble with the court. Then I do an evaluation and send it over to the audit department, where they—"

"And everything has to be done a certain way according to your state checklist. Not one deviation. No opportunities for innovation or efficiencies. It just seems like something the market could manage better," he said smugly.

Straining to keep the sharpness from her voice, she replied, "Oh, I'd love to see the market tackle the homeless problem. Unfortunately, Wall Street isn't interested in feeding people who can't pay. Or in building them homes. That's why caring for them falls to the state. We pay plenty of private contractors to do that, but we can't just write them a check and walk away. That would be irresponsible." Summer glanced nervously at the others, hoping she wasn't breaking a house rule by challenging Jonathan's views. Politics and mealtime weren't always the best companions, particularly when she was a guest in someone else's home.

"Yeah, Jon," Jeremy said. "What's the market plan for that?"

"A freer market would open up more opportunities so people wouldn't be losing their jobs and homes in the first place. If you don't have homeless people, you don't have homeless problems."

His tone wasn't confrontational, but there was an air of uninformed arrogance that got under her skin. Still, it wasn't her place to call bullshit. The siblings could do that.

"Do you plan on hiring schizophrenic panhandlers off the street when you open up your new law office?" Jeremy asked.

"Look, I know there are some people out there who legitimately need help. But even in a city like San Francisco, that should be in the dozens, not thousands. People aren't going to take responsibility for themselves if they know the state will."

"They didn't choose to end up there, you know. Not everybody had the chance to go to Stanford," Jeremy said.

Allison stood and high-fived her brother across the table.

"Not everybody, but you certainly did," Jonathan said, his voice dripping with disdain. "Both of you. It's not my fault you didn't have the grades to get in."

Jeremy rolled his eyes. "Nor the desire."

"No, I didn't have the grades," Allison shot back. "In case you forgot, I got accepted there too, but they rescinded it because my father murdered seven people during my senior year and my grades went into the toilet. Not that it would've made any difference. You got all the big money for college, so Jeremy and I ended up at Cal-Davis. Other than that, yeah, we had exactly the same opportunity as you."

"Stop it, please." Ellis sighed heavily and buried her face in her hands. "Can we talk about something a little more festive?"

Summer exchanged an anxious glance with Bruno. Clearly he was as uncomfortable as she, though he didn't have to feel guilty for escalating the conflict. She carved a piece of beef tenderloin and waved it with her fork. "This is delicious, Ellis."

"Thank you. My boys don't agree on everything, but I can never go wrong with bacon."

A barely audible snort from Allison registered her protest.

Coming here had been a mistake, Summer decided. She had no business horning in on a family holiday. Never mind that Ellis had practically insisted. No one wanted their dirty laundry wrung out in front of a virtual stranger.

The conversation abruptly shifted to the topic of Sacramento, and even Jonathan admitted he might end up living in the capital someday if he opted for a political career. Funny he didn't seem to connect the fact that politics was the ultimate bureaucratic job.

"Don't take offense," Ellis said, directing that to Summer, "but what I miss most is the culture. The theater, the ballet, the museums."

"We have those things too. But you're right, not as much." Sacramento wasn't exactly a stop on the Bolshoi tour, and the Crocker Museum couldn't compete for the same prestigious collections on exhibit at the San Francisco Museum of Modern Art. But anyone looking for fine art could find it. Besides, the City was an easy day trip.

"I like it here," Jeremy said. "And I like having Mom here too. It's safer, cheaper, quieter. The City's great, but I didn't like Mom being there by herself."

"I'll drink to that," Jonathan said, raising his glass of iced tea.

While the family exchanged gifts after dinner, Summer busied herself with the dishes, glad to be free of the tension.

"Hey, here's one for the jailbird," Allison shouted from the living room, holding up what looked like a shirt box.

Summer sought out Ellis, who was on the couch whistling innocently. "I thought we agreed no gifts."

"It's not a big deal. I saw it and thought of you."

Summer slid her finger through the tape and neatly straightened the folds in the wrapping paper.

"Just rip it!" Allison shouted.

It was a heather gray T-shirt emblazoned with the words, *Friends Don't Let Friends Watch Fox News.* "I love it. I'm going to wear it to work out, and I'll try to get there five minutes before Gene Steele and hide the remote."

Jonathan was the only one who didn't seem to find the gag gift funny. On the contrary, he was visibly agitated, and within moments, announced he needed to leave.

Summer took the opportunity to slip out as well, still wishing she'd taken a pass on the whole day. It was three thirty. Queenie and Sam's house party kicked off at four. She hadn't formally RSVP'd, but their invitation had been insistent.

After three hours with the Rowanbury siblings, even Rita looked manageable.

* * *

A rainbow flag hung from a pole above the porch at the modest ranch house in the area known as Arden-Arcade. It was a middle-class neighborhood with well-kept lawns and mature trees, the same one where Summer and Rita had lived for twelve of their tumultuous years.

"Look who it is!" Queenie met her on the front porch with a hug that nearly cracked her spine. The woman didn't know her strength. "I'm glad you decided to come. And I hope you're starving. Sam made enough lasagna to feed the whole neighborhood."

Summer wasn't hungry at all, but she'd make room for Sam's lasagna. "Are you kidding? I could smell it when I turned the corner."

The living room was packed with familiar faces. Courtney, Norma, Vicki, plus a few she hadn't seen lately because they didn't come to the potlucks. All were watching basketball, the Sacramento Kings taking on the Lakers. Couples mostly, but a handful of straggling singles like herself. Summer greeted them all, though one face was missing, and she gave Queenie a tentative look.

"In the kitchen with Sam…drinking club soda, as a matter of fact."

She was glad to hear it, though she couldn't quite suss out Queenie's implications. After their talk the other day, she was hopeful they'd given up on their efforts to push her back to Rita. It was beyond her why their friends had been so eager to see them back together given the stormy nature of their relationship.

With a deep breath, she continued to the back of the house to find Rita bent over a magazine at the kitchen table. She wore tan slacks and a dark green cowl-neck sweater with oversized hoop earrings. It was far dressier than what the others wore, and she'd even tamed her wild red hair.

"Something smells awfully good back here."

"Summer!" Sam was carving a tray of pasta. She dropped her spatula and opened her arms for a hug. "Merry Christmas."

"Same to you." She turned to Rita, who was on her feet, clearly in hopes of getting the same greeting. The moment they embraced, Sam dashed out of the room, no doubt to give them space Summer didn't want.

"I was worried you wouldn't come," Rita said solemnly.

"What you said at Muntean's about us being friends…I've been thinking about what that would look like." She dropped her arms and took a step backward. "For sure it means we ought to be able to hang out with our friends without dragging them into any more drama. We can do that, right?"

Rita passed the first test simply by not getting defensive. "I'm still not drinking."

Summer nodded her affirmation, careful not to show too much gusto. She couldn't let her approval be the pot of gold at the end of Rita's rainbow.

"And I stopped by your house again the other night—sober. I just wanted to tell you that I heard you loud and clear. No more laying it all on you."

She couldn't let on that she'd seen her.

"I talked to the kids this morning," Rita said. "They all said to tell you Merry Christmas."

The "kids," now grown and starting families of their own, belonged to Rita's older sister. One of Summer's favorite memories was gathering at the Finnegan home on Christmas Day to watch them open presents. "Hi back to all of them."

"You can still see them, you know. They know we're split up, but I told them it wouldn't bother me if they called you or whatever."

That brought a smile…because Summer had seen them several times already. "I ran into Cheri a couple of weeks ago at the mall. She had the baby with her. What a sweetie."

So far it was the best conversation she'd had with Rita since well before they sold the house. If they could get through the day without a melodramatic scene, they just might be able to make a friendship work.

"Summer, I owe you an apology…a real one." Her chin quivered slightly. "I've made it my New Year's resolution to stop being such a pain in the ass. I hope you mean that about us being friends."

"Sure." She hated sounding so brusque, but there was danger in showing Rita too much approval. "I appreciate you saying that. I'm sorry for all the ways I've hurt you. It would be nice to feel like that's behind us."

Sam returned to the kitchen and her lasagna, breaking the tension and giving Summer a window to leave.

Back in the living room, she squeezed between Queenie and their friend Toni, a capitol police officer originally from LA, and the only one in the room pulling for the Lakers. The camaraderie was palpable, a stark divergence from the family tension in Ellis's apartment. This was where Summer felt most at home—surrounded by women she'd known for years. People she understood innately because of their shared experience as lesbians. Friends who'd seen her and Rita through dark times.

Ellis Keene would probably never be comfortable in a room like this. She hadn't grown up feeling out of place, hadn't been the target of venomous insults, hadn't been denied the basic rights most people took for granted. At heart, she was a San Francisco socialite, the liberal version of a Stepford Wife. No matter how easily she'd handled Summer's overt flirtations, she couldn't possibly feel a kinship with these women.

Would she rather hang out with her friends, or with Ellis's squabbling kids? No contest.

CHAPTER THIRTEEN

"I thought I was going to lose my mind." Ellis had been ranting to Summer all the way to Modesto about what a slob her daughter was. Their week together in the tight quarters of the River Woods apartment had driven both of them to the brink.

"At least it's over with. You can send her to Cancun for spring break."

"I wish." She grew increasingly nervous as they neared the fairgrounds. "Do I really want to do this?"

"Turnabout is fair play. I met your family. Now you have to meet mine." Summer wore the same outfit she'd had on the night they first met—jeans and a white shirt with boots. The only difference was that her wire-rimmed glasses had darkened in the sun.

Ellis made note of the parking row in the large field adjacent to the exhibit hall, an open warehouse with a concrete floor. She'd never been to a fairgrounds in her life, not even this one in her home town.

"I have to warn you, my mom is kind of trippy."

"What does that even mean? Is she going to feed me brownies with pot?"

"Nah, they don't grow that anymore." Summer grinned. "But they can probably tell us where to get some if you're interested."

"Whose trippy now?" She actually was eager to meet a couple of old-time hippies. Her journalistic nose smelled an interesting backstory, one she'd probably never have the chance to write in Sacramento. Perhaps Gil would be willing to run it in the San Francisco magazine for some extra cash.

Summer paid their cover charge of five dollars each and they strolled down the first line of booths. Neon art, healing magnets, CDs that played dripping water and harps.

Looking ahead, Ellis spotted an older couple she knew instantly to be the Winslows. The gentleman was tall and lanky, dressed in khaki work pants and a blue flannel shirt. In other attire, he might have passed as a college professor with his wavy salt and pepper hair and dark eyes. His wife was the picture of what Summer might look like in twenty years, with the same stone gray eyes and fair skin. Her long white hair was tied in a single thick braid that hung to the middle of her back. She wore jeans and what appeared to be a hand-knit sweater and scarf.

Her suspicions were confirmed when Summer quickened her pace to greet them with a hug.

"Mama and Daddy, I want you to meet a friend of mine. Not a girlfriend though, so you don't have to give her the third degree," she added swiftly. "This is Ellis Keene. She lives in the building next door to me, and she hates Fox News as much as we do."

"Then she's good enough for us," the man boomed, extending his hand. "Rupert Winslow, and this is my wife Rosemary."

Behind Rupert were rows of wooden bowls and sculptures. "Oh my gosh, did you make these? They're gorgeous." She picked up a polished basket of several grains of wood woven in an intricate pattern.

"You have great taste, young lady. That's one of my favorites."

"It's stunning. Look at this detail."

"And now it's yours."

"Oh, I couldn't." She'd already noticed his groupings, and the nearest placard read *$400 and up*. She wanted to buy something to show her appreciation for his work, but had no business looking at something so expensive. A small table clock caught her eye, and on a shelf that said forty dollars. "This…this is beautiful, but I insist on paying for it."

Rupert looked at Summer and tipped his head. "Tell her." Then he went about wrapping the basket with paper and tape.

"You're getting the basket. There's no point in arguing. He's giving it to you because you recognized what a special piece it was."

"And I'm giving you something too," Rosemary stated as she scanned her array of crystals and stones. "I just don't know what yet. Have a seat."

Ellis perched on a stool beside the table, noticing a display of pamphlets for each astrology sign. Sure enough, Rosemary asked her birthday, and if she had any idea of her traits as a Taurus.

"They say bulls are stubborn. I don't know about that, but I'm loyal."

"Could be you're loyal because you're too stubborn to let go. Let me have your hand, dear."

Summer flashed her a smile and drew closer to hear the assessment.

With her eyes closed, Rosemary caressed her fingers. "I find you resistant to change…maybe because you fear the unknown. Does that sound familiar?"

Resigned to change was more like it, she thought. "I don't always embrace it if that's what you mean. But it's inevitable sometimes, so eventually I accept it."

"You're generous. You think more of others than you do yourself."

That certainly was true as far as her children were concerned.

"And you're a very passionate lover."

Ellis's jaw dropped before she broke into a smile. She was by no means a prude, but having her sexuality openly proclaimed caught her off guard—especially when she noticed Summer's blush. Probably embarrassed by her mother's candor.

Rosemary ran her hand through a tray of stones, settling on a brown one with deep green streaks. "You need the boulder opal. Hold it here to your chest. That's your Anahata."

"Your heart chakra," Summer explained.

The oval stone was smooth, and though it felt cold at first, it warmed in only seconds. "Is this going to harden my heart?" she asked, only half joking.

"Just the opposite," Rosemary explained. "The opal gives off subtle vibrations that communicate with your chakra. Held to your Anahata, it enhances your emotional equilibrium. Keeps you from becoming too…too anything. It also fuels your passion, but that's thought to be a side effect of emotional stability."

"It's just what I need. Seriously." The last word she offered almost tongue-in-cheek. "So how am I supposed to use this?"

Rosemary reached inside her sweater to what could only have been her bra, and produced a shiny green stone with deep red splotches. "You keep it close to your heart. I bet you could find a jeweler here who could whip it into a necklace if you wanted to wear it that way. I use this unakite whenever we do a show because it sharpens my mental senses…helps me see what others need. But when we're in the car I use the kunzite—it's good for circulation."

Ellis's fitted shirt had a chest pocket. "Could I just drop it in here?"

"That'll work," Summer said. Then to her mother, she added, "Her eyes are glazing over, Mama. She's a first-timer, you know. You don't want to give her too much too soon."

"I'm done for now. Except…" She swept her hand again across the tray, this time presenting her with a flat blue-green stone the size of quarter. "Take this one too."

"A turquoise?"

"It's called a chrysocolla." She folded it into Ellis's hand and pressed it to her chest. "For when you find yourself remembering painful things."

Suddenly it felt like an ambush. She swung her head toward Summer, who was rapidly shaking her head, her wide-eyed look proclaiming her surprise as well.

"Mama, we're kind of hungry. There's a taco truck outside. You want us to bring you something?"

The whole exchange had seemingly flown over Rupert's head. He pulled his wallet from his hip pocket and passed his daughter a few bills.

Ellis slid off the stool and started toward the exit on her own.

* * *

The way Ellis was marching, Summer fully expected her to turn for the car as soon as they stepped outside. "I swear to God, Ellis. I never said a word to her. Or to anybody. I was as shocked as you were."

"How could she have known that? Do I have it stamped on my forehead?"

"All I can tell you is she's like that. Scares the hell out of me sometimes. I never got away with anything my whole life. It's almost like she knew about it even before I did it."

Ellis slowed, eventually turning toward an open picnic table. The bright sun had brought the temperature up enough to make sitting outside bearable. "Tell me the truth—is there anything to all that crystal and chakra business? I never knew anyone who took that stuff seriously." The edge in her voice was gone.

"Do they help? Between us, probably not…at least not the way Mama thinks they do. But it could be there's a placebo effect." She pointed to the pocket where Ellis had dropped the opal. "As long as you know that's in there, you might stop and think about what it means to have emotional equilibrium. Focusing on it could make you feel like it's helping."

"I guess we'll see."

"I carried a green tourmaline for a long time. It's supposed to help you feel compassion. I thought if I could understand why Rita had so much trouble saying no to alcohol, I'd be able to help her." She reached into the pocket of her jeans and pulled out a dark brown stone with rivulets of gold and black. "But then I started carrying a tiger eye. It's good for your willpower. I used it to quit Rita."

Ellis took it and rubbed the smooth surface with her thumb. "And you still need it?"

After spending part of Christmas Day with Rita—and for the first time not getting into a quarrel—she was starting to feel they'd turned a corner, just as Queenie and Sam had surmised. "Let's just say I'm hedging my bets."

"I don't suppose there's one of these for money?"

Summer smiled with relief at hearing Ellis's lighter tone. "There's one for everything. But watch out for Mama. She'll send you out of here with so many stones, you'll need a wheelbarrow to carry them all. And whatever you do, don't get her started on aromatherapy. She'll have you bathing in grapefruit and sandalwood."

"I like sandalwood incense. I'm afraid to ask what that says about me."

"Actually…it's sometimes prescribed for people who have difficulty with sexual arousal. And I did not just make that up."

Ellis laughed. "I guess that explains why I'm such a passionate lover."

Just what Summer needed—more mental images of Ellis making love.

Christmas Day had been a reality check, a demonstration of how different they were in myriad ways. She could lay it on as thick as she wanted, but it wasn't going to change Ellis into a woman who liked women. The most she might ever hope for was a fling, something Ellis might yield to in order to satisfy her curiosity. That wasn't enough. In fact, she'd rather not cross that line if it meant sharing something special—then losing it.

* * *

The rest of the afternoon passed pleasantly for Ellis as she and Summer sat in a pair of lawn chairs watching the Winslows share their wares with fairgrounds visitors. Both were obviously devoted to their respective crafts, and they were better than average salespeople.

As she listened to Rosemary interact with potential customers, she began to believe the woman's insight came from an extraordinary sense of empathy. It made perfect sense that someone self-trained in reading people's emotions could deduce she was dealing with trauma in her life. Most days she could see it staring back at her from the mirror.

When the time came to head back to Sacramento, she enthusiastically accepted the Winslow's invitation to see them again the next time they came to a nearby fair. Allison would probably enjoy learning about stones and chakra.

"I have to admit I nearly cracked up when your mom said Tarot reading was bunk."

"I know. She doesn't get the irony at all." Summer had lowered the driver's side window a smidgen, causing her wavy hair to blow forward all around her face. "Thanks for indulging her. Daddy and I have learned over the years just to nod along."

Ellis couldn't resist reaching over to brush the hair out of her eyes. "She's interesting. And she's right, you know. My emotional equilibrium can use all the help it can get."

After fourteen months, she still awakened some days feeling the brunt of the tragedy, wishing she could go back in time just for a day to ask the questions that might have led her to discover Bruce's fragile mental state. Why hadn't she noticed he'd stopped wanting to socialize with people from his office? That he never talked about his coworkers? That he'd put a padlock on the tool cabinet in the garage after years of leaving it unguarded?

And then other days she celebrated the ways she'd recovered her life and taken charge. An interesting job in a new city. An apartment all her own. Summer, who made her feel it was okay to have fun again, okay to care about someone. And then there was the tantalizing undercurrent to their relationship.

"It won't hurt my feelings if you put your stones in a drawer. I won't tell Mama."

"No, I like what you said about hedging your bets. There's no harm in carrying them."

Now that she'd admitted to herself—and to her son—that she was intrigued by Summer's overtures, she'd been watching for more. Compliments, innuendos. Anything that continued their flirtations of a week ago. Nothing...which she found disappointing.

Had she read it wrong? Perhaps what Summer had meant was that lesbians *in general* would find her attractive. It could have been she thought Ellis needed an ego boost and it was her job as a friend to provide it.

Whatever the reason, she was almost aloof, leaving Ellis embarrassed by her assumptions. She'd have to straighten things out with Jeremy, chalk it up to second thoughts. Thank goodness she hadn't told anyone else. Now she just needed to let Summer know she hadn't taken her seriously.

"Maybe your mother's stones will spark something for Rex Brenneman. Nothing else seems to."

She could have sworn she heard Summer blow out a breath of disgust. "Have you heard any more from him?"

"He comes through the office and says hi. It's possible he thinks the ball's in my court. Maybe it is."

Summer drove in silence for several minutes, staring intently at the road ahead. Finally she said, "You know, if it isn't happening with Rex after this long, maybe there's nothing there. You shouldn't feel like you have to force the issue."

She had a point. Rex didn't have to be the default position if Summer wasn't interested in a relationship. There were other possibilities—men she hadn't yet met—including no one at all. It wasn't as if she were itching to get back into the game.

"Got any plans for next Friday?" Summer asked.

"Not yet. What do you have in mind?"

"You said you missed the culture in San Francisco. How about we go see *Swan Lake* at the Community Center Theater?"

"The ballet?" Of course the ballet. "Are you kidding? I'd love to."

"Good, since I already bought the tickets online. Front row balcony. I figured we could see everything from there."

"Perfect! How much were they?" She'd float her groceries on a credit card if she had to.

"My treat. You had me over for Christmas dinner."

"That's not a fair trade...unless your family comes out on stage and gets into a wrestling match."

"It wasn't that bad. Besides, your kids are practically still teenagers. I didn't expect them to behave like diplomats."

"You're being generous." She'd scolded both Allison and Jeremy and vowed to do the same with Jonathan. "But one dinner isn't enough. You have to let me do something else."

"Okay." Summer drew an enormous breath and blew it out, not taking her eyes from the road. "How about wearing that black dress again? The one you wore when you went out with Rex."

* * *

Ellis sank lower into her warm tub, inhaling the zesty aroma of the grapefruit essence Rosemary had given her to add to her bath. There were worse things than believing in the metaphysical benefits of essential oils.

Summer had vanquished all her doubts with her bold request that she wear her black dress again. No amount of playfulness would let either of them laugh it off now. The ballet would be their first date.

And the wildest part—Ellis found it tantalizing. What was it about Summer that had her questioning everything she thought she knew about herself? A woman asking her out on a date. Her response should have been a lighthearted laugh, a demure thank you and a polite decline. Yet she'd been practically begging her to ask. Years ago a dalliance like this would have been scandalous, but who would bat an eye today if she got involved with another woman?

Allison and Jonathan, for starters. They could freak out and try some kind of intervention. Therapy, anti-depressants. Involuntary commitment to a psychiatric hospital.

Now she was just being melodramatic. They might not care at all. Maybe they'd even like handing their mother off so someone else would take care of her.

But why was she doing this if she wasn't a lesbian? Or maybe the better question was why she found the idea of being with Summer so arousing. Maybe she was bisexual. The continuum.

No, it was a pendulum. People who were monogamous stayed in one place for a long time, but it didn't define them. Sometimes they fell in love with someone who happened to be the same gender.

She abruptly lifted the plug on the tub and leapt out into the cool air, jolting her body almost as much as her mind when it heard her use the word "love."

After briskly drying off, she donned a thick terry robe, retrieved her cell phone from the kitchen counter and returned to her bedroom.

Only one person could help sort her feelings. One person who'd been part of her life for thirty years, who knew her secrets and dreams. Who had the guts to tell her to go for it—or that she'd lost her mind.

Her last words to Roxanne had been hurled with hurt and frustration. She'd never meant to cut her off forever.

Her anxiety grew by the third ring and she braced for voice mail.

"Ellis?" Her friend's excitement was unmistakable.

"Oh, Roxanne…it is so, so good to hear your voice. I've missed you like crazy."

"Me too, sweetie. I think about you all the time."

Ellis relaxed instantly amidst a wave of relief. "I'm so sorry for all the things I said when you were getting on the plane that day. It wasn't your fault."

"I know that. It was hard not to call you as soon as I got home, but I figured you needed some space. I knew you'd call when you were ready. Besides, I've been keeping up with you through Jeremy."

Her heart warmed so much she thought she might cry.

For the next half hour, they caught up on the major details of their lives—Ellis's move to Sacramento and her new job,

Roxanne's recent decision to become chief information officer at one of the state's largest health care companies.

"You'd actually leave the dot-com merry-go-round?"

"In a heartbeat. That next bubble…it's out there. I can feel it. And this whole house of cards is going to come crashing down again. Besides, I'm sick of things like not being able to be there when my best friend needs me because I have a trade show halfway around the world. But first, I have a ton of vacation days. There's a beach out there with my name on it."

"You deserve that," Ellis said, feeling six months' worth of anguish fall away. It was good to talk to Roxanne again, especially to hear her own up to her shortcomings about not being there for her. "Where's your new job located? Will you have to move?"

"Their headquarters is in Walnut Creek. That's a killer commute, so I'll probably sell my house and rent something on that side of the Bay."

"That's barely an hour from here! We can start meeting for lunch again." Her excitement waned as she remembered her work schedule. "Except I'm just an office grunt now. Something tells me they aren't going to let me run off for a four-hour lunch."

"We'll figure something out. Like I said, it's time for me to shift my priorities. Enough of these twenty-something programming geeks. I need some *real* people in my life."

"I'm so happy for you, Roxanne."

Her whole reason for reaching out had been to rekindle their friendship so she could pick Roxanne's brain about Summer. Instead, she found herself rediscovering what it meant to *be* a friend. Roxanne was in the mood to celebrate, and deserved to focus on herself right now.

Besides, it wasn't advice she needed as far as Summer was concerned—it was approval. Or so she'd thought. A completely bogus proposition. At forty-eight years old, she hardly needed permission for anything.

CHAPTER FOURTEEN

Ellis stood before her bathroom mirror, alternately dangling a diamond earring from one ear and a gold hoop from the other. Her cell phone lay on the counter, its speaker activated. "Honey, I can't hear you. It sounds like you're standing in traffic."

"I'm waiting for a bus," Jonathan shouted back. "I need to get to the library. I've got a paper due next week."

"Oh, Jonathan. It's Saturday night. You should be out with your friends." There was such a thing as being too conscientious, she thought, and it described him to a T.

"Stanford isn't just any university, Mom. All my friends are busting their butts too."

Comments like that were why Jeremy and Allison found their brother pretentious at times. But he was right about Stanford. They had no idea how hard he had to work to stand out in a sea of overachievers.

"Any word yet on law school, honey? I thought they'd decide by now. People have to make plans."

"A couple of my friends got rejection letters last week, so I should hear something soon."

"But *you* didn't get one. We should take that as a good sign. I don't tell you often enough—"

"Here's my bus, Mom. Gotta go."

"…how proud I am of you," she said to her dead phone. At least he'd finally returned her call.

Jonathan's single-minded quest to get into Stanford Law School had sustained him through their tragedy, but she worried sometimes about his emotional well-being. Political differences aside, he was detached from the family in a way that disturbed her. Once he got his letter—no matter what it said—she would insist he come for a weekend visit. Just the two of them.

But tonight…tonight was about Summer and the ballet. As instructed, she'd donned her black dress again, this time tightening her bra another notch to create a deeper cleavage. An extra brush of eye shadow, a touch of cologne behind her ears. Her normally straight hair fell in soft curls around her face.

Definitely the diamonds, she decided. They were a tenth anniversary gift from Bruce, though he'd eventually confessed Roxanne had picked them out to save him from making an expensive mistake. Ellis had worn them to the symphony, opera and ballet in San Francisco. Now valued at twelve thousand dollars, they were listed among the financial assets up for grabs once the attorneys worked out a settlement. Why shouldn't she enjoy them one last time?

After securing them with a firm click, she stepped back to check her overall look. She couldn't remember the last time she'd felt so beautiful. Certainly not when she'd gone out with Rex.

Summer would be dazzled. That was the whole point.

* * *

"I do love that dress," Summer said, barely holding back a wolf whistle when Ellis answered her door.

"Wow, look who's talking."

The ballet called for something special, and Summer had gone deep into her closet for a dress she'd worn two years ago to a coworker's wedding. Plum, with a clinging wrap that gathered on her left side and flared into a short flowing skirt.

"And those are the cutest shoes! They almost look like ballet slippers."

The black leather flats were all she had that qualified as dress shoes. "Yeah, I figured I should go prepared in case one of the dancers gets hurt. 'Hey you, get in there and plié!' It's like those people who wear a player's jersey to a football game."

"You never know. Did you take ballet as a little girl?"

Summer laughed. "In the commune?"

"Oh, right."

"But I had the hots for a dancer when I was at Chico State, so I've seen *Swan Lake* a couple of times. It's beautiful."

But not like Ellis was beautiful. She'd added soft curls to her usually straight hair and swept it back off her face to show off diamond earrings set in silver. It was that extra bit that Summer appreciated most—not because she cared how Ellis looked, but because Ellis cared about it. She'd clearly put extra thought into looking even more beautiful than when she'd gone to dinner with Rex. Because it was the ballet? Or because it was her? Either way, it made her feel special. This was a real date, and she was ninety percent sure Ellis knew it.

After noticing Ellis's slender heels, Summer didn't mess around with trying to park in the city garage four blocks from the theater.

The valet eyed her car scornfully as he prepared her ticket. "A Mazda Three."

"It's the prototype for the next generation of abstemious conveyance vehicles," she said.

"What did you just tell him?" Ellis asked as they strolled toward the entrance.

"That it's an economy car."

They bypassed the coat check but took a moment to look around the lobby of the Sacramento Community Center Theater. Summer put on an air of familiarity, pointing out the restrooms, bar and entrance to the box seats. In truth, she'd been to the theater only once—for an Indigo Girls concert. No ballet, no theater, no symphony. She'd quickly get interested in all three if it meant enjoying them with Ellis.

Ellis nodded her approval. "This looks nice. Very modern."

"It's not exactly the War Memorial Opera House, but it serves the purpose. And there isn't a bad seat."

"You've been to the Opera House?"

"Not for a performance. Just a tour." She decided not to add that the tour had been a field trip over thirty years ago when she was in high school in Hollister.

As they wove through the cocktail crowd toward their assigned entry, Ellis stopped short, coming face to face with a couple she obviously knew. A May-December couple, Summer noted. The woman was a waif, with long blond hair and Margaret Keane eyes. She was bound in a dark red dress that left one shoulder exposed, its collar bone protruding like a garden rake. The gentleman looked to be a good twenty years older, and wore an aged leather bomber jacket with a white shirt and yellow tie. In his hand was a black fedora.

The woman was first to speak. "Ellis! How nice to see you. I'm so excited about tonight. Don't you just love *Swan Lake*?"

"Marcie." Ellis greeted her with a light hug, and turned back to Summer. "I'd like you to meet *Vista*'s executive editor, Marcie Wagstaff. And this is our political writer, Rex Brenneman."

So this was the infamous Rex Brenneman, oozing masculinity in his unconventional attire. Clearly a man who cared a great deal about his persona. Summer couldn't help watching their reactions to seeing one another.

"And this is my neighbor, Summer Winslow."

Ouch! Yes, they happened to live near one another. And they'd shared a ride to the ballet because it was good for the environment.

Summer smiled blankly as the three of them exchanged chitchat, and then mumbled a polite "Nice to meet you" in response to theirs when they parted. If there was one good thing about that particular humiliation, it was that Rex and Marcie had no idea she'd just been kneecapped. For that matter, she wasn't sure Ellis was aware of it either.

Ellis waited until they reached their seat to break the awkward silence. "Summer, I'm sorry. I was so shocked to see both of them, I just froze. And obviously I said something idiotic."

"It wasn't idiotic. I *am* your neighbor."

"You're more than my neighbor. You know that, don't you?" She put her hand on Summer's forearm and leaned close enough to share her perfume. "You're my friend, and…and you mean a lot to me. I just didn't feel like telling them that."

Summer hadn't exactly expected a *True Romance* confession, though being introduced as a friend instead of a neighbor shouldn't have been so difficult. At least Ellis realized how awful it had sounded. At this point there was nothing to be gained from making her feel worse about what she'd done.

She laid her hand on top of Ellis's. "It's okay. In case you haven't noticed, you mean a lot to me too. And I get to pat myself on the back because you're here with me instead of Indiana Jones."

Ellis laughed. "No, no. It's a trilby, not a fedora. Not sure quite what he's going for. London Jones, maybe."

Summer knew. He wanted women to think he had swash in his buckle.

The theater lights flashed to call the curtain and they took their last few minutes to scan the Playbill for information on the ballet company.

All the while, Summer grappled with a nagging doubt, one she couldn't keep to herself a moment longer. "Ellis, does this feel like a date to you? Whatever you say is fine. I just need to know so I can get my head around it."

The lights went down, shushing the crowd, and a high-pitched woodwind melody pierced the quiet hall.

For a moment it seemed Ellis would hide beneath the music, deferring her response until her silence ultimately put the question to rest. But then her hand fell over the armrest into Summer's lap, and their fingers intertwined.

* * *

The moment the performance ended, Ellis shrugged into her knee-length coat and buried her hands in her pockets. She had no idea where Marcie and Rex were sitting. It was one thing to hold hands in a darkened theater, and quite another to walk out that way and increase the risk of being seen.

It wasn't shame or embarrassment about being out with a woman—she told herself that over and over—but a desire to keep parts of her personal life private. She simply wasn't interested in talking to anyone about her relationship with Summer. Certainly not before she knew what to say.

"I hope you enjoyed that," Summer said. "I sure did."

"It was lovely."

What the performance lacked in grandness, it made up for in intimacy. It was nearly flawless, and Ellis was impressed by the Sacramento audience's show of appreciation. She and Bruce had been members of the Dancer's Circle for the San Francisco Ballet, a five-thousand-dollar annual gift. She'd noted in the program that she could guarantee box seats here at the Community Center Theater for the season for a few hundred dollars. If only she had a few hundred dollars.

Summer returned from handing her ticket to the valet. "I have to admit I don't make myself get out to a lot of shows or performances downtown, but I'm always glad when I do."

"We can do this anytime as far as I'm concerned." While Ellis had enjoyed the program thoroughly, the significance of the evening was never far from her thoughts. She was officially almost in a lesbian relationship. Summer had given her a golden chance to back out—*whatever you say is fine*—and she'd made the decision to set aside her qualms.

In all her rumination about dating a woman, she'd imagined it happening within the confines of River Woods. Not in public and not where people from work would see them together.

And definitely not where she'd have to explain herself to her children.

That was messed up. If she couldn't bring herself to show Summer affection in public, she had no business getting involved with her in the first place. Yet she wasn't ready to make that decision. Summer was fun, interesting. And appealing in a way Ellis hadn't experienced with another woman.

With another woman. Everything new about tonight had that tacked onto the end of it.

"Did you happen to notice any of the shows coming this spring?" Summer asked, a slight tremor in her voice, as though she was nervous about something.

And why wouldn't she be? Ellis realized she'd hardly spoken on the ride home, and not at all since Summer suggested they do this again. "I saw *The Sound of Music* is next month. Then *West Side Story*. I like both of those."

"And then *Hair*. I know every word to all the songs."

"If you go to that one, be sure to wear something tie-dyed in case they rip you out of the audience. 'You there! Get up here and burn this flag.'"

Summer laughed. "My luck they'd want me for the finale where everybody comes out naked."

"You could pull that off. You're so tiny, I don't think anyone would even see you unless they were on the front row." The instant the words left her lips, she panicked that Summer might ask where she'd want to sit.

"I'll look online and see if I can grab tickets for those."

"You should hold off until I check my budget. Remember, I've got two kids in college."

Ellis noted the dashboard clock as they pulled into River Woods. Twenty after ten. Late enough to call it a night...and early enough not to.

"I know a great little place for coffee," Summer said as she turned off the engine. "Or we can say goodnight right here and it'll still be a perfect evening."

Her instincts favored the latter, but there was something far stronger that compelled her to ignore them. Enticement. Curiosity about how far she was willing to go. There was a powerful aura of taboo, of danger, and yet she felt safe with Summer. In control.

"Coffee would be nice."

They started for the apartment, but Summer stopped at the edge of the walkway. "Here we are again, all dressed up. If you want to change first, I can wait. Or not. It's up to you."

Ellis took a moment to appreciate Summer's chic look. It was unusual to see her in a dress, but there was no hint she was uncomfortable in it. A change into their casual clothes might shift the whole tenor of the evening, perhaps even signaling the end of their date.

If she were standing out here with a man—like Rex Brenneman—it wouldn't even be a question. So why was this any different? "No, I like you in that."

But it *was* different. She would never have gone inside with Rex.

CHAPTER FIFTEEN

Sitting on the couch with one foot tucked underneath, Ellis tortured her with a bare thigh, courtesy of the stretchy fabric of her black dress. The thought of what lay beneath that fabric, only inches from view, was even more tantalizing.

Summer had bypassed the artificial fireplace in favor of an oldies music channel on her cable TV. It played low in the background, but loud enough they both could recognize songs from their high school and college years.

Ellis moaned. "This one brings back so many memories. My freshman year at Berkeley. We used to hit all the dance clubs. Everybody had fake IDs, but my friends and I were into dancing, not drinking."

Appropriately, the song was Whitney Houston's "I Wanna Dance With Somebody." As they shimmied and mouthed the words, Summer tried to envision Ellis in a college bar.

"What were you like in college? Let me guess. Long hair. All the latest fashions. Lots of guys hanging around."

"Skinny as a rail. I'd only been out of braces for a year." Ellis's curls had fallen, and she tucked the floppy strands behind her ears. "I wore my hair long until my boys were born. Jeremy was so bad about pulling it, I cut it all the way to my chin so he couldn't reach it. It's been like this for the last twenty-two years."

"It looks great. I'm jealous actually. Every time I see you, every single hair is in place, even in the gym. Mine gets wilder as it grows. It takes me about fifteen minutes with a hot comb to make it stay out of my eyes."

"Are you kidding me? Your hair is beautiful. You should let it go, let it curl all over." Ellis leaned over and brushed her bangs from where they'd slid beneath her lenses. "And I love the color."

"Got a thing for gray hair, eh?"

"It seems I do."

Subtle but thrilling, since it was Ellis's first overt admission that she was attracted to her *that* way. She'd shown a few signs, like taking her hand in the theater, but there was nothing quite like hearing it from her lips. From her agreement to come inside instead of returning to her apartment, she clearly wanted more from their evening. But how much more?

"How'd we do on our first date?" Summer asked. "Or to put it another way, will there be more?"

"We did fine." Ellis smiled softly but the furrow of her brow told a different story. "Except I freaked out about running into Rex and Marcie. I wish that hadn't happened."

"Same here if you want to know the truth. I wanted you all to myself tonight." She scooted as close as she could given the angle of Ellis's bent knee. It wasn't enough for an embrace, but there was something to be said for sitting face to face. She took a hand and brought it to her lips for a gentle kiss. "I've got a major crush on you, Ellis Keene. I know I joke around about it, but that's only because I've been too much of a coward to be serious. I think you're an amazing woman."

She caressed Summer's cheek with her knuckles, their hands still joined. "I knew you were joking around, but I always believed you meant what you said."

"Oh, I did. I want to be at the front of your line. I think about you pretty much all the time. At work, in the car...when

I lie down at night." She gently stroked the inside of Ellis's forearm, a spot that on herself was especially sensitive.

The gentle notes of an acoustic guitar filled a stretch of silence. Summer recognized it even before she heard Roberta Flack's sultry voice. *Apropos*, she thought. A "first time" for all the tender moments in their relationship.

"I love this song," Ellis said quietly.

"Dance with me." Summer didn't wait for an answer, tugging her to her feet and into the tight space between the coffee table and the TV.

At barely five feet tall, she was accustomed to being shorter than her dance partner. Her natural inclination was to reach upward, but when Ellis grasped her shoulders, she slid her arms around her waist.

"Which one of us is supposed to lead?" Ellis asked.

"Don't think about it. Just enjoy the music." Tucked into Ellis's neck, her head filled with the muted fragrance she'd noticed earlier. She didn't know one perfume from another, but this was faintly sweet, distinctly feminine. Delicious.

They tipped from side to side in a clockwise circle with all the deliberateness of a lullaby.

Summer was drowning in sensations. The fragrance, the warm breath against her ear, the subtle contours of Ellis's back beneath her fingertips. Unable to resist satisfying another sense, she brushed her lips against the supple skin of her neck, and was rewarded by a soft moan and a tilting of the head that exposed a long sinewy muscle.

Arms tightened around her shoulders, bringing their bodies together from thigh to breast.

Roberta sang soulfully of the first trembling kiss, filling Summer with desire she couldn't control. The moment felt so right for that.

She slithered one hand between them, all the way to the back of Ellis's neck. With just the slightest pressure, she drew her closer and grazed her lips to the corners of her mouth. Barely touching, then withdrawing. Returning to find a gentle tongue that pried her lips apart.

Who was leading? No one…everyone.

They'd stopped dancing.

As their kiss grew more heated, Summer allowed her other hand to roam. A continuous caress mapping the curve of her waist from her hip to just beneath her breast.

All the while, she followed in her mind's eye the path of Ellis's hands. At first her fingers laced through Summer's hair as if holding her head in place. But then her sculpted nails gently traced behind her ears to her shoulders…before drawing her into a firm embrace.

The romantic ballad raised the stakes dramatically with a reverent, almost aching, tribute to lovemaking.

Summer's fingertips found their way to the plunge of Ellis's neckline, and before she knew it, she was delving into her cleavage. Inside the lace of her bra. To the underside of her breast. Suddenly she caught her breath and withdrew to place her hand in the center of Ellis's chest.

And gently nudged her away.

With her mouth parted and eyes half closed, there was no mistaking Ellis's look of desire—which quickly turned to confusion.

Summer shook her head. "I'm so sorry. I can't hurry through this, not with you. It's too important." More than that, she needed to know there would be no regrets from Ellis about getting carried away. Not because Summer was noble. Because she needed to guard her feelings. It would crush her for Ellis to have second thoughts after making love.

Ellis took a step back, folding her arms around her own waist as though guarding herself. "Of all the possibilities I imagined for tonight, that one wasn't even on the list."

"Don't get the wrong idea. I'm more than ready to take you down the hall right now." She ignored the protective stance and hugged her again. "But I don't want to do that just because it's getting so warm in here. I need you to think hard about what you want. If we do the wrong thing, it could hurt our friendship, and I'm not willing to give that up if it's just for a fling."

"It isn't friendship I'm feeling, Summer. I don't kiss my friends the way I just kissed you." She lowered her hands and returned the embrace. "If you need to wait till my head's totally clear, that could be a very long time. I've never been in these shoes before. I was trying to let myself be in the moment."

"And I'm sure that moment would have been amazing. I hope it *will* be amazing. It just…I felt like I might have pushed you into something you weren't ready for. I guess I need to hear you say you're sure." She looked up to find Ellis's mouth too close to resist and gave her one more peck on the lips. "You probably should go now before I change my mind. Because you are one damn fine kisser. And I am one weak-willed lesbian."

* * *

"I'm not going anywhere," Ellis said firmly.

She didn't want to be protected from her feelings. What she wanted next was as clear to her as any decision she'd ever made. She'd known exactly what she was doing. Every subtle step she'd taken so far—the black dress, the deeper cleavage, showing off her thigh—had readied her for the moment.

Nor did she fear the fallout. So what if it turned out to be a fling? There was no law that said they couldn't be friends afterward.

"You want to hear me say I'm sure? Fine, I'm sure of what I want right now. I want you."

This time she initiated the kiss, but it was no simple peck. She backed up her words, covering Summer's mouth with the force of her desire, leaving no room for doubt.

When their kiss finally broke, Summer met her eyes with a smoldering gaze. "That's all I needed to know." She led her to the bedroom, turning out lights along the way.

Her resolve grew along with her excitement as Summer clicked on the bedside lamp and lay her glasses on the table. Then she folded back the light green comforter to reveal yellow cotton sheets with floral pillowcases. It was hardly the den of a seductress, but rather the intimate retreat of a down-to-earth woman.

Ellis turned her back to show her zipper. "Care to do the honors?"

The zipper fell slowly, with warm lips following the trail. She kicked off her shoes and stepped out of her dress, glad she'd chosen the lacy black slip. By the time she turned around, Summer was tossing her own dress on a nearby chair. Her beige bra and panties matched the tone of her skin, making her appear almost nude.

They embraced again, dancing without music in a steady glide to the bed, where they rolled as one to the center. Ellis held on, her body suddenly surging with heat. One hand cradled her back while the other slid beneath her slip, raising it above the curve of her hip. Their lips never parted.

She was ready to be touched. To be ravaged. To have her breasts sucked and bitten. To feel Summer's tongue between her legs.

With an upward surge, she pushed Summer aside long enough to pull her slip off.

The moment she lay back down, Summer released the clasp on her bra and pulled it away. She cupped a breast but she was too gentle, too cautious. Ellis writhed, gasped and thrust her chest upward until Summer got the message, lowering her lips to draw a nipple into her mouth.

"Yes," she hissed between clenched teeth. "I love that...I love that...I love that."

Summer responded to her urgency, shifting lower so she could knead both breasts while raking her nipples with her teeth. She stopped only for a moment so she too could remove her bra.

Ellis caught a glimpse in the brief window their bodies were apart. Summer had small breasts with tight aureoles. And then bare skin that slid smoothly across hers without the prickles of chest hair.

She opened her legs to feel Summer settle her body between them. It was only a matter of moments before the tug on her waistband, and she dug her heels into the bed to raise herself high enough that Summer could remove her panties.

"God, you're gorgeous."

Summer slipped out of hers as well and returned to kiss her, dropping a thigh between her legs. Her body...small and light as it rested atop her. So different from Bruce.

Their kiss now was delicate, their skin gliding together like satin. Mesmerizing.

But delicate wasn't what she needed. She thought at first Summer would make her wait, kiss her slowly again to build up their desire. But then her mouth drifted downward again. To her neck, her shoulder. Back to her breast. And lower.

Summer's tongue left a cool moist trail across her navel. Then she looped her arms, first one and then the other, around Ellis's thighs and nuzzled her mound.

Ellis panted with anticipation. Her legs were apart, but Summer hadn't yet opened her. Hadn't seen her desire. Hadn't tasted her want.

At first she teased, her tongue dancing around the source of her wetness. Then she delved inside before parting her with a single languid stroke.

"Oh God." Ellis squeezed her eyes tightly shut and threw her arms above her head.

Summer read her cues, her tongue swirling in response to the guttural cries and rolling of her hips. As she caressed the inner folds, she shifted her hands to cup Ellis's bottom and lift her off the bed.

The constant stroking...the arching of her back. A faint tingle as Summer grazed the shaft of her clitoris...never quite touching it until finally she took it between her lips and sucked it in rapid, gentle bursts.

Ellis erupted, letting out an urgent moan as the waves pounded through her. Louder, not caring who heard, drowning all of her doubts.

She was still throbbing when Summer slipped a finger inside and returned to lick all around her most sensitive spot in a way that made her crave another release.

Two more...then three. Summer was relentless, backing off and teasing her around the edges before honing in to take her again. Ellis finally stopped her after number four—she was too sensitive, too spent.

Summer crawled slowly up her body, caressing with her mouth all the same places as before, as if on rewind. They finished with a long slow kiss, feathery soft and flavored with her essence.

How long had it been since she'd had four orgasms in a row...and none of them by her own hand? Not since her early years with Bruce had she felt so desired.

She shivered against the cool air when Summer moved away to pull up the comforter.

"Get under here with me."

Feeling a touch of self-consciousness, she covered her breasts with her arms as she sat up. It was silly, she knew, but moving around exposed was different from baring herself in the heat of sex.

Summer stretched alongside her and propped her head on one elbow. With her other hand, she traced Ellis's brow and pushed a strand of hair from her face. "I'm so glad you didn't leave." The blanket was pulled up underneath her arm so it covered her breasts but left her chest and shoulders exposed. With her wavy hair askew and the tender smile, she looked deceptively delicate.

Ellis knew better.

It was impossible not to recognize her experience with other women. Had she always been a tireless lover bent on pleasing her partner? Was she expressing her feelings or showing off her sexual prowess?

Another thought inched its way to the forefront, one she hadn't allowed herself to dwell on as she'd contemplated this night. How would she return Summer's touch?

Sex was to be shared. How many nights had Bruce left her to satisfy herself before she'd finally gotten the moxie to call him on it? She couldn't leave Summer wanting that way.

Except her utter lack of experience pretty much guaranteed it would be a disaster. She couldn't possibly do what Summer had done because...why? Because she didn't know the tricks, the technique. It would frustrate both of them.

"Are you all right?" Summer asked.

Ellis had no idea how long she'd been silent. "I'm fine. I just feel drained...like all the energy that's been building up inside of me for weeks just ran out." It was true she was spent, but saying so was her way of lowering Summer's expectations for more. Maybe she'd even suggest they go to sleep.

"I'm not surprised. It was intense."

"That's one word for it. I haven't come four times in a night since I was twenty-two."

"Now that's a shame." Summer stretched over and kissed her on the forehead. "But you better get used to it again, because I find it pretty hard to stop when every little thing I do gets such a lovely response."

"Because you know what you're doing." Here was her opening. "Unlike some people."

Summer continued her caress, a fingertip massage of her face and neck. It was serene, clearly meant to calm rather than arouse. "All I did was show you how I feel. When you're ready to do that, you won't have any doubts about what to do. You'll do whatever you want, whatever your feelings tell you. I can promise you already, anything you do will feel wonderful because it's you. And until you're ready, you shouldn't worry about it. I'm as happy as I can be."

Was it really that simple? All she had to do was take what she wanted. Everything else would take care of itself.

* * *

It was all Summer could do to keep her hands from wandering below the blanket to caress and soothe Ellis as she recovered from her release. The luxurious feel of their bare skin touching from shoulder to toe was too much stimulation to allow her to relax. Surely there were more ways to make Ellis whimper with pleasure, and cry out as she came. She intended to find them all.

"Can you turn out the light?" Ellis asked softly. Her eyes were closed and her body had gone still.

Summer rolled away and stretched to click off the bedside lamp. When she returned, she was surprised to feel a hand on her shoulder urging her onto her back.

Interesting that Ellis had wanted the lights out. To avoid seeing...or being seen? Now she was the one perched above, apparently ready to take charge. Ever so lightly she raked her nails across Summer's jaw and neck. "I'm taking you at your word. Anything I want to do."

"I'm yours."

Ellis closed the inches between them, nuzzling until she found Summer's mouth. The deepest kiss, mixed with the intoxicating feel of their breasts brushing together, and the graze of soft hair against her hip.

Though burning with excitement, Summer lay as still as possible while Ellis traced the line of her collarbone with her fingertips. As her hands drifted lower, she followed with her lips. Light kisses all over her chest.

Finally Ellis touched her breast, kneading it gently and stroking the nipple. She hovered close, her silky hair heightening the sensations as it swept across her skin.

The instant Summer felt warm lips touch her nipple, she drew a deep breath that hissed between her teeth. "Oh, yes."

As Ellis lavished her attention on one breast, Summer clutched the other. Twisting, pinching, pulling the nipple until it felt rock hard. With only a subtle shift of her torso, she directed Ellis to take it in her mouth.

She did, raking it with her teeth almost to the point of discomfort before sucking it fully between her lips. Her fingers traveled slowly downward, pausing to circle her navel, and then tickle the hair just below. The teasing continued for a couple of minutes, long enough for her to wonder if Ellis was uncertain what to do next.

Summer rolled toward her slightly, bending a knee in a way that opened her legs. An invitation that went unanswered. After several seconds, she intertwined their fingers and began to steadily stroke herself.

She was wet with desire, and together they spread it the length of her labia. And then gradually she withdrew her hand.

Ellis continued to explore, now with long, confident strokes that pressed into her crevices and coated her with moisture. Each time a finger neared her clitoris, Summer twitched with anticipation, gasping to let her know she liked it.

In the dim green light of her bedside phone, she could see Ellis's eyes closed in concentration. Her breathing was uneven... she was focused.

Summer edged away slightly to escape too much pressure. She could take direct contact with a tongue, but not this way. She gently guided Ellis's hand off-center, where every caress drew the hood across her clitoris and caused her to tingle. "That...exactly that."

As Ellis continued her touch, Summer began a slow rolling of her hips. She was feeling more intensity with every rise, and arching higher off the bed. Her moans, her grunts, her sighs sounded as though they were coming from someone else.

A sudden warmth enveloped her as the vibrations started. Thousands of contractions in a span of only a few seconds punctuated with a long, low growl of pleasure. When her climax passed its peak, she collapsed and pulled Ellis on top of her, where they both lay breathing hard.

As they nestled, she captured Ellis's hand and moved it back to her center. "Can you feel that? Feel what you did."

Ellis cupped her snugly while kissing her neck and ear. "I had help."

"You didn't need help. Touching myself...it's something I like to do. This is the room where I let you in on my secrets and show you the real me. You can do that too."

"I think I already have."

"Oh, no you haven't. Not by a long shot." Summer drew her back down for another kiss. "We're just getting started."

CHAPTER SIXTEEN

Summer stared dismally at the contents of her refrigerator, coming to terms with what *wasn't* there—no bacon, no pancake syrup, no lox, no melon—nothing for a special breakfast to commemorate their first morning together.

It wasn't even daylight yet, but she'd slipped out of bed quietly so as not to disturb Ellis, who'd apparently enjoyed a restful night after their lovemaking. At some point she'd gotten up for the bathroom. Before returning to bed, she'd donned her slip again, a point Summer wasn't going to overthink. Perhaps she'd simply been cold. At any rate, they'd slept close enough to touch throughout the night, and at one point had held hands.

There was no point in ruminating on Ellis's reactions. She had every right to wake up doubtful or confused today. It was the first time in twenty-some years she'd been with someone other than her husband. That was more than a milestone—it was a passage.

But a larger passage was happening too. The way they'd kissed *after* making love—deep and yet tender—was all the proof Summer needed that their night together was about more than sex. They were falling in love.

The sound of the bathroom door closing signaled that Ellis was up, and she brewed a fresh cup of coffee for her.

"You look like a woman who needs her coffee in the morning," Summer said, smiling as she presented the mug.

She'd washed away her makeup from the night before, leaving her face puffy and pink. The purloined robe from the closet barely reached her thighs, and she was wearing a pair of Summer's fuchsia gym socks. "I should have thought this through last night."

"It's a bold look."

Ellis set the coffee on the counter and backed Summer into a corner of the kitchen where she couldn't escape if she'd wanted to. There she delivered a long minty kiss.

The moment she finished, she retrieved her mug and shuffled wordlessly into the living room.

"Wow, you keep that up and I'm really going to like you in the morning." Summer followed and found her sitting on the couch hugging herself. "Are you cold?"

"I'll warm up in a minute." Ellis patted the couch beside her. "I was surprised when I woke up this morning. I mean earlier, while you were still asleep."

"No wonder. A strange bed with someone beside you for the first time in ages."

"That's what surprised me. I couldn't get over how normal it felt."

Of course. Their apartment layouts were virtually identical, except for the extra bedroom. "Because everything's so similar. It was like waking up in your own bed."

Ellis groaned and rolled her eyes dramatically. "Will you stop being so practical? I'm trying to give you a compliment. I should have been freaking out, at least a little. But I didn't because I feel so comfortable with you."

"Ohhh." Yes, Summer was falling in love. Any woman who could scold and flatter her at the same time was a woman after her own heart. "And I'm supposed to say I felt the same way, which happens to be true. That I was comfortable waking up with you because it felt like you belonged there."

"And now you get to notch your bedpost." The words were playful, but there was a hint of cynicism in her tone.

"No way, I'm not a notcher. Even if I were, last night didn't feel much like a notch to me." She took the mug from her hands and set it on the coffee table. "Make a lap, woman."

Ellis complied, and Summer straddled her so they were face to face.

"You get no more coffee until you hear this and tell me you understand. Ready?"

"We'll see."

"I find you gorgeous. And sexy. And…and beguiling. Don't you love that word? I love that word."

"Beguiling." Ellis squinted at her with what looked like exaggerated skepticism. "It isn't something I hear a lot."

"That's what makes it special. If that was all you were to me, I might just notch the bedpost." She clasped Ellis's hands with both of hers and pressed them against her chest. "But the best things about you are inside here. You're kind, you care about other people. And you're the strongest woman I've ever met. Being with you does something to me. When I was touching you last night…when we were kissing." She drew in a deep breath for the courage it would take to admit this. "It wasn't about sex, Ellis. I was making love with you."

That L-word. As scary as it was, she was glad to have finally put her feelings out there.

Ellis pierced her with a gaze through narrowed eyes, and wriggled her hands free to cup Summer's cheeks. "I felt the same way."

Summer laughed nervously. "God, what a relief!"

"For a whole night I felt like my old self, back when I was happy. Back when I didn't have so much to worry about." Ellis finished by pulling her in for a kiss.

Though they'd both tiptoed around the "three little words," it was clear to Summer the feelings were there. It was only a matter of time before they confessed to more.

"So can I have my coffee back now?"

Summer vacated her lap and handed her the mug.

"Now I need you to do me a favor," Ellis said. "Go over to my apartment and bring me back some clothes. If I walk back over there at eleven o'clock on a Saturday morning in my little black dress, everyone in the complex will think I'm a hooker."

* * *

Summer burst through the door carrying jeans and a dress shirt, both on hangers, and a pair of brown loafers.

"What in the world? I told you to bring my yoga pants and sneakers."

"You're lucky you got anything. I almost got caught."

"Caught by whom?"

"Somebody's at your house. I think it's Allison. There's a backpack on the couch, and a jacket that looks like hers." Her voice shook with excitement. "Whoever it is was in your shower with the bathroom door shut. I didn't mess around with finding what you told me to get. This stuff was right there in your closet so I grabbed it and got the hell out of there."

Why on earth was Allison at her apartment? More importantly, why had she shown up without—

"Oh, crap! I forgot to turn my phone back on after the ballet." Her hands shook as she checked it. Nine missed calls and four voice mails, which she listened to in succession. "I have to go."

"What is it? Why is she there?"

"She's there because I didn't answer my phone," Ellis said testily, immediately feeling guilty for snapping at Summer. Of all the nights for Allison to need her, why had she chosen the one night she wasn't there? "Sorry. Apparently she got worried this morning because I still wasn't picking up. She needs to talk to me about something important."

She made a quick detour into the shower to wash away the smell of a night of sex. A longstanding habit, one that actually didn't feel so pressing after sex with another woman, but she wasn't taking any chances.

"What am I going to tell my daughter about being out all night?"

Summer fell across the bed to watch her get dressed. "I take it the truth is off the table."

"I'm not ready to talk about this yet. At least not with her. Or Jonathan. They both have too much on their plates with school."

"But you'll talk with Jeremy?"

Ellis tugged her skinny jeans over last night's panties and squatted to stretch them out. "I already did. Before Christmas."

"Now there's a story I want to hear."

"It's going to have to wait." She set her dress heels and slip on the bedside chair with her dress. "I'll get these later. Wish me luck."

Summer walked her to the door and stood on her tiptoes to plant a quick kiss. "You could always say we got home from the ballet last night and your neighbors were having a loud party."

It was an excellent lie, one she practiced to herself on the short walk to her apartment.

The alternative was to grow a spine and tell the truth. Why not? One of her sons was on board, albeit a bit skeptical. Allison was a chip off the old block, an enlightened liberal who let people be who they were. She'd be able to see how good Summer was for her.

Or maybe she should just let her kids figure it out on their own. It wasn't as if they were entitled to know everything about her personal life. What person their age wanted to know about their mother's sexual proclivities anyway?

She pushed open her front door to a sight Summer must have found frightening—the TV was on, as were the lights in the kitchen. Had she walked in on this without warning, she'd have thought someone had broken in.

"Hello?"

The only answer was the sound of a toilet flushing from the master bath.

"Who's here?"

The bathroom door opened. "Mom?" Allison emerged, her wet hair having soaked the shoulders of her T-shirt.

"Allison. What are you doing here?"

"Where have you been? I was calling you all night."

"So I just heard." She held up her phone. "I went to the ballet last night. I forgot to turn my phone back on. Is everything all right? Did something happen? How did you even get here?"

"Jeremy picked me up at the dorm about an hour ago. By the way, I'm staying the night. I need some time away from my roommate. She's on my last nerve. Thank God she's leaving next quarter for an internship. Let's just hope I don't get somebody worse." As she talked, she squeezed her hair with a towel and padded barefoot into the kitchen.

"Of course you can stay." And of course she'd have to make a quick call to Summer telling her their weekend plans—to lie around naked and discover ways to please one another—were off.

"So where have you been? Jeremy knocked on your door at seven o'clock this morning and you were gone already." Allison suddenly whipped around, her eyes wide. "Oh, my God! Did you have a date? You spent the night with somebody! No, wait. I don't want to know. That's too weird. Don't tell me."

Faced with a moment of truth or deflection, Ellis felt the courage drain from her body. "Sorry to disappoint you, but I can explain myself without being weird. It so happens we got home last night and my neighbors were having a wild party. Cars everywhere, music blaring. I could feel their bass through the wall." Because a decent lie had to be believable. "Summer suggested I stay over at her place. That struck me as a good idea, considering. I'd never have gotten any sleep over here."

"Ugh, it sounds almost as bad as the dorm." Allison didn't seem to care that she'd spent the night at Summer's. Why should she? Would it even occur to her that staying all night with a lesbian was out of the ordinary? She seemed far more focused on getting the precise amount of almond butter spread to all four corners of a vegan cracker. "I need to talk to you about something. It's important."

"Obviously." Ellis felt conspicuous wearing a dress shirt with jeans…and loafers without socks. It was unthinkable that her daughter wouldn't notice so many pieces out of place. "But hold that thought. I need to use the bathroom."

"It's kind of a mess in there," Allison called behind her.

A mammoth understatement. The floor was strewn with towels and Allison's clothes, her toiletries spread across the vanity top. For the first time Ellis could remember, she bristled at feeling her privacy invaded. She had a guest room with a full bath. So what if Allison liked her walk-in shower better?

Summer answered on the first ring.

"We have to cancel everything until tomorrow afternoon. Allison's staying the night." She went on to explain how her daughter was escaping an annoying roommate. "I'm sorry. She needs to talk about something. Oh, and I used your party excuse, so be sure you back me up."

Evading her daughter made her uneasy. She'd always tried to be the kind of mother her children could talk to. Though she'd tried to spare them from things that hurt—their cousin who did drugs, the teacher who thought Jeremy needed counseling to overcome his sexuality—it wasn't in her to hide important facets of her life.

With a toilet flush and a spray of the faucet, she disguised her real reason for retreating to the bathroom. When she emerged, Allison was sitting on a barstool with her hands folded.

"So what is this very important thing you need to talk about?" She set up her coffeepot to brew a cup, then began wiping the counter of her daughter's crumbs.

Allison finished chewing her culinary masterpiece and tossed her napkin in the general direction of the trashcan. "I need a car."

Ka-ching!

"Oh, honey." This was bad, bad news for her bank account. Another obligation in addition to three more years of tuition. What's more, she couldn't buy her daughter a cheap clunker after Bruce had lavished their sons with a pair of fancy sport sedans on the day they graduated high school. The fact that the family money was now tied up and possibly gone was irrelevant to her sense of fairness.

"Please don't say no yet, Mom. Let me tell you why I need it." Her first reason—so she could get a part-time job and drive to work—was nearly a deal breaker.

"Allison, there will be plenty of time in your life for work. Right now I want you to focus on your studies." She wasn't going to have another child get sidetracked and drop out of college.

"But what about a summer job? You don't want me lying around on your couch for three months watching stupid stuff on TV."

She shuddered to think of her daughter living with her during the summer break. They'd barely survived the week at Christmas. Three months in this tiny space would have them at each other's throats.

"Jeremy thinks it's a good idea. He hates it when I ask you for money."

"This isn't your brother's concern." She recalled the conversation she'd overheard on the night she moved in. "Jeremy didn't stay in college long enough to know what it's like when you really have to apply yourself. You're only a freshman. Trust me, it gets harder every year. If you don't believe me, ask Jonathan."

Allison scowled at the mention of her other brother. "I'm not like Jon. All he cares about is brown-nosing his professors so he can get into law school. I want to have a life too."

"I wish you wouldn't be so hard on him."

"And I wish you wouldn't throw him in my face all the time. He does that enough by himself."

They weren't quite shouting, but they were loud enough for Ellis to worry about the thin walls. She poured her coffee and stirred in the cream while willing herself to calm down.

"I don't mean for it to feel like I'm throwing Jonathan in your face, honey. But there's no need for you to criticize him the way you do. You're a better person than that. Can he be a little self-absorbed? Yes, but just because he has different views and priorities doesn't mean he doesn't deserve your respect."

Jonathan had flat out told her he didn't care how Allison and Jeremy treated him. He was happy to avoid them, but she wasn't going to let that happen. They were a family, and after all they'd been through together, she couldn't allow them to drift apart.

"I respect him…and I love him because he's my brother." Her tone was sufficiently contrite. She'd always responded best to appeals to her better nature. "But forget Jon, okay? Let's get back to my reasons for needing a car. I have to move off campus next year. The dorms are mostly for freshmen."

"You said you'd find an apartment on the bus route."

"Fine, I'll ride the bus to class, but come on. I'll have to go grocery shopping too. That's a hassle on the bus, and I can't expect my roommates to drive me around all the time. Besides, it gets dark at five o'clock in the wintertime. You wouldn't want me waiting at some bus stop after dark, would you?"

Ellis knew if she pushed back hard enough, Allison would relent. All three of her kids were well aware of her precarious financial situation, but she'd promised herself never to let her daughter feel shortchanged just because she had the bad luck to be born third. It didn't matter if the money wasn't there. She'd have to find it.

"I promise I will buy you a car this summer." She could take out a loan or trade in her own luxury SUV for two lesser models. "Now that we have that settled, I need you to clean up your mess in my bathroom. And in the future, please use the guest bath."

"Aye-aye, captain." She even added a salute as she walked past her on her way down the hall. When she reached the bathroom, she shouted, "So you stayed the night with Summer? Bet that was weird."

She pretended not to hear.

CHAPTER SEVENTEEN

There was one positive thing to say for the day—it wasn't quite as bad as Christmas. Allison and Jeremy appeared to get along reasonably well, so there wasn't any squabbling. Bruno was polite as always. But Ellis clearly looked nervous about the whole affair. Not today's affair, apparently—the one they'd started two nights ago.

Summer still felt out of place among the Rowanburys. The strangest part was knowing Jeremy was aware she was seeing his mother, but sworn to secrecy. Since he'd surely told Bruno, that left Allison as the only one in the dark. It felt deceitful, and she hoped Ellis would talk to her soon.

According to Ellis, her invitation to join the family today had been Jeremy's idea, ostensibly to thank her for taking their mother in during the wild party that hadn't actually happened. At least that's what they'd told Allison. In truth, he'd suggested it so they'd all have the chance to get to know each other better.

All in all, it wasn't a bad way to spend a rainy Sunday afternoon. Summer knew she'd need to build her own bond with the whole family if she and Ellis were going to have something meaningful. At least Jonathan wasn't there to put everyone on edge.

"I know! Let's play Spoons," Allison said. She raced to the kitchen and collected four spoons from the drawer.

"Where are the cards, Mom?" Jeremy asked.

"Where did we leave them at Christmas?" Ellis fished around in a kitchen drawer. "Here we go."

It was uncanny to Summer how quickly everyone brightened. Clearly this was a game they played often.

"I'm not sure I know what Spoons is," she said.

Bruno fetched a side chair from the bedroom and added it to the circular dining table. "Just the bloodiest game ever invented. At least the way these guys play."

The object, it seemed, was to pass the cards around the table one at a time until someone collected four of a kind. That person grabbed a spoon from the center of the table, after which the other four players had to race for one of the three remaining spoons. Whoever failed to get one got an S, then a P, and so on until they spelled out the whole word. Then they took away a chair and a spoon. The game was played until only one remained.

"I'm afraid to ask what makes this so bloody."

"Watch those two," Jeremy warned, indicating his mother and sister. "Their fingernails can kill."

By the time they'd finished the third hand, Summer's knuckle had been gouged by none other than Ellis. It was indeed a raucous game, hilarious at times. Much better than watching TV, and an easy way to get to know the various personalities without having to make strained conversation.

"I wonder what your noisy neighbors are thinking now, Mom," Allison said. "I bet they won't have any more loud parties. Or maybe they'll think it's okay because you make a lot of noise too. Good thing Summer has a spare room for you."

Summer looked over her cards at Ellis, whose face had turned red. "I know what you're up to, Allison. Stop your chattering and quit trying to distract everybody."

She drew the Queen of Clubs to complete her set and surreptitiously removed a spoon, all the while passing cards on as if she were still playing. It was several seconds before anyone noticed one of the spoons was missing. Then the rush was on. The last one flew off the table, resulting in Ellis and Bruno diving on the floor.

"That was sneaky," Allison wailed.

"Who cares? I'm bleeding."

* * *

Ellis huddled next to Jeremy and Bruno on the couch so she could keep her voice low. Allison was in the guest bedroom packing her things to return to campus.

"It was fun, don't you think?"

"I like her," Bruno declared. He and Summer had hit it off, joking throughout the afternoon and bonding over their status as state employees.

Jeremy was less emphatic. "So do I, but whether we like her or not isn't the issue. It's how you feel, Mom."

"But it matters to me what you think. Not just of Summer but all of it. You know her a little better now. It's not like we're going to run off and get married or anything, but she could be around whenever you guys come over. How will you feel about her being a part of our lives?"

At the peak of their card game, with everyone having fun, she'd gotten the sudden feeling everything would fall into place. The move to Sacramento had been a family decision. Now that she was on her own, her children wanted her to live in a safe place, be financially secure, have someone to lean on. Implicit to those things was putting the trauma of the shooting behind her so she could begin a new life. They should welcome the fact that she'd fallen in love with someone decent who treated her well.

"I'm okay with it," Jeremy finally said, this time with a little more enthusiasm. "But you ought to ask yourself honestly if you are, because it doesn't really look like it from where I'm sitting."

She slumped against him, frustrated that he refused to believe she knew her own feelings.

"Seriously, Mom. I went through this, so I know how it is. If you were totally okay with it, you wouldn't be whispering. You'd own it. You definitely wouldn't be asking Bruno and me not to say anything in front of Allison, like it's a big secret you're ashamed of."

"What's a big secret?" Allison tossed her backpack toward the door and walked around the couch to face everyone.

A chill gripped Ellis as Jeremy jumped to his feet and nudged Bruno toward the door. "We're going to go, Mom. Thanks for lunch. So long, Allie."

Allison barely acknowledged him, her steely gaze fixed on Ellis. "What's he talking about? What secret are you not telling me?"

Ellis threw her head back and sighed. "Get your things. I'll tell you in the car."

Maybe it was best her hand had been forced, since she hadn't been able to get up the nerve to start the conversation on her own. And Jeremy was right. She couldn't treat her relationship with Summer as if she were ashamed of it.

"I'm all ears, Mom," Allison said as she buckled her seatbelt.

"Can you please just let me get out of the parking lot?" She stopped near the exit, shrugged out of her raincoat and tossed it in the back seat. The exercise gave her an extra minute to think. In fact, she dragged her feet for several more minutes until they were clear of stoplights and proceeding smoothly down Interstate 80. Davis was only a fifteen-minute drive away.

"Quit stalling, Mom. I want to know what's going on."

"I was planning on telling you. Not this weekend necessarily, but soon. I just wanted to be sure…and I'm not totally sure, but mostly." The last words she blurted impulsively to give herself cover in case all hell broke loose. "Let me put it this way. I'm sure about now but not about the future."

Allison groaned. "Just tell me."

"I'm trying!" Trying to find the words was more like it. "It's about Summer. She and I…we've started seeing each other."

From the corner of her eye, she saw her daughter's jaw drop.

"No fucking way."

"Allison!"

"Oh, come on! I just found out my mother's dating a lesbian. What did you expect me to say?"

"I expect you to be civil and treat me with respect." She'd assumed Allison would have questions, but never had she expected this level of dismay. "Why does this upset you? You never had a problem with Jeremy being gay."

"Jeremy's not my mother." She pulled the hood of her sweatshirt up and turned toward the window. "Christ, can't I have just one normal parent?"

To be compared so flippantly to Bruce was like a vicious slap. At that moment, Ellis wanted nothing more than to step on the gas and get to Davis as quickly as possible so she could push her daughter out on the curb. Allison knew better than to think she could get away with talking like that. The fact that she'd intended her words to hurt made them that much harder to stomach.

"I'm going to forgive you for saying that because I love you. And I know you're going to feel awful when you think it over and realize how ugly you just sounded."

"Whatever."

"Is that all I get? Whatever?"

The speedometer showed her doing nearly ninety. She had no recollection of shifting to the far left lane, and she slowed immediately and fell in with the flow of traffic. At the same time, her temper calmed and she formulated a different approach.

"Sweetheart, help me understand what the problem is. It's obvious you like Summer. Jeremy and Bruno like her too. She's a very nice person."

"That was before I found out she hits on women who aren't gay. That shit's creepy as hell." An unusually vicious tone.

"Why? Because she's a woman?" It offended her to realize she was being judged. "Would you think it was creepy if a man were hitting on me instead? What if I didn't like it? Because I'll have you know I get that too sometimes, and I've got to tell you—those are the people who creep me out, not Summer. She's never been anything but respectful. And you should give me enough credit to know when I appreciate someone's attention and when I don't."

"But you're not gay, Mom. I have lots of lesbian friends who know better than to hit on me."

Ellis moved over again, this time into the slowest lane. Between watching the road and trying to see her daughter's face, she had no business going so fast.

"Honey, what makes you so sure it was her hitting on me and not the other way around? I happen to find her attractive. I don't know why that is, but it is. I've never felt that way about another woman before. It's because it's her."

"That's fucking absurd. Just get me back to my dorm. I don't care how fast you drive. I don't even care if we get in a wreck."

She'd seen this kind of anger and pessimism directed at Bruce after the shooting, but had never been on the receiving end. "Please get a grip on yourself. Whatever you think of me right now, it's not worth all this hostility."

Allison answered with brooding silence until they pulled onto the street next to her dorm. As the car slowed, she snatched her backpack from the back seat and readied for her escape. "Just do whatever you want, Mom. You're going to anyway. It's obvious you went to Jeremy and got his seal of approval, but you didn't bother to ask me what I thought. You just dumped it on me like you'd made up your mind already. It's always Jeremy. I bet he's loving this. Are you doing it so you can be gay just like him? Wait till Jon hears about this. He's going to go ballistic."

In a surge of anger, Ellis hit the brakes harder than she had to, slinging both of them forward. It was one thing for her daughter to grouse about her own persecution complex, but quite another to threaten to tell her brother the news. "It's not your place to say anything to Jonathan. I will talk to him when I'm ready. I don't want you disrupting his studies."

"Like you just disrupted mine? Seriously, Mom. Wasn't it enough that Dad fucked up my senior year and got me knocked out of Stanford? Now I'm finally getting my shit together, and you dump this on me. Just forget about the car, okay? I'll probably end up flunking out anyway. I'll just get a waitress job and a bus pass. Or was that your plan all along? You couldn't make anything of yourself so you don't want me to either." She bolted from the car and slammed the door behind her.

Ellis sat stunned as she watched Allison stomp toward the dorm. She'd never seen her daughter so unhinged—not even when her father had murdered seven people.

* * *

Summer divided the contents of her crockpot into five small containers. Chicken and wild rice soup, one of her favorites. And now it would be lunch for the next week, because Ellis had declined her invitation to share it.

That something was amiss was obvious from her sullen voice and her cool response to an invitation to come over for the evening. It was a far cry from her cheery mood earlier when she'd whispered goodbye at the door and added a hint about getting together later—minus the distractions.

Summer wanted to give her the benefit of the doubt, but couldn't shake the feeling that whatever had happened in the meantime likely had something to do with her. Especially since Ellis was willing to see her, but only in her own apartment. It didn't take a genius to know she intended to avoid a repeat of Friday night.

When Ellis met her at the door, Summer knew instantly her suspicions were correct. A scowl had replaced the smile that was there earlier, and her reluctant shuffle in her house slippers gave the impression she was marching to the gallows.

"I don't know what happened, but it can't possibly be as bad as you think it is."

"My daughter hates me and wants to drop out of school and possibly kill herself in a car wreck." She looked over her shoulder at the clock above the kitchen bar. "And by now, Jonathan probably does too."

She'd scrubbed her face of makeup and changed into knit pants and an oversized, worn T-shirt. Her hair was pulled back in a tie, though some of it didn't quite reach and fell loosely around her cheeks. If Summer had to guess, it was a deliberate effort not to look attractive. A wasted effort.

"You told her about us?"

"Not intentionally. She overheard me talking with Jeremy and Bruno." Ellis plopped on the couch and let out a dramatic sigh. "Honestly, I thought she *might* be a little skeptical, but I never expected her to fly into a rage. You wouldn't believe the hateful words that came out of her mouth."

Noting Ellis's body language—folded arms with her legs crossed in an almost-lotus pose—Summer didn't think it a good idea to sit close. She positioned herself at the far end of the couch and listened as Ellis recounted the ride back to Davis. It was difficult to reconcile the friendly young woman from this afternoon with the one she now described.

"I have no idea what's driving this. I've never known her to be so judgmental…and she hasn't gone off on me like that since she was fourteen. That got her grounded for a month, but I can't exactly do that now, can I? This makes no sense at all."

Summer didn't dare offer her true opinion, as it likely would be difficult for Ellis to hear. Allison needed professional help to deal with what her father had done. The trauma of coping for so long had left her fragile, unable to handle any more disruption in her life. "She probably just needs some time. I remember when I started coming out to people. Mama and Daddy were like, no big deal. In fact, they both said they already knew. But my best friend from high school freaked out, and so did her parents. That was it for us. It's a shock for some people. Most of them come around though. I bet Jeremy went through that with his friends too."

Ellis was staring blankly across the room, but she turned and nodded at the mention of her son. "She also accused me of having a favorite child—Jeremy. Trust me, no mother wants to hear something like that. My whole life has been a balancing act for those kids. You could add up their Christmas presents every year—all three of them would be within a dollar of each other."

Summer was reasonably sure Allison had insulted her during her tirade, but she could handle it. She was more worried about

Ellis having to listen to that sort of vile contempt from her own daughter. "Don't take it to heart. People say things they don't mean when they're upset."

"But why does this bother her so much? That's what I can't understand."

"Because it's different. And maybe because her whole life's been turned upside down, and now she's just trying to find some stability. This threatens that." She took a chance and scooted close enough to pull Ellis's hand into her lap. "Who knows? She might have reacted the same way if you'd told her you were seeing a man."

"I asked her that." Ellis sighed loudly and shook her head. "It was definitely about you being a woman. She said it was creepy. Her word, not mine. She even asked me if I was doing this so I could be like Jeremy. That's just crazy."

Summer was in no position to offer advice. She didn't know a thing about kids, nor the Rowanbury family dynamic. All she could do was offer support. "If you want my two cents, you did the right thing being honest with her. A lot of people have been conditioned to feel ashamed, so they expect to be bashed when they finally tell the people close to them. Allison will respect you for insisting on your own dignity. Maybe not now, but someday."

Ellis frowned and nibbled at her lower lip. "I kicked myself all the way home for not being more careful when I was talking to Jeremy and Bruno. She might have been okay if we'd kept it to ourselves for a while. But right now…this is a horrible time for her to have to deal with this. I can't blame her for feeling like everything's gone off the rails."

It was understandable she was being protective of Allison, but Summer was picking up more—the beginnings of regret.

"Look, sweetheart. Everybody pushes back against news they don't want to hear. It's only natural. She's been through so many changes…her father, losing her high school friends, college. It wouldn't matter who you were seeing. As far as she's concerned, it's just one more change. You know she'll adapt."

"Maybe, but what worries me is what she'll do in the meantime. She's so smart—probably the smartest of my three—but she came close to not even graduating from high school because of what Bruce did. She shuts down. No, it's worse than that. She screws up on purpose, like she's punishing herself and everyone else. I was so glad when she got to college and finally shook it off. I don't want her to fall apart again."

From her self-destructive behavior, the girl was deeply troubled. But Summer's heart broke most for Ellis, who clearly was crushed by the rift. Her despair over Allison was but a narrow window into what she must have suffered from her husband's savage act.

"I'm so sorry for what you're going through. What can I do?"

It scared her to realize Ellis couldn't look at her as she answered. "I'm her mother. I'm supposed to protect her. In her mind, this is as bad as what her father did." She held up her hands to ward off the protest already on Summer's lips. "Not that us seeing each other is wrong. But it's having the same effect on her."

"Because she's lost all perspective. It's a jolt to find out your mom is seeing a woman, but only at first. Especially with somebody as open-minded as Allison. The problem is it calls up all the old emotions from when everything in her life changed." That was dangerously close to psychobabble, she realized, brushing Ellis's cheek with her knuckles. "I shouldn't be talking out of my ass. You know Allison best."

Ellis gave her a pained look. "I'm worried about her."

"Of course you are. So just tell me how you want to handle this." They could pull back and see each other only in private. Stolen moments were better than none. "I'm willing to talk to her if you think it would help."

"No!" she said emphatically. "There's no telling what she'd say to you. The way she is right now, it would be awful."

"I've seen this before, Ellis. Allison will come around eventually. The person she is deep down won't be able to live with herself for taking away your happiness."

"I think we need to step back…"

No no no no! "Step back? You mean…not see each other when she's around?"

Ellis turned to face her, wearing the same solemn look as the night she'd told the story of Bruce's rampage. "You know how I feel about you, right? Everything we said about making love… it's all still true."

There was definitely a *but* coming.

"But I can't think about myself when one of my kids is hurting this much. It just isn't possible."

Summer knew exactly what was coming next, and it filled her with dread.

"I can't do this. I just can't. I need to call her and tell her we aren't seeing each other anymore…that we talked it over and decided to just be friends."

"Friends." Her instincts for self-preservation kicked in, prompting her to withdraw her hand and stiffen. She wouldn't grovel in front of someone who was callous enough to toss her aside at the first sign of trouble. "Why not just neighbors?"

"Summer, please don't be like that. I don't have any choice."

"Of course you have a choice. You could stand up for yourself. For us. You could try to find a way to bring her along. Get her some professional help to figure out why she's taking her anger out on you." She leapt up and started toward the door, brimming with frustration. "You have lots of choices, Ellis. Why are you going with the most extreme?"

"It isn't extreme to want to keep her from hurting herself."

That was Rita's *modus operandi*—to stop drinking for a short while and threaten to start again if Summer didn't come back. To moan about how life wasn't worth living without her. "That's called emotional blackmail. The only way to beat it is to ignore it."

Ellis sprang from the couch like a striking snake, the cords in her neck tightened with anger. "I don't care what it's called. I don't take chances when it comes to my kids."

Summer whirled away, using all her willpower to resist slamming the door.

CHAPTER EIGHTEEN

Ellis seethed at the tinny sound of pop music seeping from the headphones of the woman in the next cubicle. Between that and the putrid smell of someone's tuna sandwich, she was ready to scream. Why couldn't people keep their obnoxious habits to themselves?

She picked up the next assignment from her inbox, a printed Word document clipped to the reporter's notes. It was a promotional feature for the entertainment section, an interview with Tamara Tinsley. Fresh off a stint on Broadway as Cosette in *Les Misérables*, she was coming to Sacramento as Maria in the national tour of *The Sound of Music*.

Summer had presented her with a pair tickets for that, and for the next two shows as well. The only reasonable thing to do was give them back, and if she wouldn't accept them, to pay her whatever they cost. Maybe Gil would agree to let her do some freelance articles, something she could work on after hours and on the weekend. A few hundred extra bucks would come in handy.

Her chances for preserving even a friendship with Summer were slim, given how they'd avoided each other completely for the past three days. She'd even skipped her workout, fearing she'd be humiliated if she walked into the fitness room only to have Summer pick up and leave without a word.

It was true what Summer had said. Allison probably could benefit from talking to a therapist, especially if she was threatening self-destructive behavior. That wasn't coping—it was a cry for help, made worse by her continued refusal to reply to the half-dozen messages Ellis had left urging her to call.

Summer hadn't deserved such an unyielding response, though the emotional exchange had exposed the shallowness of her feelings. You didn't walk out in a huff if the relationship was worth fighting for. Ellis had only been concerned about her daughter. Had Summer not stormed out, they might have calmed down and explored some of those other options.

Who was she trying to kid? This wasn't Summer's fault. She'd walked out because Ellis had told her she couldn't see her anymore. It wasn't over though…at least not as far as her heart was concerned.

Maybe it wasn't too late to salvage what they'd started, even if it were only an agreement to stay close for now and keep their possibilities open while Allison dealt with her issues. Neither of them had said anything overly cruel or malicious that couldn't be forgiven. It all depended on whether or not Summer felt the same sense of loss. Or was she relieved to have gotten out before little differences became big problems? Only by talking again could they find out.

Ellis toyed with her phone, puzzling over how to say that in a pithy text message. *Been thinking about us all w—*

Her cell phone, set to vibrate, rumbled in her hand. It was her attorney's office in San Francisco. "May I please speak to Mrs. Rowanbury?"

She resisted the urge to correct the woman, since her conversation was open to everyone in the adjacent cubicles. The *Vista* staff didn't need to know she'd changed her name.

"I've been asked to schedule a meeting with you. Could you make tomorrow morning at nine o'clock?"

That was a horrible time to drive into the City across the Bay Bridge. "I'd prefer a bit later...ten thirty? And can you tell me what this is regarding?"

"I'm afraid not. I've only been instructed to schedule the appointment for nine."

Resigned to leaving her home at six a.m., she scribbled the time on her notepad as though it weren't instantly burned into her head. After over a year of wrangling, she was more than ready for some movement on her case. At this point the outcome almost didn't matter—she just wanted the whole affair behind her.

Her downward fall since Bruce's death was nothing short of remarkable—from a lively three-story homestead to a cramped apartment where she lived alone. From lunching in North Beach and Woodside to leftovers in Rubbermaid. From being her own boss to working on the lowest rung of the ladder.

For a brief window, Summer had given her a reason to look toward the future. Now she'd have to add another heartbreak to that list. Unless...

Angie appeared in her cubicle with her usual stack of folders, which she carried all the time to dole out at the first sign of an empty inbox. "Here's the photo that goes with the Tamara Tinsley interview. Clip that to the rest of it when you're done."

Ellis needed to concentrate on her work. Not on Summer, nor Allison. She scanned the notes and typed Tinsley's name into her search engine. The feature was mostly background with a few quotes. MFA from Boston Conservatory...twenty-six years old. Except her official bio had her birthday as February first, which meant she'd be twenty-seven by the time they went to press on the next issue. She scribbled a note in the margin.

The article referred to Tinsley as a blonde, and the attached photo showed her as such—but in her role as Cosette. Ellis had seen her in *Phantom* and remembered her as a brunette, and in fact, there were no other photos online of her as a blonde. *Need photo as brunette.*

There wasn't much more by way of facts to verify. According to the notes, the interview had been conducted over the phone, and the reporter presumably had a recording. That was their standard practice in case something needed to be verified. As best she could, Ellis matched the quotes to the gist of the scratchy notes to ensure Tinsley wasn't being misquoted or taken out of context.

The final question, however, raised a red flag. Among several roles Tinsley indicated she'd love to play was Sally Bowles in *Cabaret*. Peculiar she'd chosen that one because Bowles was an alto, whereas Tinsley was a soprano. Not just a soprano, but a lyric coloratura—the lightest of all sopranos. Why would she want to sing a role as brash as Bowles?

There was nothing in the notes about *Cabaret*. In fact, the question wasn't even listed in the interview.

With growing suspicion, Ellis reread the article. Other than a handful of quotes, it was a bland regurgitation of mundane production info—direction, choreography, number of cities on the tour—nothing that couldn't be found on the theater company's website. Her doubts were confirmed when she Googled one of the quotes and found it in Houston's city magazine. Another was purloined from the *Hollywood Reporter*, and the quote about *Cabaret* was actually from one of Tinsley's costars in *Les Miz*.

The entire article had been fabricated. Cobbled together from snippets found on the web by a freelance writer who'd probably never picked up his phone to conduct an interview in the first place.

"Angie?"

Her supervisor returned. Reluctantly, it seemed, as she herself was busy trying to make sense of a feature article on Sacramento's growing network of bike trails. "This is a mess. I can't tell if the miles are one way or round trip. Or if there's a fee to ride through the park. Our readers won't be able to make sense of this."

"Let me show you this." Ellis hated to pile on more bad news, but she couldn't let this freelance entertainment reporter get away with repackaging content from other published sources. "What do you want me to do?"

"Hmm…we'll have to strike that last paragraph, since she wasn't the one who said it. But see what you can do about boosting the word count. That one has to come in at five hundred."

"That's it? It's not even our interview."

Angie shrugged. "We do that sometimes. Just check the wording and make sure it doesn't say we actually talked to her."

A fake interview. Like the supermarket gossip rags that told outrageous tales around a tiny quote or paparazzi photo taken completely out of context. *Angelina Tells Brad's Gay Lover 'No More!'*

"Did *Vista* really pay someone to do this? It's worse than an eighth grader's book report."

Angie chuckled. "One-fifty apiece, I think. Some of them aren't even that good. But they fill the pages. And they leave more resources for the important stuff."

Ellis could only shake her head. In a matter of minutes, her view of *Sacramento Vista* had tumbled from that of a prestigious local news source to a tabloid. It was depressing…and yet, it was a treasure trove of opportunity. Three of these a month would cover her daughter's car payment.

* * *

The movement of the dreamcatcher caught Summer's eye as warm air began flowing from the air duct in the ceiling. As a child, she'd gone to sleep many nights under its hypnotic sway from a small electric fan in her bedroom. *It catches all the bad dreams*, her mother had said. Which made it pretty useless in her office, except as a calming focal point when she took a break from her work.

For the past three days, her "breaks" were merely breaks in concentration as she rehashed the ugly confrontation. She'd all but backed Ellis into a corner by getting angry at the first hint of her cracking resolve. Had she discussed things calmly instead of flouting her indignation, they might have found a way forward. Instead she'd forced her to side with her daughter and now was left with nothing.

Rita would have called that throwing out the baby with the bathwater. That had been one of her favorite arguments as she insisted her drinking was only a small problem, certainly not serious enough to cause a break up. *You're always overreacting.*

It hadn't been the case with Rita, but she couldn't escape feeling this time it was. She was too impatient, too proud.

The worst part was knowing she'd piled even more stress on top of a woman who'd already been through enough to last a hundred lifetimes. So much for wanting to support her no matter what—she'd failed that test.

Alythea appeared in the doorway of her office waving a document. "You want to know how these people are going to solve the homeless problem? By giving them salmonella."

"Who's that?"

"This place in San Jose…the Good Way Kitchen. They were cited three times last year for health code violations and neglected to report it in their grant renewal application. Not one word."

"Don't they realize we compare those reports?"

"Funny you should say that." Alythea put a hand on her hip and held out the document. "I always thought we did, but apparently not this time."

Summer got a sinking feeling she'd missed something. "Is that my recommendation?"

"Uh-huh." Her boss did sassy better than anyone on the planet.

"Sorry. Give it back. I'll fix it." Apparently she'd allowed herself to be mesmerized by more than the dreamcatcher.

"I already did. I just came in here to see what's up with your head. You haven't set foot outside this office all week." As she talked, she strolled around the small space, stopping to give the dreamcatcher a spin. "Rita bothering you again?"

"No, I haven't seen her."

"Your new lady then. What's her name?"

Nothing like wearing her heart on her sleeve. "Ellis. Ellis Keene. Except she's not my new lady, at least not anymore." She spilled out a sanitized version designed to preserve the story of Bruce—her daughter was dealing with other emotional problems and couldn't handle the idea of her mother getting involved with someone.

"Someone in general, or someone who happened to be of the female persuasion?"

Summer nodded, chuckling in spite of herself at her choice of words. "Could have been. The problem was I got impatient because I felt like she was letting her daughter control her. I knew better, but I shot my mouth off."

"How could you know better? You don't have children."

"No, but I have friends who do, including you. You'd never let anybody come between you and Nemy."

The situation with Ellis gave her a whole new respect for Queenie, who'd helped raise Sam's two boys from the time they were in elementary school. It was more than a responsibility. It called for sacrifice and a willingness to take a back seat to whatever the kids needed from their mom. Even when the "kid" wasn't a kid anymore.

"Sorry I let that one slide through. I can write them a menacing letter if you want me to—given my current mood, I should be able to pull that off with no trouble at all."

"Forget it. I already called their contact person and told them to resubmit." Alythea lingered in the doorway for a few more seconds, as if contemplating whether or not more was needed to make her point. She had the perfect touch as a supervisor, a velvet hammer that got results without scolding or ridicule.

"Don't worry, Alythea. I'll get my head back in the game."

She was spending too much emotional energy on Ellis. If she couldn't manage her train of thought at work, she'd have to find a resolution—a way to smooth things over so they at least could be friends. That would have been a far more adult response than stomping out.

* * *

"What did you think of *Swan Lake*?"

The baritone voice startled Ellis and she spun around on her rickety chair.

"Sorry. Guess I should have knocked." Rex smiled and rapped his knuckles against the fabric of her cubicle wall. His tie was askew and his sleeves rolled up, but what really stood out was the absence of his bomber jacket. That meant he was working in his office instead of on his beat in the capitol.

"I thought it was lovely. The woman who danced Odette was in *Don Quixote* in San Francisco a couple of years ago." She folded her hands across her chest dramatically, determined to make this conversation about the ballet and not the woman she'd gone with. "*So* talented. Did you know the San Francisco Ballet was the first American company to perform *Swan Lake*? Nineteen-forty."

"I did not know that," he answered emphatically.

Ellis recognized she was being mocked and smiled sheepishly. "I get carried away. I was glad to see you were a fan of the ballet."

That was possibly the stupidest thing she could have said. Why would she be glad unless she wanted him to invite her to another?

"To be honest, I don't know a lot about it. I like the symphony though. Marcie had an extra ticket...her boyfriend had to go to New York or something. Or maybe that's just what he told her because he didn't want to go. Anyway, she called me at the last minute. Probably payback from last year when I dragged her to a rubber chicken awards dinner." He seemed to be going out of his way to explain away his presence with their boss.

"You'll have to take my word for it then. It was a beautiful performance."

"I appreciated how athletic all the dancers were. Maybe we should go into San Francisco some weekend and see another one. Then you can educate me on everything I'm missing."

Just as she'd feared. Another date, this one with the apparent brazen presumption they'd spend the weekend together in the

City. What happened to his measured approach, the one where he'd all but promised to wait for her to say she was ready for more? Or maybe he thought she'd just done that.

The surrounding cubicles had gone quiet. No typing, no rustling of papers, no phone calls. She pictured Angie and the other assistant editors with their ears pressed against the flimsy walls.

"What I should do is get back to work." Still holding eye contact with Rex, she added, "Isn't that right, Angie?"

She'd thought it would send Rex on his way, but instead, he stepped closer, lowering his lips to her ear to whisper, "Meet me downstairs for coffee in five minutes. There's something I need to talk to you about."

Ellis felt her stomach drop. He'd practically asked her to come away with him for a weekend in front of their coworkers with no regard for her privacy. Now he had something so secretive she had to leave the building to hear it. He'd want to know who Summer was. Maybe he'd seen them holding hands.

Her whole body shook as she mindlessly shuffled the notes on Tamara Tinsley. She already hated how the others made it their business to eavesdrop on her personal conversations. Now there would be more whispers, including gossip about Summer.

She remembered the text message she'd started earlier. They needed to talk it out, but now there was a wrinkle in her schedule with the trip to the attorney in San Francisco, which she also needed to clear with Marcie. The weekend ahead was further complicated by Allison, who could show up at any time.

It crossed her mind to ignore Rex's request. To let him spin his wheels outside, working himself into a lather over what he obviously thought was a scandalous secret. What right did he have to comment on her personal life?

No, until she got this settled, she wouldn't be able to focus on her work. The moment she heard Angie pick up her phone, she pulled on her jacket and left.

True to his word, Rex actually meant coffee. He met her just outside the main lobby with a white cup from the cafe. "You look like a skinny latte."

She took it without a word of thanks. "What did you need to talk to me about?"

He tipped his head away from the entrance. "Let's walk."

"I don't need to walk. I need to know what was so secret you couldn't say it in my office. Or yours, for that matter."

"You know how those gossips listen to everything. I didn't think you'd want them to hear this." Ignoring her protests, he took her elbow and guided her down the sidewalk. "Marcie told me something the other night I thought you ought to know. Said she'd gotten a call from an attorney in San Francisco. He asked for a salary affidavit. He didn't say why, but I presume they're going after your future earnings."

Ellis thought she might be sick. In a handful of words, he'd told her everything. He knew all about her. All about Bruce. And the wrongful death claims.

She bit her lip hard and stared into the street, so angry she was afraid to speak.

"Marcie doesn't know what it's about, Ellis. She only mentioned it to me because she was worried you'd skipped out on some creditors."

"Why did she think it was any of your business?"

He shrugged. "Because she's young and reckless and thinks every detail of life belongs on a Facebook page. It was a lousy thing to do."

"I'm sure you were happy to set her straight."

"I didn't tell her anything." His compassionate look was even more convincing than his words, as though it genuinely pained him to tell her the news. "Except that I had an idea what it was about, but I didn't want to break your confidence. I told her I knew for a fact you hadn't done anything wrong. That's all she knows."

Whether Marcie knew the truth or not was less important than the news itself. That was why her attorney wanted to see her, to prepare her for the worst. The families of Bruce's victims weren't satisfied with taking every dime she and Bruce had put away, every piece of property they'd owned together. They were preparing for a judgment that would punish her well into the future. She'd never get out from under their wrath.

"Look, Ellis. I'm sorry I didn't tell you I knew who you were. I should have done that when we went out to dinner. I was hoping you'd eventually trust me enough to open up."

It was all she could do not to laugh. "You wanted me to trust you? After you went digging into my life like I was one of your assemblymen on the take? That's the opposite of trust."

He shook his head. "I didn't look you up. I already knew who you were." Clearly exasperated, he leaned against the brick wall with his knee bent and one hand in his pocket. "After the shooting, I did some preliminary work on a column about the families of the victims, something to tie in with a gun bill that was being talked about in the judiciary committee. The bill died so I never followed up. But your name was on my list of people to interview."

"As Ellis Rowanbury."

He grimaced and took a sip of his coffee. "I got copies of all the relevant documents for my column. Your maiden name's listed on your husband's death certificate. I recognized you as soon as you introduced yourself and said you'd just moved from San Francisco."

Which he should have mentioned sooner. "Who else knows?"

"No one, as far as I'm concerned. I only meant to give you a heads-up about the lawyer so you wouldn't be blindsided in case Marcie said something."

Marcie was the least of her worries.

"For what it's worth, Ellis, I'm here if you ever need to talk. Not as a reporter, as a friend. I know what they're trying to do to you. You don't deserve it."

If anyone at *Vista* other than Gil Martino had to know about her past, she at least was glad it was someone with enough compassion to keep it quiet.

"Thank you, Rex. Right now the only person I feel like talking to is my attorney."

CHAPTER NINETEEN

The lobby of the Sherrill Legal Group had an unobstructed view of the Transamerica Pyramid. It struck Ellis as fitting that she was forced to stare at it while she waited for the receptionist to send her back for her consultation.

Myron Sherrill had approached her the morning after the shooting with an offer to represent Bruce's estate. She'd been taken aback by his eager solicitation until he made it clear it would take an aggressive attorney to prevent the plaintiffs from taking every penny she had. The firm's fee was thirty percent of whatever they salvaged.

Bruce had earned several million dollars in his twenty-five-year career as a money manager, and he'd invested their income wisely. In addition to their financial instruments, they'd owned outright their five-bedroom house in Diamond Heights and a vacation home on the Russian River. All of their assets were being targeted for total liquidation by the surviving family members of Bruce's victims. If Rex was correct, they were going after her paltry wages as well.

Sherrill had hoped for an early ruling that put only half those assets at risk—Bruce's half. When the judge went against them, they requested arbitration and Sherrill assigned junior associate Brittany Zimmer to her case, a clear signal he didn't expect a lucrative outcome.

The receptionist, a small Asian woman who could have been forty or sixty, rose and directed her into a hallway. "Ms. Zimmer is ready for you now. Fourth door on the right."

She entered a small interior office, more proof of Zimmer's lowly position in the pecking order. It was decorated—if one could call it that—with a plain cherry desk and credenza, and two matching armchairs. A fake fichus tree in the corner gave the room its only color.

Zimmer looked to be in her early thirties, with long dark hair, a round face and a wide, toothy smile. She rose and placed both hands on her lower back to support her swollen belly. Eight months along was Ellis's guess. If it were less, the woman was in for misery. Or triplets.

"Mrs. Rowanbury, please have a seat."

"You first," she answered with a nervous chuckle. "And I go by Keene now, my maiden name. You should have a record of that. Myron Sherrill handled the paperwork."

"Oh yes, I'm sorry." She arranged several documents on her desk so she could study them all at once and passed a single page to Ellis, a summary of talking points. "Thank you for coming in so quickly. I got your email saying you were concerned about the plaintiffs contacting your employer to document your income."

"Can they actually come after my future wages? Mr. Sherrill indicated my exposed worth was established on the day Bruce died."

"It was, but keep in mind the withdrawals you've already made from the estate. That potentially increases your personal obligation going forward."

Tuition and moving expenses. She understood that in theory, but Sherrill had been confident the arbitrator would allow those expenditures in the final judgment. If not, the worst that could happen was she'd be required to pay it back to the estate—the same way she'd have paid it had she borrowed the money. No real difference in the long run, he'd said.

"I spoke with Mr. Cox this morning," Zimmer went on, referencing the lead attorney for the families. "What his clients want is an assurance that you and your family won't come out of this better off financially than their families. I'm sure that sounds vindictive, but it's merely another argument for maximizing their payout. As you probably know, many wrongful death cases turn on emotional grounds. This introduces the concept of shared hardship—if they have to work harder and go into debt to provide for their families, they want you to do the same."

Put that way, it wasn't an unreasonable position. It was unseemly to argue her innocence to seven families who also were blameless.

"What does that mean for my case? Are we getting any closer to resolving this?"

"In fact we are. We've finally had some movement from your homeowners insurance company. They've agreed in principle to a payout. That's great news. Just an initial offer, but now that they're finally at the table, the plaintiffs are ready to propose a settlement with us. Several of them are starting to experience financial hardship and we can use that to our favor to force a settlement that gives them an immediate payout. Then they can turn their guns on building management and the security company."

Ellis dropped her jaw with horror. Of all the metaphors Zimmer might have chosen, she went with a shootout.

"Oh, my God! Mrs. Keene, I'm so sorry." The woman's pregnant glow turned blazing red and she took a deep swig from a water bottle on her desk. "I should have had more presence of mind than to say something like that. I deeply apologize."

"It's...unfortunate." What else could she say? It wasn't in her nature to scold people who weren't her kids, no matter how thoughtless their behavior. "When you say immediate, what does that mean? Are we ready to make an offer?"

Ellis hardly cared anymore about the settlement. If they took every dime, so be it. She just wanted it finished so she could get on with her life.

"They've already made one. It's tentative though, depending on how you feel about the equity of the split. That's why I wanted to meet today." She handed over a second document with a summary of the terms. It divided her total assets by eight—one part for each victim and one for her.

"If it's equity they want," Ellis said, "I can live with that."

That actually was a better outcome than she'd anticipated. Between their investment accounts and the sale of their houses, the estate was quite large. Even if the law firm took thirty percent of her portion, she'd be left with enough to cover Allison's tuition and start a modest nest egg. That was far more than she'd hoped for.

"We'll proceed then. With your signature, we can present it to the arbitrator as early as tomorrow." Zimmer sounded almost eager, as though Sherrill had given her the directive to close the case no matter the terms. That made sense in light of her condition, especially if she was planning an extended maternity leave. The firm probably considered the settlement a money-loser for them at this point.

For Ellis, it had been an albatross. The idea that it might finally be lifted made her feel like celebrating for the first time since the shooting. Then her heart sank to realize she couldn't call the one person she wanted most to tell.

* * *

The fog crested the ridge at Pacifica, marring an otherwise sunny ride south along the 280 to Woodside. It was fitting they should have lunch at Buck's one more time before Roxanne left Silicon Valley for her new job.

The memory of her last drive along this route came at her in vicious spurts. The radio report, the frantic calls, the police officer who'd finally answered Bruce's phone. It was a silent anniversary, one she refused to mark—the day her life changed forever.

Tears welled up as the rustic restaurant triggered long-lost recollections of happy times. She'd barely composed herself when the sight of her friend threatened to break her down again.

Roxanne leapt from a bench near the door and greeted her with the warmest hug they'd ever shared. For a full thirty seconds, they squeezed one another tightly until Ellis finally shed a tear.

"I am so sorry," Roxanne murmured.

"For what? I'm the one who should be apologizing."

"For not being there when you needed me most. For not calling you anyway." She finally released the hug and held Ellis at arm's length. "It's a travesty we haven't seen each other in so long. And I promise never to let this much time go by again."

"Same here." She got her first good look at her longtime friend, who'd eschewed her power suit for designer jeans and a blazer. "You look like you're ready to go on vacation."

"I'm heading to a beach in Thailand, but not till tonight. I've got the whole afternoon and I want to know everything. How's life in the capital? How are the kids? How's work?"

They walked arm in arm to a table in the corner beneath a sloping hardwood ceiling, where they ordered wine and perused the lunch menu.

"I'm more interested in you," Ellis said. "How did it feel to jump off the Silicon Valley hamster wheel?"

"Oh no, you don't. We talked all about me on the phone the other night. It's your turn. What did your attorney say about the case?"

Ellis shared the high points, including her hope it would be over soon.

"It's so unfair what they're doing to you."

She waved off the remark. "I'm over it. It finally hit me today that most of those people are just fighting for their kids. I'd be doing exactly the same thing. If money makes them feel better, then I'll feel better if they have it."

"You're way more magnanimous than I'd be. Tell me about your kids."

"Jonathan's supposed to hear about law school this week, so that'll be another worry off my plate. He's a nervous wreck but I'm not. His grades are outstanding. And Allison likes UC-Davis. She made the Dean's List first quarter, speaking of outstanding grades. It's easier for her to focus now that she's out of the City."

It didn't feel right to share her suspicions about her daughter's emotional struggles. That was a private family matter.

"And what about my Jeremy? I haven't talked to him since October." He'd always been Roxanne's favorite.

"Still in love with Bruno. Enjoying his work."

The past year's strain on their friendship dissipated with every update, every anecdote that bolstered how satisfied she was with her new life in Sacramento.

Satisfied? Only a few days ago, she would have said happy.

They were briefly interrupted by a waitress delivering their lunch, a pair of decadent turkey melts on sourdough. Roxanne had already insisted on picking up the tab, and for once, Ellis didn't argue.

"And so what else? Have you made any new friends?"

"Yes, one very good friend. A woman who lives in the next building." Her *neighbor*, she recalled with shame. "We work out together in the fitness room…have coffee together. She's an interesting woman. I've enjoyed getting to know her."

She wanted very badly to tell Roxanne about Summer, that she'd fallen in love. Except there was nothing to tell now that their relationship had come apart. It couldn't possibly have been love if she was willing to walk away from it for Allison.

"And I'll have you know I actually went on a date." Pushing aside her thoughts of Summer, she shared the details of her dinner with Rex, ending with his disturbing mention of the Transamerica Pyramid. "Needless to say, that freaked me out."

"Is this Rex Brenneman, the political columnist?"

"You've heard of him?"

"He interviewed me over the phone a few years back about a political contribution I made. Had me scared shitless I'd done something illegal."

Ellis laughed. She could well imagine Rex intimidating the hell out of everyone he spoke to. "If you had, I'm sure he'd have printed it. The man's a bulldog."

"A handsome bulldog. He was one of *Chron Magazine*'s Most Eligible Bachelors in Northern California." She patted Ellis's hand. "And *you* went out with him."

"I hadn't realized he was such a catch. I can see why though. He's very nice…to me, anyway." She thought of how he tormented her coworkers. "Too bad there wasn't anything between us. At least I didn't feel it."

"Of course you didn't, sweetie. That's going to take some time. It hasn't been that long since Bruce died. Obviously you're not ready."

Bruce had nothing to do with the readiness of her feelings. As she'd lain in bed with Summer, she hadn't given her wounds a thought. "I don't think that's it. The truth is I was seeing someone else too, but we're a little on the outs right now. It sure felt like I was ready for that…but it's complicated. We have issues to work out. Maybe too many…but maybe not."

It was surprising to hear herself characterize her relationship with Summer as though their parting might be temporary. For all she knew, Summer had washed her hands of her. Plus there was no indication Allison would lighten up. She still hadn't responded to her messages.

Roxanne lit up with delight. "This sounds juicy. Spill it."

Her sudden willingness to talk about Summer was spurred by excitement, just as when she'd rushed to tell Jeremy. "You aren't going to believe this, Roxie. I had trouble believing it myself. I've been seeing my friend, the woman who lives in my apartment complex."

Roxanne laughed. "Now there's an idea. Imagine how fast men would shape up if we threatened to leave them altogether."

It was hard enough to say it the first time. Now she had to be more convincing.

"Roxie, I'm serious. The woman I've been working out with, she's a lesbian. She started flirting with me. Not in a creepy way, just…" She recalled her daughter's description and made certain to note she wasn't offended in any way. "She'd say things like how nice I looked, and she joked around that if I ever decided to date women, she wanted to be at the front of the line. It wasn't pushy or anything. Next thing I knew I was thinking about her all the time. This has never happened to me before."

"Oh, honey." Roxanne reached over and squeezed her hand. "I'm sure it's nothing. Of course lesbians are going to think you're lovely—because you are. But men think so too. We all like getting compliments, no matter where they come from. You started thinking about moving on from Bruce and she happened to be there. So did Rex Brenneman, by the way. I'm telling you, he's a catch. You need to give him another chance. Once you get out and start dating more, you'll be back to your old self."

"It wasn't just a fluke. It was real." She put both hands over her heart. "I felt something for her. It's not like you and me. We're friends and that's all there is to it. I love you dearly. But it never crossed my mind to want to kiss you, or—"

"Have you slept with her?"

The words seemed to echo throughout the dining room and she felt her face grow hot. "Yes," she whispered, looking about surreptitiously.

"And?" Roxanne's look of surprise was replaced by casual amusement.

This was her oldest friend, the one with whom she'd traded dozens of tales of her sexual romps, including intimate details of her life with Bruce. Girl talk, usually shared over a bottle of wine.

Ellis leaned closer and kept her voice low. "Would you believe seven times in one night?"

Roxanne made no effort to be quiet. "Get out of here!"

"Cross my heart. Only two for her, but that's because I'm just a novice." As soon as she said it, she felt guilty for trivializing their lovemaking.

"I need to give this lesbian business a try. What's this woman's number?"

"It wasn't just sex. We were such good friends…and before I knew it I was falling in love."

"Oh, don't be ridiculous. You're as straight as I am."

"That's what I always thought too." Though her tone was serious now, she didn't want this to turn into a heavy conversation. It served no purpose to argue over something Roxanne couldn't understand. "But it turns out I might not be."

"I've known you thirty years, Ellis, and I'm telling you— ain't no way." She waved a hand dismissively before taking a monstrous bite of her sandwich.

"I would have said the same thing, but I swear this is different. The problem right now is Allison's freaking out. Jeremy's cool with it though. He likes her."

"Of course he does. It validates his choice. But I'm with Allison on this one."

"His *choice*?" Now she was irritated.

"Not for Jeremy. It's his orientation." She was at least mildly contrite. "But it isn't *yours*, sweetie. You spent twenty-five years with Bruce, and I know for a fact you were happy with him."

It was probably no use to share her theory that sexuality could shift for anyone. Roxanne would surely insist it would never shift for her.

"Listen to me, Ellis. I personally don't care what people do in the privacy of their bedrooms. Whatever floats their boat. But you're in a vulnerable place right now. You shouldn't let anyone—not a man, woman or dog—take advantage of that." She stopped eating and took her hand. "I'm not saying you shouldn't enjoy it. Seven times in one night? Go for it."

Typical Roxanne, decisive and strident. And take no prisoners along the way. She always processed information quickly, instinctively arriving at conclusions far more quickly than her peers. Then she was ready to move on to the next topic. It was a trait that served her well in her career, but it wasn't always conducive to sensitive talks.

None of that mattered to Ellis. She had her best friend back.

CHAPTER TWENTY

Without looking up, Summer fell into step with a small group of pedestrians at the crossing, trusting them to save her from herself. She was too busy texting to watch for traffic lights.

I miss my friend. Can we talk tonight?

Her thumb hovered over the *Send* key, but at the last second, she hit *Cancel*. Though the handwriting was on the wall—there would be no romance with Ellis—she wasn't ready to admit it.

She'd made no overtures since the weekend, despite the intensive soul-searching that reminded her of how she'd come to the decision to leave Rita once and for all. In one column were the reasons she should try again to persuade Ellis to give their relationship another chance. At the top of that list was the fact that both of them had said they were in love. Real, honest love, or so it seemed. Add to that their compatibility and genuine friendship, and it was hard even to see the other side.

But those things obviously hadn't carried much weight with Ellis. Her quick, decisive retreat was enough to make Summer doubt the veracity of her feelings, as if their fling had been purely sexual. In a moment of indignation, she'd even imagined Ellis checking "bi-curious experience" off her bucket list.

There was nothing to be gained by thinking the worst. Besides, she knew better. It was an impossible set of circumstances that left Ellis feeling she had to choose between her own needs and desires and those of her daughter. Instead of piling on to her worries, a real friend would support whatever she felt she had to do.

Ellis might well ignore any of her messages anyway—and for good reason—but Summer had to think this through for a way forward. Their breakup had left her miserable.

Had she known she'd still be undecided today, she'd have postponed her lunch with Sam Lotti to another day. That would have freed her to wait outside the *Vista* building and try to talk to Ellis in person. The worst that could happen was Ellis refusing to see her. Since that was already the case, there was nothing to lose.

Sam waved through the window of Vallejo's, where she sat at a table for two.

With her text message deleted, Summer resolved to set aside her cell phone, at least long enough to enjoy lunch. "How's it going, Sam? You look great, woman."

Like Summer, Sam worked for the state, but two blocks away in the Department of Water Resources. Her transformation for work was remarkable. She wore a black skirt and jacket over a silk blouse, accented with silver jewelry and red lipstick. It was quite a contrast to the laid-back jeans and sweaters she wore at home. Like two completely different people, and Summer enjoyed them both.

"You're not so bad yourself. We clean up well for a couple of scruffy dykes, right?"

"Hey, speak for yourself." Summer wasn't quite so decked out, but her gray slacks and navy tunic were a far cry from what she wore to hang out. She recalled her words to Ellis. "If I could get away with it, I'd wear pajamas to work."

"You and me both." Sam looked over her shoulder at the bustling cafe. "I ordered you the chicken tacos like you said. You were right about this place being a madhouse at lunch."

Within moments, their hustling waiter delivered two taco baskets and deposited the check face down on the table.

"Thanks for meeting me," Summer said. "I feel like every time we see each other, there's a million people around. We don't get enough chance to talk, you and me."

Besides the perpetual presence of Rita, there was also the fact that Queenie had a forceful personality that dwarfed those around her. Sam, on the other hand, was laid back and thoughtful. When she expressed an opinion, it was certain to be measured.

After her recognition of Queenie's role in raising Sam's boys, Summer had found herself wondering how they'd handled it. While she wanted to know how Queenie had managed her role as stepmom, it struck her that Sam was the one who'd have the most insight into what Ellis needed. Besides, Sam was more discreet and less likely to worry aloud about how any of this might impact Rita.

"I've got something on my mind…maybe you can help me sort it out."

"Something to do with Rita?" Sam asked.

"Not this time, believe it or not…although everything I do seems to affect her in one way or another. She'd probably go ballistic over this." If she wanted Sam's honest advice, she'd have to be up front about why. "Before I spill my guts here, I need to ask you to keep this under your hat for a while. I don't mind if you tell Queenie, but I don't want all our friends knowing, especially Rita."

Sam stopped eating and smiled wryly. "You must be seeing somebody."

"Yes…no. I was, but we hit a wall. I met somebody and we got to be good friends. Then we slept together and it all went to hell." That wasn't a fair characterization. "Not that sleeping together screwed it up…it just makes it weird to be friends now."

"Who is she?"

"Nobody you know. My neighbor." She nearly laughed at the irony of describing Ellis merely as her neighbor. "She moved here last fall from San Francisco. She's got three kids, but they're all grown, college-age. They still come around a lot though."

"Lucky her. I wish mine did." Both of her boys had joined the military right out of high school. One was in North Carolina, the other in Germany. "I take it she's straight...or at least she thought she was."

"Yeah, but I never got the vibe that it bothered her. She's a widow...forty-eight and a hardcore liberal. Plus one of her sons is gay, so she has zero problems with it."

"You like her kids?"

"Yeah, they're okay. But her daughter's not too happy about her mom seeing another woman. That's what set everything off."

Sam began a steady nod, her face taking on a faraway expression. No doubt she was remembering her own issues with Queenie. "Been there, done that. You should have seen my boys when Queenie and I first started seeing each other. They were so jealous. I'd put them to bed and we'd start making out on the couch. Next thing you know, one of them had a bad dream or needed a drink of water...whatever they could do to get between us. Hell, I couldn't sit down without one of them crawling into my lap."

"But it wasn't because she was a woman, was it? Your boys were little."

"True, but that might not be your real issue either. Could be her daughter's just freaking out because she's jealous."

She hadn't considered the jealous angle. It made a lot more sense than getting upset over her mom seeing another woman. "That's exactly why I wanted to pick your brain. I knew you'd get this."

As Sam raised her taco to her lips, it collapsed, dumping half the ingredients back in her basket.

"Happens to me every time," Summer said, handing her a plastic fork from a bin on their table. "But why would she care if her daughter's jealous? She doesn't even live there."

"It doesn't matter where they live. Moms are hardwired to put their kids first. If Queenie hadn't accepted that, we wouldn't have made it. It took her a couple of years to adapt, but she worked at it. What made her a great stepmom was learning to love my boys practically as much as I did. And once they got used to her being there and figured out they could depend on her, they started loving her back."

"I get that, but I'm not talking about packing lunches and tucking them in at night. Her daughter's a freshman in college. She doesn't even live at home anymore."

"She's still Mama's baby girl. You're going to have to forge a relationship with her if you want one with her mom."

Summer nibbled on a tortilla chip, imagining what a friendship with Allison would look like. "I think we'd get along just fine once she got past the whole 'my mom's acting like a lesbian' part. The real issue is I can't get her mom to see that. She's ready to drop everything at the first sign of trouble." Admittedly, that was an oversimplification, but she couldn't go into Allison's emotional struggles without divulging the family's story.

"There's the rub then. Sounds like you might not be dealing with the kid at all. Could be Mom's not as open-minded about this as you think. If she was comfortable in her own skin, she wouldn't let her daughter push her around like that."

Of course. It was a point she hadn't considered. Ellis wasn't merely giving in to placate Allison. She was using Allison as a rationale to cover her own doubts. What's more, those doubts could be about anything, not just her sexuality.

"Damn." This changed everything. "I hadn't thought about it but you might be right. This might not be about her daughter at all. If that's how she feels, there's nothing I can do."

"Sure there is. Talk to her. Find out what her issues are."

Summer came to an aching realization. "Sam, I can't pressure her into going where she doesn't want to go. If it's not her, it's not her."

The decent thing to do was to back off completely from a sexual or romantic interest. From the moment Summer had learned about the shooting, she'd known Ellis needed a friend who would listen and back her up. Instead of doing that, she'd walked out without even trying to save their friendship.

Now all she had was a pile of regrets. She couldn't pretend not to know the sweetness of her kiss, nor the loveliness of touching her. But she could try to push those memories to a cherished place...and be the friend Ellis needed.

* * *

Lunch with Roxanne had drained all of her emotional energy. From anxious to elated to deflated in the time it took to eat a one-course meal. One thing was certain—she didn't have it in her to drive north on I-280 back into the City. There were other ways to get around the Bay, and one of them took her through Palo Alto.

At four in the afternoon, the day was already wearing on her physically. Not only had she left home at six a.m., she'd stayed at her office past nine the night before to bank some of the hours she expected to miss.

She'd spare an hour or so for Jonathan though. His apartment was only minutes off the freeway on Sand Hill Road. She hadn't visited in almost a year, not since delivering the boxed contents of his old bedroom in her SUV. It was more than a little ironic that his share of a student apartment next to Stanford University was as much as her rent in River Woods. She wasn't sure how he'd manage next year without her financial help, but he was confident he'd find a way.

Nearly every space in the complex was taken, and two were occupied by Volkswagen sedans—one silver, one metallic gray. She couldn't recall which was his. After squeezing her SUV into a space marked *Compact*, she managed to slither out without bumping the car next to hers.

The apartments were laid out in townhouse fashion with the living area on the first floor and three tiny bedrooms upstairs. It took two buzzes to bring someone downstairs to the door.

"Hi." The young man who answered had short, neat hair like Jonathan's, but he dressed more like Jeremy, in jeans with a heavy metal band T-shirt.

"Hello, I'm Jonathan Rowanbury's mom. He wouldn't happen to be home, would he?" She probably should have called, but in the back of her mind, she'd been afraid he'd discourage her from coming.

"Uh…" He frowned and glanced nervously over his shoulder up the stairs. "Jon doesn't live here anymore."

Stunned, she stepped back to make sure she had the right building.

"Hey, Hurston! When did Rowanbury move out?"

A buff, shirtless teenager bounded down the stairs. "Sometime last summer. Whenever Pope moved in."

Surely Jonathan had told her that and somehow she hadn't processed it. Last summer had been the most hectic time of her life…packing up the house, finding a job and a new place to live, getting Allison ready to go off to college.

"You wouldn't happen to know where he moved?"

"Somewhere down in the South Bay," said the boy called Hurston. "I know he was taking some classes at San Jose State so he could get his grades back up. They told him he could reapply after a year."

Ellis braced herself against the door frame as a wave of nausea threatened to bring up her lunch.

"You all right, ma'am?"

A silent nod was all she could manage. She returned to sit in her car, where the magnitude of Jonathan's betrayal caused her to burst into tears. He'd been lying to her since last summer, maybe longer—following his father's deceptive ways to perfection. There was no dean's list, no pending graduation nor imminent reply to his law school application.

Jonathan, the strong one. The one whose resolve and focus had seemingly gotten him through the tragedy on an even keel. It was all a lie—he'd taken it harder than anyone.

* * *

Summer sprang to answer an insistent knock at the door and stopped herself. It was a mere seven hours ago that she'd told Sam she'd been seeing someone. If Sam had broken her word not to say anything, there was a good chance this was Rita.

When the knocking became pounding, she reluctantly gave in, remembering how Rita had behaved the night the police were called. She swung the door open to find not Rita but Ellis, her hands in the pockets of her blazer and a look of utter dejection on her face.

"Come in. Is everything okay?" It was clear she was upset, and Summer instinctively held out her arms.

Ellis fell into them, and in only moments, dissolved into sobs. "Just hold me for a minute…please." It was twice that long before her tears finally subsided, leaving her face red and swollen. "Jonathan's been lying to me. Just like Bruce. All this time telling me how great he was doing at Stanford. I found out this afternoon he got kicked out last summer."

It was a horrible thing for him to do in the wake of his father's deceit, yet Summer felt nothing but compassion for the poor boy. Bruce Rowanbury was responsible for this, just as he'd rendered Allison emotionally incapable of handling changes in her mother's life. After more than a year, Ellis was still picking up the pieces, and likely would until her children faced down their grief.

Devastated and with nowhere to turn, Ellis needed her to step up and be a friend. Listen and take her side.

No matter how much Summer hurt from being pushed aside, she couldn't deny the love she felt. If friendship was all Ellis wanted, she'd be the best friend she could be. No innuendo, no references to their intimacy, no pressuring for more.

She guided Ellis to the couch and sat close. For once, she resisted her natural inclination to caress her hands.

Jon's story was eerie for how closely it tracked with his father's duplicity. Surely he knew what a terrifying impact it would have on his mother if she found out—and that she'd torment herself with visions of him spiraling out of control and turning to violence.

"What is it that makes the people I love feel like they can't talk to me? Am I that difficult to deal with? I know I can be stubborn sometimes, but I'm not a monster."

"This has nothing to do with you, Ellis." It was easy to imagine Bruce too had been a proud and arrogant man, expecting more of himself than he could deliver, and incapable of admitting his failure. "Jonathan's used to being at the top. I could hear it in his voice. Now he's probably embarrassed. He was trying to fix this before anyone found out."

Sitting together so close felt achingly familiar, and it was all she could do not to draw Ellis back into her arms. This was no time to risk rejection.

"Just like his father," Ellis went on. "What did they think would happen if they told me? Did they think I'd stop loving them? That I'd ridicule them?"

"If anything's to blame, it's probably testosterone. Or blame it on society for making rules about how *real* men are supposed to act. Jonathan's school problems happened because he couldn't cope with what his father did. But lying to you about where he was? That's on him."

Ellis looked as though she might start crying again.

"This will work out." She wiped Ellis' cheek with her thumb, all the while wishing she could kiss the tears away. "You just need to talk to him. Let him know you found out. Tell him it's all okay, that you're there for him."

"I tried to call him but he won't answer."

"He can't hide forever. Talking to you could be just what he needs to release the pressure valve."

"Maybe you're right." She squeezed Summer's hand. "My life is so full of drama. Are you sure you even want a friend like me?"

Summer had almost convinced herself she could accept being only friends, but hearing Ellis use the actual words was downright depressing. It was almost as though they'd never even been lovers.

"I want a friend *exactly* like you." She smiled bravely. "One of these days, I'll be the one needing a shoulder to cry on. And I'll turn to you because you're the strongest woman I know."

Ellis gave her a dubious look. "I don't know where you get this stuff. If there's one thing I'm not, it's strong."

"You're selling yourself way short. Look how you pulled yourself up after Bruce. New city, new job. You held it together when most people would have come apart."

She finally smiled, albeit weakly. "You're good to me. And good *for* me too."

Though her heart hurt with longing for the tenderness they'd shared only a week ago, Summer knew she could do this. All she had to do was forget.

* * *

All in all, the visit with Summer had gone better than Ellis expected. Though for someone who'd lamented how hard it was to quit Rita, she'd had no trouble quitting this time. Instant nothing. After a whole week of being ignored, Ellis had worried she might not even open the door.

Now that they'd broken the ice, it would be easier to see her again…to work out, to share dinner. Clearly their romance was over, so there was no point in trying to reason with Allison. Summer—who'd described herself as "touchy-feely" with nearly everyone—hadn't even held her hand.

As she drew back the covers on her bed, her phone chimed and displayed Jonathan's photo. Only seven hours after her first urgent message asking him to call, and two hours after the one she'd amended to add, "no matter how late."

Despite her hours of practice on what to say, she felt a dip in her confidence until she heard the echo of Summer's words. *Because you're strong.* The stakes were too high to be anything but.

"Hi, sweetie."

"Sorry I couldn't call earlier, Mom. They won't let us talk on our cell phones in the library."

Which library would that be? No, she wouldn't trap him in his web of lies. He didn't need more humiliation on top of what he already felt.

"Jonathan, I went to the City this morning to meet with the attorneys. I'm starting to see some light at the end of the tunnel."

She shared the tentative terms of the agreement, including the fact that she'd come out of it in better financial shape than expected. "Then I met Roxanne for lunch in Woodside. Since I was so close to Palo Alto, I stopped by your apartment. They told me you didn't live there anymore."

With practiced calm, he immediately answered, "I was going to tell you the next time we talked. I moved in with a friend of mine on the other side of—"

"It's okay, honey. The boys said they thought you were taking some catch-up classes at San Jose State." She concentrated in order to keep all traces of judgment out of her voice, emphasizing instead her love and compassion. "I called the dean's office at Stanford this afternoon. They wouldn't tell me anything specific—so I'll need you to fill in the blanks—but they did explain what happens when a student goes on suspension. I'm sure this is a difficult time for you, and I thought you'd appreciate hearing how much I love you."

After a long, pained silence, he sniffed loudly and his story spilled out in a stumbling voice. His academic progress at Stanford had ground to a halt after the shooting. First probation, then provisional status and finally suspension. He was eligible for reinstatement after a year, provided he could prove himself capable of completing his degree.

"What kind of progress are you making now?"

"Not as much as I'd like." Besides carrying a slate of political science and economics classes, he was working evenings and weekends stocking shelves at a Target store. "That's why I couldn't call earlier…and why I couldn't stay long at Christmas. I had to get ready for Black Monday."

Ellis surprised herself by laughing. "That must have been horrible. I won't go anywhere near the stores on days like that."

"Anyway, I decided to drop two of my classes. I figured it was better to get two A's than four C's."

"Tell me what you're studying."

It was the best conversation she'd had with Jonathan in years, and one of the few times since high school, she realized, they'd talked one on one for more than just a couple of minutes. Little by little, his voice relaxed, as though she'd lifted the weight of the world off his shoulders. Exactly as Summer had predicted.

"I guess Allison and Jeremy are going to bust my chops over this."

"They don't need to know, honey. We can keep this between you and me."

"Nah, that's okay. It's too stressful trying to keep it secret. Go ahead and tell them."

It was a relief to hear him reject his father's ways. "No, you should be the one to tell them. And I want you to quit your job. Focus on your classes and rack up those A's. We'll find a way to cover another year of school."

"But that's not fair to Allison and Jeremy."

"Jonathan, after this settlement, I won't have much going into retirement, so someone will have to take care of me in my old age. My plan is to get you through law school. You wouldn't let your mother live on the streets, would you?"

He laughed, the first time in ages she could recall.

"So like it or not, young man, you've just made a deal with the devil."

"You got it." His phone beeped, and he explained that his battery was dying. He seemed genuinely sad their call was ending. "I love you big, Mom."

Her heart swelled to hear him utter the phrase from his childhood. "I love you big too. Nothing will ever change that. And I want you to come see me as soon as you can. I miss you."

Summer was right about how she'd feel—that she'd pulled her son back from the brink. The next time he came to see her, she'd plant the seed of having him apply to law schools besides Stanford. His quest to be the smartest, the best of the best, was his undoing.

She was reminded of her own career ambitions, how she came to realize she never would have survived the high pressure of a job like Roxanne's. Some people were cut out for that. But not her, and perhaps not Jonathan.

Now if only she could get her daughter to return her call. In the course of her hour-long conversation, there was no indication Allison had told her brother about Summer. Perhaps she'd reconsidered her shameful behavior. Not that it mattered at this point—her sexual relationship with Summer was history.

CHAPTER TWENTY-ONE

Summer squirmed in her chair in an effort to stretch the muscles around her spine. Two and a half hours was too long to sit without a break, especially for a dry lecture on something as mundane as new paperwork protocols. As if the subject matter weren't boring enough, the Deputy Secretary of Health and Human Services apparently had practiced several delivery styles and chosen the one guaranteed to put the entire room to sleep. His speech was a halting monotone, with most sentences separated by filler words. *Uh…um…you know.*

"I think my blood flow has stopped," Alythea whispered. "Stab me in the heart and let's see."

"I can't. My arms went numb about an hour ago."

"Are there questions?" the speaker asked, apparently having caught their murmuring.

The worst part was not knowing when it would end. Another hour? Two, or even three? It was possible the deputy secretary would stretch the presentation out to the end of their workday, oblivious to the fact that funding cycles were rigid—a delay of even one day on the Sacramento end could mean a whole month of funding lost for a program desperate for money. Skipping an afternoon of work wasn't an option when they were up against a deadline for allocations.

Years ago, Summer had practiced meditation as a means of decluttering her mind. She'd focus on the tiny things that distracted her throughout a typical day, envisioning each one on a slip of paper she'd burn until only smoke and ash remained.

She tried it from her chair, starting with the deputy secretary and his lecture. In her mind's eye, she was back at her desk closing out the paperwork that would speed funding to the state's homeless shelters.

This mind-numbing training was coming at a huge personal cost—Ellis had texted with an offer to take her out for sushi after their workout to thank her for lending a shoulder while she cried over Jonathan. Instead, she'd be stuck in her office until eight o'clock at the earliest.

Still, the invitation had come as a welcome surprise. She'd assumed they'd work out the terms of their friendship gradually, but Ellis appeared to be picking up where they left off. From the look of it, Sam had hit the nail on the head—it was Ellis who had the real problem, not Allison. Now that the romantic and sexual aspects were off the table, she was happy again.

Summer wouldn't be able to recover as quickly. It would take weeks if not months of measuring her words and expressions, of checking her hands to make sure she wasn't sending the wrong message. Eventually she'd get her emotions back where they belonged.

"Before we…you know…get to the next half…um…unless anyone has a question, we should…uh… take a short break. "

A collective groan went up from the room to learn their purgatory was only half finished. Yet the mention of a break caused people to shift in their seats as they collected purses, water bottles and notes in preparation for dashing out the door. Anyone who dared delay their break by asking a question would probably find slashed tires later.

* * *

Ellis had a love-hate relationship with Rex's columns. She loved reading them because they were interesting, but hated being the one to tell him the presiding justice of the third division spelled his name McGuiness, not McGuinness. That the campaign finance bill was an Assembly bill, not a Senate bill. That the governor signed it last April, not March.

It wasn't that he'd be irked at being corrected. She was more worried he'd dropped those errors in there intentionally to see if the assistant editor would catch them—which meant there might be more. No wonder the others didn't like him. For a guy who could be so nice, he also was a bit of a jerk.

Her phone chimed with a message, Summer finally returning her text. *In meeting since lunchtime…will have to work late. Sorry.*

Or so she said. Ellis had felt certain the awkwardness was behind them after their emotional talk. The problem was they'd addressed Jonathan's issues, not their own. Summer had stepped up when she was needed, but it was all too clear she had no intention of going back to the way things were. *Working late.* Next she'd be coming down with something. Making excuses, playing games.

Ellis had no patience for that. It was childish to punish someone with the silent treatment. If Summer had changed her feelings, she should say so.

It certainly would solve a lot of problems, like mollifying Allison. Like not having to dread the day she introduced Summer to her parents, her brother and her in-laws. Like no longer having to face the internal confusion about who she was.

The realization of how much easier life would be should have brought a surge of relief. Instead her overriding emotion was a painful sense of loss, along with the fear that she'd never be able to trust her feelings about anyone again.

Within moments of tossing Rex's article into her outbox, he appeared to pick it up. "Good afternoon. I hope I didn't screw up too much. I never want to make you work too hard."

She chuckled, appreciating the distraction from her melancholy. "It's the same amount of work whether you screw up or not. If you fill your column with facts, I have to verify them."

"Good point." Given his rolled-up sleeves and loosened tie, he'd been working in the office rather than on his beat at the capitol. As he scanned her notes, his eyebrows arched in surprise. "Only one *n* in McGuiness? Are you sure about that?"

"Now you're fact-checking the fact-checker?" She swatted his forearm with her pencil. "And then what? We arm wrestle?"

Grinning broadly, he threw up both of his hands in surrender. "Okay, okay. I trust you."

After his heads-up on the attorney calling Marcie, she'd begun looking at him in a different light. He definitely was an ally at *Vista*, and even a potential friend. It was funny how her nervousness around him had ceased after she started seeing Summer, because she no longer considered his interest in her a viable option.

Perhaps that would change. Roxanne would be over the moon if she started seeing Rex. He truly was handsome. And very smart...and cosmopolitan. She could do a lot worse.

Unfortunately, her litany of his finer qualities failed to move the needle. At least not the way Summer had.

He perched on the edge of her desk and lowered his face even with hers so he could whisper. "By the way, I wrangled a couple of box seats at the Opera House for tomorrow night. They're dancing *Giselle*. You interested?"

She was flooded instantly with memories of her nights at the ballet with Bruce. His smart tuxedo, her cocktail dress and finest jewelry. The elderly Grossmans, who'd shared their box for years. The feeling of privilege at being part of San Francisco's arts crowd.

"I don't need to know right this second," he went on. "But maybe by the end of the day?"

It took her several seconds to fully process that he was asking her on another date...perhaps even an overnight date. "Thank you, I...I'll have to check with my kids to make sure they aren't coming by this weekend. My daughter and I...we're going through kind of a rough patch right now, and we might need some time to smooth it out. You know how that is."

"You bet I do."

Her response credibly delayed her having to answer, and also laid the groundwork for why she'd have to decline. Eventually she'd find the words to tell Rex she appreciated him as a friend.

The way she appreciated Summer as a friend. What a miserable thought.

It was only a week ago she'd felt the excitement climbing, that she'd known within a matter of days they'd make the leap to sharing a bed. There had been no need to manufacture her feelings the way she'd tried to do with Rex. If anything, she'd been nervous about the idea of getting romantically involved with a woman, but her feelings for Summer were too powerful to overcome.

That's what she'd thrown away in answer to Allison's outburst. All at once she felt a sense of urgency to know if there might ever be a chance to get it back—or had she ruined it forever? They needed to talk…another late-night visit. It was Friday, a day they'd come to set aside for each other.

The only place where she could make a private call was the ladies' room off the main hallway near the elevator bank, outside the *Vista* offices. Four stalls, all empty.

She expected to reach voice mail, and was momentarily taken aback when Summer answered her call.

"I…I thought you were in a meeting."

"He let us out for a break, thank God. There was a mad dash for the bathroom. But we have to go back for who knows how long. And half the people on our floor are going to have to work late tonight to get our paperwork out the door. Otherwise we miss the funding cycle."

She was protesting too much, Ellis thought. Since when did state workers stay overtime? "So I guess dinner's out for tonight."

"Sorry."

After several awkward seconds, it was apparent she wasn't going to suggest another time. "Summer, are you avoiding me?"

"No! Of course not. Why would you think that?"

"Because I practically had to break down your door last night to get you to talk to me. You haven't been to the fitness room all week. No calls, no texts. Nothing. It's like we aren't even friends anymore." She was tempted to challenge her story about the long meeting and having to work late too, but that would put Summer on the defensive. "I was hoping after last night that we were okay again."

"We are." A deep sigh was followed by what sounded like a door closing. "I didn't mean for you to think I didn't want to be your friend. I just thought you could use a little space…that maybe we both could."

Both of them.

"That's informative. I hadn't realized I was crowding you."

"I didn't mean it that way."

"Let me be clear, Summer." She sharpened her tone to make it known she was irritated. "Honesty matters to me—*a lot*. I've been on the wrong end of someone keeping secrets, and I don't want to go through that again. So if there's something I should know about how you feel, I suggest you tell it to me straight."

"I'm not being dishonest. I'm just…" She sighed again loudly. "I was crazy about you—that's me being honest, okay? Crazy about you. But I could see how hard it was for you to deal with Allison, and I didn't want you to feel like I was forcing something on you that you couldn't handle. All that got me thinking…it took a few days to figure out what I wanted, but I got clear on it last night when you were at my place. I want to be your friend, Ellis. Nothing more, nothing less."

So there it was. Summer was finished with the intimate aspects of their relationship. And Ellis had done this to herself.

"We can talk some more tomorrow if you want to, but right now I have to go."

A painful lump formed in the back of Ellis's throat. "Don't put yourself out."

The heavy door swung open with a *swoosh*, and Angie Alvarez dashed into the first stall, in too big a hurry even to look her way. "Blessed Mother of the Baby Jesus. I didn't think I was going to make it. That man wouldn't let me off the phone."

Ellis dabbed the corners of her eyes and exited before Angie could see her.

She returned to her cubicle intent on getting back to work. Her next assignment was a review of Sacramento's newest restaurant, the Brasserie Capitale. Virtually all the menu items were in French, incorporating various accents, carets and cedillas. A fact-checker's nightmare.

So their lovemaking had turned out to be a notch on the bedpost after all.

The lead on her pencil snapped and she tossed it against the wall of her cubicle. How was she supposed to concentrate with Summer's stark decision playing on a loop in her head. *Your friend…nothing more, nothing less.*

She shoved the desk, sending her chair rolling backward, and sprang to her feet.

Rex's office was in the corner opposite Marcie's, and every surface was covered with folders, books or notepads. He was peering at his computer screen with his reading glasses atop his head, but he jumped up immediately to clear a chair.

"It's okay. I can't stay but a minute. I just wanted to say I checked with my kids. They aren't planning to come over this weekend, so if your invitation to the ballet is still open, I'd love to go."

He flashed a wide smile. "That's great. Would you…like to stay the night in the city?"

She froze for a moment, waiting to see if he'd clarify the terms of their date. He didn't, which was a clarification in and of itself.

Summer didn't care what she did. *Your friend…nothing more, nothing less.* They were finished.

"That would be lovely."

* * *

"Aaaiiiii!" Summer let out a muffled scream and pounded her desk with frustration.

She should be flogged for her careless choice of words— *nothing more, nothing less.* It must have sounded so flippant.

After Ellis's appearance at her door the night before, she'd felt sure they were on the right track. It was easy to be her friend, and she firmly believed the day would come when she'd need someone and Ellis would be there for her.

But then one glib remark meant to underscore her resolve had come out like *take it or leave it*. Now she could only hope Ellis would give her the chance to explain herself.

Then again, what could she possibly say? There weren't many ways to admit she was merely going through the motions of being friends while her heart was aching for more. That she was bravely committed to getting up every morning and hoping it hurt less, and that she dreaded the day Ellis found someone else to love. All of that was true, but it would only put pressure on Ellis to return her feelings. More likely, it would make her uncomfortable because she couldn't.

Alythea knocked and entered her office simultaneously. "Don't think you're going to hide out in here and miss the second half of this training. If he holds us up one minute on account of you being late, I'm going to kick your butt."

"Get in line," she said brusquely, pushing past her friend in the doorway.

"What is up with you?" Each word was punctuated with a half-beat pause.

"Sorry…personal problems."

"Which person?"

"Ellis. I can't seem to do anything right." They opted for the stairs instead of the elevator, and it caused her words to bounce off the concrete walls. "No matter what comes out of my mouth, she's guaranteed to take it the wrong way."

Alythea huffed and shook her head. "I'm starting to think this woman might not be worth the trouble. I've known you, what? Eighteen years? Next to Julius, you're the most easy-going person I know. If she can't see that, it's because she's spoiling for an argument. Nemy's worthless husband did that all the time." The man was so emotionally abusive to their daughter that Alythea and Julius had paid for the attorney to facilitate the divorce.

Summer didn't want to believe something like that about Ellis. "No, it's a trust issue. She was on the wrong end of a horrible situation. Imagine the worst kind of deception in the world and multiply it times a million. You don't recover from something like that overnight. I honestly think I can help her if she'll let me."

They reached the conference room, where the deputy secretary was returning to the podium. Alythea grabbed her arm to stop her at the door. "It took us two years to convince Nemy she had to leave that SOB. You know why? Because you can't save somebody who doesn't want to be saved."

Alythea had Ellis all wrong, but Summer was powerless to fix her perception without giving away the horrible secret. "She wants it...and she deserves it." *No matter how long it takes.*

CHAPTER TWENTY-TWO

Ellis counted out all of her quarters to feed the meter, hoping an hour and twenty minutes would be enough to reason with her daughter. She'd heard from Jeremy that Allison was out with her friends late on Friday night, so she was sure to be sleeping in. If she wasn't going to return calls, she should expect to be roused from her bed.

She tugged her wool blazer around her against the morning chill. Her jeans were slightly worn and her shirttail flapping freely in the fashion of the day, but no one would mistake her for anything other than a mom, especially as she headed into the dorm.

Currant Hall was one of several brightly-colored rectangular buildings positioned inside Tercero, the residential center of the Davis campus. There wasn't a soul in the lobby or on the elevator, not surprising for seven forty-five on a Saturday morning. She'd been to Allison's room only once—on moving day last fall—but remembered it as being on the third floor, next to last room on the left. Just to be safe, she verified the number from Allison's campus address before knocking.

"Go away," her daughter moaned from inside.

Ellis tried the door and found it unlocked. They'd have to talk about that. A quick glance showed a lump in one bed and the other neatly made, its occupant gone. "Allison?"

"Mom?" She frowned as she pushed herself up in bed, looking as though she'd had quite a night. Bloodshot eyes, streaked makeup, wild hair, and she was wearing only panties and a tank top. Her jeans, sweater and shoes lay in a pile on the floor. "What are you doing here?"

"We need to talk."

"Now?"

"It wasn't my first choice, but you wouldn't return my calls."

Allison grunted. "I was going to."

"And now I've saved you the trouble." She was tempted to launch into a lecture on how inconsiderate Allison had been to ignore her, to say nothing of her tantrum last weekend. But that wasn't why she'd come. "I've been worried all week you were going to do something foolish to punish me. I hope those were just angry words."

From the open textbooks, laptop and notepad on the desk, it was clear she hadn't given up on her studies. That was a relief.

"I haven't dropped out of school, if that's what you were worried about."

"Among other things." She sat on the edge of the roommate's bed, being careful not to muss it. "Allison, I still don't understand why you got so upset. We don't have to talk about that now, but I hope we will eventually. I don't need to know everything you think and do—nor do I want to—but I can't allow you to pull away from me like that."

Left unsaid was why, but she was sure Allison could fill in the blanks. Her failure to engage at a deeper level with Bruce had enabled his frustrations to fester.

"Jon called me yesterday…told me all about getting kicked out of Stanford." Allison cracked a cynical smile. "You're having a pretty shitty week, huh Mom?"

"Tell me about it." Ellis managed a light chuckle. "My daughter goes off on me…I find my son in a totally different college than the one I thought I'd sent him to. And I broke up with somebody I cared about."

"You didn't have to do that." She had the decency to look guilty. "I talked it over with Jeremy a couple of days ago. He basically said if I didn't accept you and Summer, it meant I didn't accept him and Bruno either. So I was going to call today and tell you it was okay."

Ellis was proud of her son and grateful for his support. It didn't escape her that his word on this carried more weight with Allison than her own. She'd had years to adjust to him being gay and only minutes to think of her mother in that vein.

"Thank you for your permission, but I'd already decided not to let you choose those things for me. I've never done that for you and I never will."

Allison sighed and swung her legs out of the covers. Then she slid into her jeans and padded barefoot to the door, apparently on her way to the bathroom. Without turning around, she said, "I want you to be happy, Mom."

She didn't know whether to be furious or relieved. It hardly mattered now that Summer was no longer interested in a romantic relationship. Furthermore, she was acting as childishly as Allison had last weekend. Ellis would never understand people who preferred the silent treatment over talking something out, but at least she didn't have to guess about how they felt. Bruce never showed anger at all, while inside he was seething at the world.

Her daughter returned and took a plastic bottle of orange juice from a small refrigerator under her desk. "You want one of these?"

"No, thank you. I had breakfast at home. Would you like to go out?"

She shook her head.

"Honey, I'm glad you talked to your brothers. That makes what I have to say easier."

Allison looked at her warily.

"We've been through so much, the four of us. Between you and Jonathan especially, I realize now that I dropped the ball.

I was wrapped up with the attorneys, with getting the house ready to sell. And I was numb, just like you. I thought we all were strong enough—and close enough—that we could get each other through what happened. We were there for each other. We cried a lot and we hugged. You remember those nights you came and crawled into my bed?"

Her eyes filling, Allison nodded.

"You'd think I'd know my own kids better than I did. I should have seen how hard it was, especially for you and Jonathan... thank goodness Jeremy had Bruno. I should have gotten you the help you needed. I see you carrying all this anger around and I know it's my fault for not dealing with it the right way."

"It's not your fault, Mom. You weren't the one who killed seven innocent people." She wiped her eyes with the back of her hand.

"But my responsibility is you. Always you. That's why I broke things off with Summer. I could see how much it upset you. It's my job as a mother to care more about you than myself."

"Whatever." At least it was said without attitude.

"Honey, you're a freshman in college now. Can you please try to speak in complete sentences?"

"Whatever...you say...is obviously how you see it." It was crude, but nonetheless properly constructed. "I don't remember getting my way every time I got upset. Why was this time different?"

"Because you were threatening to flunk out of school, for starters. That nearly happened in high school, so I knew damn good and well you might do it again. And not caring if you're in a car wreck? I can't have you go off feeling like that."

Allison shrugged. "It was just words. I was mostly pissed because you told Jeremy but not me."

"I would have told you." She had trouble believing the reaction would have been any different but wanted to give her daughter the benefit of the doubt. "It doesn't matter now."

"Whatever." She quickly added, "You want to do is fine."

"What I want is for you to deal with your anger." And for Jonathan to regain his ability to focus. Blinking back tears that welled at the thought of her children's struggles, Ellis continued, "I could use some help with this too, sweetie. If you're willing, I'd like us to go together to see someone. The boys too if they feel like they need it. None of us deserves to feel this way. More than anything, I want you all to have the future you planned for yourselves before this horrible thing happened."

Allison was crying openly now, and Ellis joined her on the bed for a hug. It broke her heart to see her daughter come apart, but if they followed through—and she'd see to it they did—they were finally on the road to recovery.

* * *

Summer was drenched in sweat after forty-five minutes at full speed on the elliptical. She didn't usually go this long, but was paying penance for having missed her workout three days in a row. It was surprisingly quiet but for the grind of her machine. She hadn't expected to have the fitness room to herself on a Saturday morning.

Nor had she expected to peek out at seven thirty and find Ellis's car already gone. That left her kicking herself for not marching over there last night and pounding on her door the way Ellis had done on Thursday.

It was a misunderstanding, plain and simple. What else could explain the dramatic change in Ellis's demeanor, from warm and open as she cried over Jon to curt and dismissive on the phone? It wasn't rational to get so upset over someone having to work late. There had to be something else going on, and she was determined to get to the bottom of it.

Her legs trembling from exertion, Summer collected a pair of dumbbells and proceeded through her upper body routine. As she wrapped up her third set, the familiar SUV pulled into the parking lot and Ellis returned to her apartment. No groceries, no packages, and most important, no kids.

Good manners called for a shower after such a sweaty workout, but Summer didn't want to risk having her leave again. She wiped down with a towel, slung it around her neck and knocked on Ellis's door.

Ellis had doffed her blazer and replaced her shoes with bedroom slippers. An unexpected smile crossed her face—not a broad grin by any means, but it was a welcome change. "You're working out early."

"Because I've been lazy all week. I was going to knock on your door and drag you with me, but your car wasn't here."

"I went to see my daughter. She wasn't returning my calls, so I had to catch her before she got out of bed. She's a captive audience in her underwear."

"How is she?" She only asked to be polite. The last thing she wanted was another fight about Allison.

"Much better than the last time I saw her. We had a long talk and a good cry." Indeed, the makeup around her eyes was smudged. "My job for next week is to call around and find a therapist who can help pull us all out of the ashes."

That was great news. Maybe Allison would learn to let go of her mother so she could live her own life.

"Want some coffee?"

"Water would be nice." Summer followed and took her usual seat at the bar. "Look, about yesterday...I don't know what I said or did to get you so upset with me. And that makes me feel awful, because I ought to know you well enough by now that I should be able to figure out when something's going to hurt you. You have to know, Ellis, I'd never do that on purpose. I care about you way too much."

Ellis passed her an ice-cold bottle of water and proceeded to set up her coffeemaker. With her back still turned, she said, "You didn't do anything wrong. I was just being oversensitive. If I had any doubts, you erased them by coming over here this morning."

It was a relief to know her stalking had paid off. "I want this friendship to work. I can't stop thinking that if we hadn't made love, we'd be sitting here laughing our butts off about something. I wouldn't be losing sleep or wracking my brain about what to say. And it's all my fault. I know it. I shouldn't have come on to you like I did."

"It's not anybody's fault unless we did something wrong." Ellis turned and leaned against the counter but continued to stare at the floor. "I think I'd feel better if you didn't regret it quite so much."

The admission caught her off-guard until Ellis finished her thought with a chuckle.

"Trust me, you don't want to go there," Summer said. "The only thing I regret is making a mess of our friendship. I feel like I took advantage of your emotions…that we should have waited a lot longer. Then there wouldn't have been any questions. And if I'd gotten to know your kids better—"

"I'm not sure it would have made any difference with Allison. She was looking for a reason to blow up and I gave it to her."

Maybe so, but it might have made a difference in the way Ellis handled it. "The doubts were yours too, Ellis. I could see it on your face. Your kids made you stop and think about it, and you probably would have stood up for yourself if you knew for sure we were doing the right thing."

Ensuing silence made her worry she'd gone too far. Or perhaps not far enough.

"But you know what? It's okay to have doubts. When I first started seeing women, I had a lot of questions too. Did I want to live a life most of society didn't approve of? Did I want to give up the chance for a family like the one my parents had? I didn't decide those things overnight."

It was killing her that Ellis hadn't answered.

"And here's the other thing. It's perfectly fine to do something and then change your mind later. So no, we didn't do anything wrong. It's okay to decide you don't want that. What matters to me more than anything is that you and I can be friends…that we can talk like this about whatever's on our mind. And we can be honest."

"Nothing more, nothing less."

So that was it. She'd taken offense at the trite characterization. "I meant that literally. That I wouldn't pressure you to do something you didn't want to do, and I wouldn't treat you like a casual acquaintance. This right here"—she jabbed the counter with her index finger—"this is us. Laying it out there for each other in a way we don't do for other people. You're special to me, and I don't want that to change just because we aren't lovers anymore."

The words tumbled out sharply, but she didn't regret her emotions, especially when Ellis leaned over and clasped her hand. "I'd be crazy to say no to a friend like you."

As they shared their first genuine smile in a week, Summer felt some of the tension dissipate, replaced by an aura of comfort and familiarity.

Ellis gave her a skeptical look. "I don't suppose you're up for another workout."

"Not on your life, but I'll cash in a raincheck for last night's dinner. You like barbecue?"

"Mmm...I can't. I'm busy tonight." She dropped her eyes and let go of Summer's hand. "I'm going into the City for the ballet...and we probably won't be back until sometime tomorrow afternoon."

It was hard not to notice she'd left out a very important detail, but easy to understand why. She undoubtedly had a date, and Summer would bet her last dollar it was with Rex Brenneman. "Sounds like fun. I know how much you miss that," she said stiffly.

"*Giselle*, one of my favorites."

"I'm sure you're dying to see the Opera House again." As for Summer, she was just dying.

* * *

Ellis's dress was two shades of plum with lace above her bra line and down the sleeves. She'd last worn it when the New York Philharmonic played Davies Symphony Hall. Almost two years ago, with Bruce. She remembered because he'd hurried back into the house to change his handkerchief to one of nearly the same shade. Not because he was meticulous about his appearance, but because she'd suggested it once in the early years of their marriage and he automatically incorporated it into his routine. Their social life, after all, was her domain.

Looking back, she wondered how much of Bruce's life had been "going through the motions." His last three years, for sure, since those were the ones in which he pretended to be an executive of a financial services company. It wasn't much of a stretch to imagine him pretending other things as well. When had he stopped loving them or caring about their lives? Certainly well before the day he brought the wrath of the world down onto their heads.

Her suitcase lay open on the bed awaiting her selection of pajamas. The practical choice was the gray satin set Jeremy and Bruno had given her for Christmas, but it hardly mattered, since she had no plans for anyone to see her in them. Surely Rex wouldn't dare suggest they share a room on only their second date.

The thought made her physically ill, nauseous with anxiety. If he were a gentleman, he'd already have booked separate rooms, but how would she handle it if he hadn't? She'd have to insist on her own. Depending on which hotel he chose, a room in the City could run upwards of five hundred dollars, which she'd be paying off for months.

Why had she said yes to an overnight date in the first place? Or any date, for that matter. The answer made her furious with herself—because she'd been frustrated by Summer's apparent lack of interest, which turned out to be a misunderstanding. It was too late to cancel. Rex would see right through the old headache excuse, and the truth might ruin their chances of working together. He was powerful enough at *Vista* to sink her possibilities for a better position, even with Gil Martino on her side.

Life would be a lot easier if she could learn to care for Rex the same way she cared for Summer. He obviously found her appealing, though she hadn't fully convinced herself his attraction went beyond the morbid fascination of dating the widow of a mass murderer. She'd be the envy of Roxanne. Jonathan would be thrilled to engage with someone so politically astute, and Allison and Jeremy could shed their worries about her getting involved with a woman.

Summer wouldn't take it well, even if jealousy weren't an issue. As a matter of principle, she was opposed to the idea of going out with someone from work. Her fallen face when she heard of the ballet plans, however, likely had nothing to do with Rex being a coworker. She was still hurting over their breakup and doing her best to put up a brave front.

Ellis recognized the look, guessing it was the same one on her face. Any excitement she felt for the chance to go back into the City for the ballet was blunted by the fact that she was going with Rex instead of Summer. If they'd gone together—even as friends—they'd have talked and laughed the whole way. No anxiety, no sense of dread. And they'd have shared a hotel room without batting an eye. The irony was breathtaking.

She rolled her suitcase to the foyer in time to see Rex's Audi pull into the guest space next to her car. To her mild surprise, he'd traded his bomber jacket for a dark suit and low-key striped tie. His trademark trilby was missing as well. It was the most handsome she'd seen him.

His face lit up in a broad smile when she opened the door. "You look lovely."

"Thank you." It came instantly, that nervous feeling that bordered on embarrassment, to know she was being scrutinized. "I hardly recognized you without your bomber jacket."

He held out his hands the way a lounge singer would on the last notes of a ballad. "Hey, it's not every day I get the chance to go to the world famous Opera House."

His admission triggered the recognition that this wasn't an ordinary outing for him. He'd already confessed to knowing little about the ballet, so he didn't just happen to have tickets for *Giselle*, as he'd suggested. His motivation obviously was to entice her out for another date.

"Let me get your bag."

She wanted badly to relax and grant herself the freedom to enjoy the evening. Only the luckiest of women landed a date with one of Northern California's most eligible bachelors.

As he stowed her suitcase in the trunk, she walked slowly toward the passenger side of the car. With each step, the feeling she was being watched grew stronger, and she turned toward Summer's apartment.

She was there, standing perfectly still with one hand on her doorknob. Going or coming, it wasn't clear. But her downcast look was obvious even from so far away.

Rex hustled to the passenger door and opened it before she could. "I checked the traffic report earlier. Nothing to worry about construction-wise, so let's hope we get there without running into a backup on the freeway. Knock on wood." He did just that, tapping the varnished inlay of the opulent dashboard.

Settling against the luxurious leather seat, she cast a wary eye toward Summer's door. She was gone.

"Our dinner reservation is at six thirty at the North Box. Have you eaten there?"

The North Box was an elegant restaurant inside the Opera House on the Mezzanine Level. She and Bruce often met friends there for dinner before the performance. How many of those same faces would see her there with Rex tonight?

"Ellis?" He prodded her as he turned out of the complex.

"Sorry, I was trying to remember which one that was," she lied. "I've eaten at so many."

How was it that Summer had chosen that exact moment to step outside? It was as though she'd waited...watching for Rex's car. That she'd come out to face the inevitability of Ellis moving on. Whatever her reason, she'd meant to be seen.

Ellis absorbed that realization with the growing awareness that she too had felt a palpable need to connect before embarking on an evening that marked the resolute end of their short-lived romance. She'd known before looking that Summer would be standing there, that they'd silently press one another one last time to ask if this was what they wanted.

"Rex, I'm so sorry...please stop the car."

CHAPTER TWENTY-THREE

Summer scrolled through the list of showtimes at Tower Theater, Sacramento's most recognized art house cinema. Subtitles required her to focus, and that would get her mind off what was arguably her worst day in a very long time. French at four, Chinese at six thirty. If her misery persisted, she could do Italian at nine. For sure, she wasn't going to sit home and punish herself with fantasies of Ellis.

The next day would be even worse because she'd wake up wondering if Ellis and Rex had slept together. If she stewed on it hard enough, it might even come as a relief if they had, since she wouldn't have to dread its eventuality. Ellis would probably tell her, and then by mutual unspoken agreement, they'd never talk about it again.

Friendship. Nothing more, nothing less.

She opened her door and froze at the sight of Ellis coming up her walk, rolling her suitcase behind.

"Were you going somewhere?" Ellis asked.

"I was…but I'm not now." She took the bag and dragged it inside, her insides fluttering with excitement. "You changed your mind."

"I decided I'd rather be here," Ellis said. "I hope that's okay."

"You know it is." Summer was afraid to presume too much, even with a suitcase in her foyer. "Was there something about Rex?"

"In a way, I guess. He wasn't you." The corner of Ellis's mouth turned up in the start of a smile, and she held out a hand. "Why would I want to be with anyone else when I can be with someone I love?"

Summer repeated every word back to herself to be sure she understood. "Oh, my gosh."

In the open foyer, there was no place to fall, no way to brace herself against the force of Ellis's sudden kiss. She gave in, arching her back and trusting Ellis to support her weight. Tongues and teeth. And hands already inside her sweater snaking up her back.

"Please don't go changing your mind again. Losing you once is more than enough."

"I'm as sure as I know how to be." Ellis took charge, tugging her down the hall toward the bedroom. With a wild swipe, she hurled the covers back as if the bed were her own. Presenting her back, she commanded, "Unzip me."

Summer didn't care that she seemed to be in a hurry. This was a whole new experience in the light of day and she intended to relish it one inch at a time. She left a trail of kisses where the skin was newly revealed. Midway down her back, she discovered a strapless bra and freed its clasp.

The dress and bra fell in a heap, followed by her slip and hose. Summer couldn't resist cupping her bare bottom. With her chin on Ellis's shoulder, she murmured, "I need you to stand right here until I'm naked."

That took hardly a moment, and the next time she stepped close, she wrapped her hands around Ellis's hips and pulled her backward. Straining for contact, she ground against the pillow-soft flesh.

"Do that to me," Ellis rasped. She flung herself across the bed face down, and bending her knees to open herself from behind.

The sight of her pretty pink labia was nearly enough to make Summer come on the spot. She pushed herself into the cleft, twisting side to side to feel the friction. There was a toy for this and she would get it—brand new with Ellis's name on it. But for now, nothing could feel this good. She parted the wet folds and slid a finger inside…then three.

Ellis rolled with excitement, tightening with every rise. Her brow furrowed, her eyes closed.

Resting all of her weight against her backside, Summer finally reached her other hand around and found Ellis's fingertips already massaging the taut bundle of nerves at the top of the slippery fold. In a matter of seconds, Ellis shuddered and cried out.

Summer wanted to hear that for the rest of her life.

* * *

Ellis lay panting on the bed, relishing the feel of Summer's smooth skin covering the length of her body. She'd come only twice before growing too sensitive, but she was sure there would be many more to follow. How could she have thought she could leave this?

Summer's head fell against her shoulder. "I love you. I think I would have died if you hadn't come back."

There might be hell to pay for that decision. Rex had managed to hold his temper, but he was far from okay with how she'd broken their date. It would have been much worse to have led him on, she reasoned. Especially since there was no chance he could compete with what she felt for Summer. "I'm back for good, so I hope you're ready for that. I'm dragging a lot of baggage."

"That's the great thing about there being two of us. I'm here to help you unpack it."

Ellis wriggled out from under the weight and tipped Summer onto her back. As they kissed, she mapped every inch of Summer's body within reach of her fingertips, including the wet hollow between her legs. Then she brought those fingers to her lips to taste the tangy essence.

The memory of what Summer had said the night they'd first made love played in her ear. *When you're ready to show how you feel, you won't have any doubts about what to do.*

Her mouth began the journey. From her sensitive neck to the rise of her breasts, where she lingered until Summer moved to touch herself.

"No, that's mine," Ellis murmured as she captured the wandering hand.

Lower…past her navel and across the smooth plane of skin that surrounded her silky curls. She knew exactly what Summer was feeling—the anticipation as she drew closer, the thrill of knowing a soft tongue would soon touch her. It was no surprise when her legs parted to invite her in.

Ellis nestled into the space and inhaled her arousal. Parting the lips with her fingers, she found the pink skin glistening. Then for the first time she tasted the softest part of a woman.

* * *

The waiter dropped off their drinks, club soda and a glass of chardonnay, and took their dinner order.

Ellis offered a toast when he left. "This was a great idea."

"You couldn't possibly think I was going to let you waste that lovely dress," Summer told her with a chuckle.

After three hours of making love and dozing beneath the warm covers, they'd showered together and called The Waterboy for a reservation. Apparently it was one of Sacramento's finest restaurants and thus a perfect place to celebrate the first night of their renewed commitment. They'd lucked into a corner table so far from the bustle of the main dining area that it gave them an aura of privacy.

Summer, having already spent her only evening dress on the night they went to the ballet, wore black slacks with a silk shirt and one of Ellis's vibrant scarves.

"I like you in those colors," Ellis said as she reached across the elegant linen tablecloth to finger the scarf. "Reds and blues make your eyes pop. Did you know that?"

"You make my eyes pop. The very first time I saw you, I had to find out who you were. And wouldn't you know it? That would be the night my ex showed up after too many drinks. I was so embarrassed."

Ellis vividly recalled her stroll along the sidewalk where she'd been retrieving something from her car.

"I thought you were so pretty," Summer said.

"You weren't so bad yourself, you know. Though you looked kind of pitiful limping around on your broken toe. Tell me again how you did that."

Summer shared the tale of "game night" at her friend Courtney's. "I want you to come with me next time. You'll have to teach them how to play Spoons. I'll bring the Band-Aids."

Ellis arched one of her eyebrows to show her skepticism, a look she'd perfected over twenty-some years of raising kids. "How do you think that'll go over? Not the Spoons...I'm talking about the part where I'm hanging out with you and all of Rita's friends."

"It could be a little tricky at first," Summer conceded. "Not at Courtney's, because Rita never goes to game night. You'll probably meet her eventually though. The lesbian community's too small to avoid somebody forever."

The lesbian community. "Am I part of that now...the lesbian community? I'm not sure I think of myself that way."

"You don't have to call yourself anything. Other people will though. We're all in neat little boxes according to the sex of the people we sleep with. Didn't you get the handbook?" There was enough cynicism in her voice to underscore that she didn't care for labels either. "I'm a lesbian though. There's a good chance you'll be lumped in with us."

"I don't care what anyone calls me. I've just never tried it on before."

Everyone Ellis knew—Roxanne, her extended family and at least two of her children—would be at a loss for words entirely, but they'd probably refer to Summer as her lesbian lover. It was amusing…the notion that she was being led astray. She had an answer for anyone who dared to criticize Summer. "Bruce."

"I beg your pardon."

She hadn't realized she'd said it aloud. "I was thinking we might need a truce, your ex and me. I'm not thrilled about the prospect of meeting her. Chances are she won't be too thrilled with meeting me either." Had she covered up her slip?

"Word will get around pretty quick. I suppose the decent thing would be for me to call her and give her a heads-up. But don't worry. I'll make sure it's a long time before the two of you cross paths."

Ellis chuckled. "And I'll do the same with my parents and brother."

"Does it make you nervous to think about telling people?" Summer reached across the table for her hand.

"Not as much as I thought, to be honest." She took a sip of her wine as she imagined her mother's confused expression, the same one she'd displayed when she learned about Jeremy. "I mean, let's face it—can I possibly shock them worse than Bruce did? By the time you've choked out, 'Hey, my husband's a mass murderer,' everything else is a breeze."

It was the first time she could recall talking about the killings without wanting to cry. In Summer, she had a chance to leave her horrible past behind.

With the lessons she'd learned, she'd make a better go of life this time around. No more handing off her financial responsibilities, no dividing their domains. They'd be partners in every sense of the word.

Summer's eyes suddenly widened at something over her shoulder. "I don't believe it."

Ellis couldn't resist turning, and saw two women striding toward a table like theirs at the other end of the restaurant. "Let me guess. One of those women is Rita."

"The tall one with the red hair. And that's not even the unbelievable part," Summer said as she ducked low in her chair. "Good, they can't see me now. The woman she's with is Tracie Carlson, the woman I went on the blind date with."

"The one with the drinking problem?"

Summer chuckled and shook her head. "I can't believe I'm saying this…they might be perfect for each other. Maybe they'll help each other quit."

"I don't think they saw us."

"We could stop by on the way out and say hello. Are you up for that?"

"If you want." From her side of the table, she had a clear view of the pair. Both were attractive, but the redhead was especially striking. "You never told me Rita was so beautiful."

"I happen to like beautiful women. You're the most beautiful woman I've ever dated."

Ellis knew better than that. Love had a way of fixing perceptions, turning ordinary people into raving beauties and handsome rogues. "I could say the same about you."

"Very funny. I'm also the richest, so you can see how far that takes you."

She shrugged. "I've been rich. It was nice. But I'd have given all of it up for a partner I could trust to be honest with me, to love me enough not to hurt me. That's better than rich."

Summer held out both hands palms up. "I'm going to be those things for you, just like you'll be them for me. If we're partners, we're equals."

With their hands clasped in a tight grip, Ellis tried to imagine Bruce—or even Rex—saying such a thing. She couldn't. It took a woman for that.

Bella Books, Inc.

Women. Books. Even Better Together.

P.O. Box 10543
Tallahassee, FL 32302

Phone: 800-729-4992
www.bellabooks.com